Little Sister

by

Wendy MacGown

Bloomington, IN Milton Keynes, UK

AuthorHouse™
1663 Liberty Drive, Suite 200
Bloomington, IN 47403
www.authorhouse.com
Phone: 1-800-839-8640

AuthorHouse™ UK Ltd.
500 Avebury Boulevard
Central Milton Keynes, MK9 2BE
www.authorhouse.co.uk
Phone: 08001974150

First published by AuthorHouse 5/2/2006

ISBN: 1-4259-2829-3 (sc)

Library of Congress Control Number: 2006902637

Printed in the United States of America
Bloomington, Indiana

This book is printed on acid-free paper.

To my Andrea

Chapter 1 – June 1995

Ying Fa cursed her sensitive nose, held her breath and hurried through the alley that connected her apartment building to the main road. The aroma of burnt onions, cooking oil and human waste mingled noxiously in the oppressive heat. A sudden loud screech rent the silence and she covered her ears.

It was Mrs. Lau, yelling at her lazy son. The harsh sound echoed off the five-story buildings on either side of her.

"Mrs. Lau, she'll never learn," she muttered. Someone would complain, and then Mrs. Lau would get a stern lecture or a rent increase, or maybe, since she refused to listen, her family would be relocated.

She quickened her pace, the clatter of sturdy black heels on the dusty pavement attesting to her haste. She shuddered in the strange dark dawn that cast its gloomy pall across the narrow alley, reminded of other families who'd disappeared from her complex, only to reappear at the market a few days' later, whispering tales of run-down squalor. At least her family knew how to keep their eyes lowered, blending in smoothly, steering clear of trouble.

They had four incomes now as well as her grandmother's retirement, making them wealthy compared with many of their neighbors.

So much gained; so much at stake. It was what her mother often said.

She stepped out onto the main street and turned left, gasping for air; and then held her breath against the stench of entrails and rotting meat from Mrs. Ji's butcher shop across the street. She moved quickly, out of its reach, and then took a sharp breath trying to calm her roiling stomach. Looking around to see that no one watched, she reached back and pulled her cotton shirt away from her sweaty back. Then, without a pause in her stride, she leaped over a smashed pineapple, long forgotten by a distracted street vendor and not yet claimed by a hungry rat.

The smells and sounds were as familiar as the taste of boiled egg dipped in soy sauce that had been her breakfast that morning. Her family had moved into their apartment five years ago, but she had lived in Maoming all her life.

Her building stood on the edge of a vast network of similar structures—four, five and six stories high. Some were crumbling; some were bright with hanging laundry, and others bamboo-covered, not yet ready for habitation. It was a city within a city, with shops and housing all patched together like a comfortable old dress.

As murky dawn crept over the buildings ahead of her, the city came awake with the sounds of car horns, bicycle bells and shouts. With its belching refineries, Maoming was China's number-one oil city, helping to push the country into its rightful place in the economic echelons of the modern world.

She raked a hand through her chin-length black hair and expelled a breath. The smog was so dense this morning that it choked her. Just moments ago at breakfast, her grandmother had bemoaned the lack of sunshine, long obliterated by the pollution.

They were complaints of the aged, though Poh Poh rarely complained—especially now.

Ying Fa hid her smile behind a hand, surrendering to the glee that filled her at the thought of her new nephew.

She turned and nodded a slight greeting at a sleepy trinket vendor who, broom in hand, had stepped out of her shop. The shriveled old woman, who mainly dealt in teapots, and was an old friend of Poh Poh's, nodded in return; and then stooped to battle the relentless dirt that had gathered on her steps.

Ying Fa's embroidery case banged against her leg as she skipped: she had almost burst out laughing. There had been a telling twinkle in the old woman's eye. Word must have spread quickly through the maze of apartment buildings.

In the wee hours of the morning, her best friend and sister-in-law, Soong Hsiao, sweaty and pale, her face glowing with joy, had delivered Anjie, her firstborn son.

Anjie was born in the green pig year, the most generous and honorable sign of the Chinese Zodiac. Grandmother said he'd be nice to a fault and have impeccable manners and taste. He'd care about his friends and family and work hard to keep everyone happy—a worthy addition to the dwindling Wong family. Meanwhile, he was round, red, angry and imminently welcome.

Even Father, usually stern and silent, had touched his smooth, rose-petal cheeks in delighted awe. Mother was already planning his one-month celebration; with Hsiao probably sleeping in contented, dreamless oblivion.

She swerved past strollers on their day off, headed to the market; and kept pace with the swiftest of walkers in the gathering foot traffic.

Poh Poh often said that Mao's gift to the country had been a swelling population of diverse opinions and needs. Although some of his programs had gone awry, creating pockets of rage and despair in their wake, hope yet lived in the birth of such innocents as Anji. Hope lived in the aged, having tasted of China's ancient glory. Hope lived in the young, eager for their chance at success.

"Wait!" she cried, spying two of her friends scurrying ahead of her beside the long, public bicycle rack. She slowed her pace, imagining the voice of her mother, Zhaodi, screeching about her lack of decorum. Then she giggled, recalling the meaning of Zhaodi's name—bring me a little brother—and thus invited a sharp look from a black-suited old man.

Swiftly, she adopted a blank expression on her smooth oval face, fearing she'd given offense, or had given herself away. One never knew where power exerted its icy grip.

Her friends Wen Baak-Hap and Huang Chung smiled back at her as they moved steadily forward. Both lived with their respective families in her building; and they all shared the building's tacked-on kitchen.

The girls were staggered in age, with Ying Fa born in the year between the other two. They'd traveled together to Huazhou City a few years earlier as eager apprentices of the Maoming Silk Factory, sharing their desire to learn how to machine embroider the gorgeous delicate silks that came from the Southern Guangdong Province. The

Maoming Silk Factory's clothing, coverlets, draperies and tablecloths were becoming increasingly popular in the West, thus the need for their skills.

Baak-Hap and Chung were first cousins and as close as sisters. Their intimate whispers had never intimidated Ying Fa; and they were glad to work together on the same factory floor.

However, she missed working beside Hsiao, her dreamy best friend, and now her sister-in-law, who had not been chosen for the special training because she couldn't concentrate.

Until about six months ago, Hsiao had been a silk weaver in another wing of the factory; but she'd kept making mistakes. Her family, who exerted great power in the city, had arranged for her transfer to a nearby social welfare institute, fearing the silk fibers made her vulnerable to colds; and considered caring for babies a few hours a day a healthier alternative.

The slight smile on Baak-Hap's plump face told her that she had already heard about Anji. Chung's narrow eyes, bright and watchful, studied Ying Fa as if looking down the end of a chopstick. Like Ying Fa, the girls wore dark trousers, black shoes and white blouses. Their faces shone from scrubbing.

Ying Fa laughed as she slipped between the girls, catching each one's arm, sure of her welcome. Chung's feigned scorn belied her generosity.

"So, Hsiao had a boy," Baak-Hap said blandly as she leaned on Ying Fa for support. A glint of jealousy and resentment flashed in the depths of her beautiful, sad eyes. Her older sister was pregnant again; desperately hoping for a boy after the last two mistakes had been quietly taken away. Ying Fa's heart went out to her childhood friend, but knew better than to speak of it. Such a shameful topic should never be broached.

"He's so skinny and quiet," Ying Fa said, still smiling. It was best not to tempt fate with the happy truth; its very utterance juicy bait for bad luck. She shuddered, imagining Anji being carried away. Such events were commonplace, yet never discussed. The thought was intolerable on such an auspicious day.

She flipped her hair back with one angry motion and picked up her pace, the sound of Anji's angry wail still resounding in her ears. Everyone in the complex would know by now that Anji was a greedy one, soon to be spoiled by Zhaodi's indulgence. He was a precious gift—the cement that would bind Hsiao far tighter to the Wong clan than any useless daughter.

Chung patted her arm in mock consolation. "Hsiao must be beside herself," she said, her deep voice made nearly inaudible by the blare of traffic. "And your mother?"

"I have a headache already from her complaints." Ying Fa grimaced. "You know how she can be." The girls laughed.

They gripped her arms tighter as they sped around the corner and then ran together to the factory compound, their legs pumping, their shiny hair bouncing.

The compound had once been the home of an aristocratic family. A high brick wall surrounded it. Two plump mulberry trees, the symbol of the factory, guarded its entrance.

Ying Fa squinted at the walls, imagining as she often did the busy family who had once lived inside: elders, babies, titled ladies and gentlemen; the eager servants scurring about while the family lay in delicious indolence. She imagined them thriving within its protective walls, enjoying the petty politics and jealousies that were inherent with living in such close, comfortable confines. As always, she kept these dangerous and old-fashioned thoughts to herself. Reminders of her own family's past happiness in such a setting would be unwise.

The girls arrived a half hour early, as was expected by Li Zuomin, the factory manager and their Communist Party Boss. He liked to be called Manager Li, though many called him "the Boss" behind his back, thinking this granted him some semblance of honor. She knew first hand that he scorned such flattery.

Manager Li ran twenty factories, choosing to begin his rounds each day at hers. He chaired many committees, chiefly those dealing with city management. Rumor had it that he was Maoming's number-three man, an important member of the inner circle. He held no favorites and trusted no one, including his powerful wife, Mrs. Li. Father had once said, in a mood of whispered confidences, that she'd maneuvered her way up the Party ladder by snatching choice committee positions and nurturing important relationships with the wives of other Party Bosses, and with the threat of her husband's powerful name.

Manager Li liked to postulate each morning on some essential mindset; but he always commented on his pleasure in seeing China's workers expressing enthusiasm for their jobs. Thus, given the scarcity of well-paying employment, the girls arrived early each day as a way to show their gratitude and respect.

Ying Fa, sandwiched between the two girls, lowered her gaze as she strode into the factory compound, seeing Tsang Anwei, the only son of Mrs. Fa, her next-door neighbor, standing at attention at his guard post, nearly handsome in his green officer's uniform. Starched and solemn, his round, hungry face was bright with sweat. He stared at her with abject longing—fool that he was.

His mother, Mrs. Fa, from the Shanghai Fas, had come to Maoming as a young girl, submitting to an arranged marriage to the much older Mr. Tsang, a minor official in the Communist Party. Mr. Tsang had died shortly after Anwei's birth; and she'd devoted much of her life to raising her sturdy son, the love of her life and her hope for a secure future.

Too bad the man was an idiot.

How could she possibly join his family, her own Wong family name becoming an appendage, a reminder of her subservience to his stodgy Tsang clan? She'd heard that in the west, women actually took their husband's family names, eliminating their past altogether.

In China, one could never eliminate the past.

Listening to Baak-Hap and Chung giggle as they slipped into the courtyard beside her, her mood turned decidedly dark. Acting like a silly monkey, Chung cast Anwei a sidelong glance and nudged her as if to transfer some of his attention onto herself.

It took all of Ying Fa's restraint to keep from rolling her eyes. Any display might encourage the oaf. "He's looking at you," she said through clenched teeth, making Chung giggle louder, one hand pressed to her reddening face. "You could do a lot worse, my friend."

Though Tsang Anwei brought honor to his family with his postion, and was certainly worthy of a girl's interest, she couldn't erase the memory of him soiling his pants in primary school and being dragged out crying by the teacher, a loss of face from which he had never recovered, as far as she was concerned.

She wasn't about to follow her mother's dictates and encourage him. Too bad he had such a nice mother. Mrs. Fa was a lovely, charming woman, who engaged her in conversation each time they shared the kitchen.

She shuddered, thinking of Anwei's thick fingers grazing her skin, his flacid childlike mouth pressed against hers, and sighed deeply. He was such a miserable little man, with no hope in her direction. Feeling sorry for him, she lifted her chin and smiled, positioning her gaze somewhere to the left of his face; and then sucked in her breath as bright red spots appeared on his cheeks, lighting his moon-like face. Like a child's doll, he nodded furiously and his eyelids creased into lines of joy.

She jerked her chin away in disgust, and with a few gentle shoves, guided her friends to their places in the courtyard. Anwei knew that her day off was Tuesdays. He'd try to finagle the same. Then he'd start following her around on her marketing errands and eat into her precious afternoons like an over weight water buffalo. It was all too horrible to contemplate.

She gazed around the courtyard, knowing by the quickly averted faces that most of the male workers had had her in their line of vision. Their beady, crab-like faces sickened her. Not one of them had even a shred of appeal. Couldn't they leave her alone?

Ignoring them all, she looked around the wondrous old compound and imagined herself its wealthy mistress, plotting revenge, sending them scurrying for cover. She'd call down the guards and have every one of them carted away for daring to look so boldly.

She straightened her shoulders, thinking of scholars on their knees, desperate for a single look; and then later, watching them recite their poems extolling her beauty to an enthralled emperor.

Her eyes cleared and she saw the drab walls that marked the confines of her existence, the broad entrance of the compound at the street end, and above it the administrative offices. Two long, parallel wings housed the factory floors, with the embroidery room on the ground floor to the left, and the assembly room above it. The opposing wing housed the weaving room on the second floor with the warehouse below it. The dining hall and bathrooms were located at the base of the courtyard, above which was a large conference room used for meetings. She'd never been inside. The barren courtyard, in which they all stood, was scrupulously clean. She breathed deeply, imagining it carpeted with a maze of pink-tipped peonies.

Morning exercises were about to commence; and even now, sleepy workers were lining up for inspection.

This was no time for daydreams. She pulled pins from her embroidery case and secured her hair, glad to have remembered them at the last moment. She was no longer a child needing her grandmother's reminders. She donned her hair net, as did the other silk embroiderers, who were just arriving for the shift.

A bright patch of sky suddenly drew her attention. Far above, the wind whipped toward the sea, leaving a clear spot in the hot June sky. The sight of it stirred an indefinable longing in her heart. Her brother, Yutang was always saying that she was too romantic, too naive. He teased that she was overly affected by the movies that came out of Hong Kong these days.

He was right, though she'd never admit it. She often fantasized about being Maria, dancing the hills of *The Sound of Music*, yearning for something beyond her reach. Like that patch of blue.

She shook her head slightly and pouted. Was she jealous of Hsiao's happiness? No, that wasn't it. As Anji's mother, Hsiao deserved to be treasured. That she'd settled on Yutang for a husband was punishment enough. Yutang had a craving for women that Hsiao could never satisfy.

She'd never be called wife if she had to settle as Hsiao had done. Though Hsiao appeared happy, she'd had to subjugate herself to fit in, to live her life as wife and daughter-in-law, and now mother.

She touched her trouser waistband, checking that her blouse was tucked in, feeling eyes watching. It took so little to set men off. Even her cautious check was probably being observed.

She wanted a man who was capable of holding a conversation, a man eager for adventure, which didn't describe even one of the men she knew. Was something wrong with her? Was she expecting too much?

Hsiao had Anji; and Zhaodi her perfect submissive daughter-in-law, an old-fashioned girl who'd bestow upon her the respect that she craved—that Ying Fa had never provided.

Zhaodi was to retire soon and finally, she had everything that her heart had ever desired. But what about her own daughter? What had she done to earn her mother's disdain?

"What's wrong?" whispered Baak-Hap, her eyes narrowed with concern.

Ying Fa smiled and shook her head slightly. "Nothing. I was just thinking about my brother."

"Oh, the skirt-chaser," Baak-Hap said, wrinkling her nose. Ying Fa stifled a laugh.

A few years ago, Baak-Hap had seen straight through Yutang's slippery charm. She'd laughed at his single undisguised attempt at her virginity, saying that his interest wouldn't last much past the first bedding; that there were plenty of bored housewives who'd love what he had to offer. Baak-Hap had brought Hsiao to tears more than once with her angry tirades.

Ying Fa looked down at the ground sharply. Such talk spoke ill of her elder brother, Hsiao and her entire family; though it was no secret that Yutang was a braggart and a playboy, always looking to advance himself. Sadly, Hsiao was learning to suffer in silence. In the end, her little son would give her more than Yutang ever could.

She stood taller, straightening her shoulders, and then dropped her arms, palms at her sides, seeing Manager Li step from behind the guard station and nod in Anwei's direction. Thickset, with a bulging stomach, Manager Li was one of the few people whose very presence could eliminate her laughter. His skin was dark and swarthy from years of hard work under the open sky. His sparse hair was gray, lank and stringy. His dead black eyes, scaning the courtyard like a shark in the depths of the sea, missed nothing.

Her grandmother once described him as ruthless in his pursuit of balance—for himself. The Cultural Revolution had destroyed his elder brother, a highly respected college professor in Beijing, while he'd profited in both wealth and status. His great misfortune had come during the government crackdown at Tien'anman Square, when his two swarthy sons had been killed.

She lowered her gaze as he approached, the spit drying in her mouth. Her heart raced, as he looked her over. Even after he moved on she remained as still as a stone. She'd seen him turn and look once, well after he'd moved on, trying to catch her unawares. She'd recently caught him looking at her with a sick longing that portly old men seemed to exhibit. Despite his power and wealth, she wasn't interested. She wouldn't marry at all, if it came to that.

What she craved was a man who could laugh—a young man who wanted to be with her, who returned her love. No angry, lecherous old man could ever meet that need.

Manager Li liked to look at all the pretty girls, sometimes going as far as touching what he should not. Poh Poh maintained that he was in love with his brother's haughty widow, Chan Yanru, who had once been beautiful. Perhaps, like many of the older men of her acquaintance, Manager Li was simply attracted to her lucky face.

Lucky? There was nothing lucky about having a pretty face, though Zhaodi claimed it was her finest attribute.

"For what?" she had asked her mother one day. "To attract Li Zuomin, a married man—what's the future in that?"

Zhaodi had remained silent: she had never been a beauty. If displeased, Manager Li could strip their family's prospects to nothing.

13

Although she liked to argue with her mother, she had always bowed to the prevailing wind, if only to assure herself and her family of a promising future. To do otherwise would be foolhardy; and she'd always trusted her elders to know what was best for her.

Despite what Zhaodi said, she had no illusions about her looks. Unlike movie actresses who were sleek and pretty, she had the figure of a peasant. And she was no one to show off. While brash Yutang lit up a room, she was content to tread discreetly around the edges; gathering ripples of smiles in her wake as she charmed one person at a time.

Like all good schoolchildren, she had spent her upper school summers lugging water, pulling weeds, and feeding the ducks at a remote farm. She'd learned humility by smiling eagerly through her toil, though every muscle in her body had ached to the point of snapping like so many twigs. Memories of the city, its smells, conveniences, noises and many delights, had silenced her complaints. She'd quickly discovered that those who did complain were rewarded with more of the same.

She couldn't keep her mind from wandering during Manager Li's droning lecture about the benefits of hard work. Distracted, she watched the night shift file silently through the courtyard and out the main entrance, their shoulders drooping, their eyes downcast, lest they earn Manager Li's notice.

What new project would Forewoman Chen assign to her today? The slight weight of the embroidery case in her pocket lifted her spirits. Maybe she'd work on children's robes or elaborate purses.

She loved working with the bright threads, sewing stitch-by-stitch, creating palates of beauty against a background of fine silk. It was a dream come true, far beyond her meager aspirations; and she was secretly thrilled that her small talent contributed to the family's income. By spring, they'd have enough saved for a motorbike or a telephone or both. Poh Poh would decide—for it was she who controlled the family's funds and made the most important decisions.

Manager Li gestured to one of the floor foremen, a skinny nervous man, who led them in a brief exercise program. When it was over, the foreman signaled the beginning of their day.

Ying Fa glanced up in time to see a slender young man following Manager Li through the doorway. Had he crept into the courtyard after the night crew; or had he been standing behind them all along? She looked at Chung questioningly.

"That's his nephew," Chung said, taking her arm. The gossip buzzed around them as they filed toward the embroidery room.

They'd been hearing for weeks about Manager Li's nephew, a recent graduate from the university in Beijing. After a year of string pulling, Li Gwai Ha was to become Manager Li's newest assistant. A Young Pioneer from the earliest grade, Gwai Ha was also a member of the Communist Party. While Manager Li's sons caused trouble in Beijing, Gwai Ha had applied himself, earning travel privileges to Changsha, Shanghai, Guangzhou and even to Hong Kong. Destined to manage his own factories, Gwai Ha required only an apprenticeship, which his uncle eagerly provided. Once back in Maoming and under his uncle's Party leadership, however, it was unlikely that he would ever be reassigned.

She regretted not seeing his face, half-remembering an older boy with a bored expression, his mother's darling, who'd gone to one of the better elementary schools on the other side of the city. Hsiao had gone to school with him for a few years, but had few memories of any encounters.

Ying Fa had caught a glimpse of him once or twice at the market; he'd been trailing his beautiful, icy mother, Chan Yanru. She had faint recollection of a delicate feminine hand raising a plump papaya to sniff; and then in an instant, her porcelain-perfect face transformed into an opera mask of horrible porportions, as she shrieked something in her Guangzhou accent about the quality of fruit in fifth-rate Maoming.

According to Poh Poh, she'd always been hard to please. Poh Poh knew her family from Guangzhou, where both women had been born and raised. Like Poh Poh, Mrs. Chan was a mahjong enthusiast. Each Wednesday night for the past two years, a small circle of women had taken turns hosting the game. With Gwai Ha at university, Mrs. Chan had taken a meager one-room apartment, quarters too small for mahjong—though according to Poh Poh, it was an excuse. She was covering up for the lack of housekeeping skills.

Upon Gwai Ha's return, she had supposedly obtained better quarters. Rumors were flying that Manager Li was conferring with a matchmaker concerning his esteemed nephew. With his sons now dead, his own mortality was like a painful boil, only to be lanced by the birth of a grandnephew. His elder brother's two daughters, as with all female relatives, were of no consequence. He needed a male child, even if it came from his elder brother's line.

Her own options were slim by comparison; matters such as these beyond her ken. Traveling to Beijing was a dream that would never come true. She considered herself fortunate to have made it as far as Huazhou; though like Gwai Ha, she'd done well in school. She'd even been a Young Pioneer in her youth, just as he had. But her income had been needed to help finance Yutang's expenses while he'd trained at Changsha's top auto mechanic school; so her education had come to an abrupt halt before she'd finished upper school.

It had been Poh Poh's decision. Wanting to please her, she'd quickly complied, telling herself that it was an honor to have a skilled trade, to be valued for her abilities. If only Yutang didn't lord it over her so much.

She took one last glimpse of the sky overhead, then entered the embroidery hall, grateful for another precious day of employment. According to Zhaodi, many uneducated girls her age turned to forced farm labor, or worse.

She took a deep breath as she scanned the familiar room. Large windows lined the courtyard-facing side, though the weak sunlight barely filtered through. Smaller windows were sparcely placed along the austere outer wall, to protect the privacy of those within. Near the door, but well away from the wall, was the forewoman's stark wooden desk, outfitted with a telephone and a filing cabinet. From the lofty ceiling above, wires dropped down to the several row of industrial embroidery machines. At the room's far end were several tables well laden with stacks of supplies, boxes of shimmering fabrics and baskets of color-coded skeins.

She closed her eyes briefly, visualizing a great hall surrounded by several comfortable apartments. She smelled incense and perfume. Placed here and there were exquisite lacquered tables laden with succulent dishes. Soft music slowed the pulses of lounging ladies draped in embroidered silks, flirting behind delicately painted fans. Bold courtiers stood about preening, brandishing glasses of ruby red wine in bejeweled hands. Servants padded in, carrying swaddled babies to adoring grandmothers.

She smiled to herself. Though life as it had existed during the classic period would never return to modern China, she dared to imagine it into existence. She moved, floating, as if she were an exquisite courtesan or a high official's treasured third wife. She smiled, bowing slightly, and took the project instruction sheet held out by Forewoman Chen.

She smiled slightly at the crafty old woman, who was about Zhaodi's age. Chen Ming was quick to find fault and quicker to gossip, and not one to indulge in the practice of imagination.

"Hsiao delivered? Everyone's healthy?" she asked in a harsh tone, her thin lips stretching into the semblance of a smile. It was said that she had turned bitter after her adoring young husband had died of cancer. Besides being left childless, she'd become the sole caretaker of a blind and ailing father-in-law.

She liked to think of Chen Ming as clever and strong, like a wary rat, a true survivor; and was proud to have made her laugh twice. Like Zhaodi, she appreciated complaint-filled theatrics.

"He cries and cries," Ying Fa said, shaking her head and frowning deeply. "I don't know how we'll survive it. He is such a noisy one."

"And Hsiao?" The forewoman's eyes were bright with interest.

"Weak as a two-day-old fish. She keeps us running with her endless demands. Get me soup. Get me a blanket." She mimicked the forewoman's smile and leaned forward slightly, her hands on her hips, unable to imagine her passive sister-in-law demanding anything. Endlessly apologetic, Hsiao's sweetness drew no one's attention.

"She'll be as fine as first caught squid," Forewoman Chen said and patted Ying Fa's arm. "As rich as spicy shrimp," she muttered. Then her expression darkened as she glanced out the open door.

Was Manager Li on his way?

"What is today's project?" Ying Fa asked quickly, gripping her instructions tightly, not daring to look at them.

"Children's robes," the forewoman hissed with a dismissive nod. She turned to Chung, looking annoyed, and handed her her instructions. "Pillow cases for you," she spat.

Chung's expression didn't change, though Ying Fa caught the slight downward turn of her mouth. In spite of the extra training, Chung had never managed to proceed beyond pillowcases, and even then, she struggled.

Ying Fa moved away fast, seeing the envy in her eyes.

Children's robes! It was a plum of a project, a sure sign of Chen Ming's confidence. She quickly buried her excitement, fearing she'd attract more jealousy as she headed to the supply area.

Amidst the chattering women, she plucked a basket from a heap on the floor and filled it with skeins. A timid stock girl followed her to her station, toting a box of robe backs.

Barely able to contain herself, her mind raced in anticipation of the project. The instructions were simple. She'd start by embroidering the backs, and then the front lefts, and finally the front rights. It was someone else's job to assemble the jackets and add the padded linings and the piping. The robes were designed in the traditional style, with frog fasteners replacing the more modern buttons, snaps or hook and eye closures that many factories used these days. It continually amazed her that before the Cultural Revolution little girls had gone blind sewing the neat, tiny stitches all by hand.

"It's a shame, really," whispered Baak-Hap, her face glowing with knowledge. She sat at a machine beside Ying Fa.

"What?" Ying Fa looked at her sharply.

"The nephew. The nephew. Where are you in that pretty head of yours?" Baak-Hap hissed as she shook her head. "Li Gwai Ha is his family's pride and joy now," she whispered. "Some say he's Manager Li's unacknowledged son, especially with the other two now gone."

"Do you think so?" Ying Fa asked. She'd heard the same from her grandmother, but couldn't picture Gwai Ha's mother stooping to become her brother-in-law's mistress. The Chan family of Guangzhou was a powerful clan: they'd thrived even during the Cultural Revolution.

She dropped several skeins into her lap, ticking off each color according to the instructions, hoping Baak-Hap would continue. Her story was far from new, but the telling infused an element of excitement into their well-ordered day.

20

She winked at Baak-Hap, then swiftly and thoroughly inspected her machine's glossy surface and the floor around it for any telltale signs of the previous night's efforts. The night crew had swept the floor and dusted her station, leaving not even a single thread to mar her work.

Chung dropped her basket beside her station in the next row and looked around furtively. "It is said that as a young man, Manager Li fell in love with his beautiful fourth cousin, Chan Yanru." Blessed with an expressive deep voice and graceful gestures, Chung was a born storyteller. The women around her exchanged pleased smiles, and glanced at her encouragingly as they prepared their machines.

Chung acknowledged them with slight smile. "Though Chan Yanru was in love with Li Zuomin," she continued, "she married his elder brother Li An, a university professor in Beijing and the pride of his family."

Ying Fa shook her head slightly. It was easy to accept Manager Li's betrayal, yet difficult to imagine a beautiful, haughty young woman like Chan Yanru had once been, truly in love with him. As with Anwei's childhood accident, how could one romanticize such realities as Manager Li's dark fleshy jowls, and the reek of his oily overripe body?

"Meanwhile, Manager Li was sent to Shanghai to manage his family's silk warehouse," Chung continued. "He was an angry man, a man of passion, undaunted by such a setback. Then it all fell apart. The Cultural Revolution had begun." Chung paused, her bright eyes gauging her rapt audience. "Books were torched. Teachers were maimed, if not killed outright, and their possessions confiscated. Chan Yanru fled Beijing. Desperate for shelter, she walked hundreds of miles, going beyond exhaustion. Month after month she pulled Li An, her beloved battered husband, behind her in a cart, desperate to reach his family's home in Maoming. Along the way, she lost track of her daughters, casting their fates to the winds. Yet despite her care, Li An never recovered. He died several years later, mindless and broken."

"It's as my grandmother says," Ying Fa whispered, glancing around through lowered lashes, trying to encourage her. Though heads were bowed over stations, not a few bright, curious eyes glinted in Chung's direction as the women threaded their machines.

"We knew of Gwai Ha as a child," Ying Fa said, after a few minutes. "Hsiao did, at least. He was an older boy, well liked by everyone, though a little on the skinny side. His mother was beautiful and doted on him too much."

"It is said that she still keeps tabs on him," Chung said with a smirk. "Even now, with her in Guangzhou and him here in Maoming, she mails him every day."

Forewoman Chen shot Chung a warning glance, thus putting an end to the morning's tale.

Blushing furiously, hoping she hadn't earned the forewoman reproach, Ying Fa reached for a scrap of silk.

Li Gwai Ha was probably haughty and distant like his mother. He'd never look in her direction. Poh Poh had heard that he was a wiz at computers, a veritable genius, and the only person his uncle would trust with the factory's books now that Beijing wanted everything computerized. Li Gwai Ha was something of a mythical figure: handsome, intelligent and worldly. Some lucky girl would catch his eye; or his uncle would find him a wife. The ensuing romance would provide them with stories for years to come.

She sighed deeply. When would her special someone appear? Marrying some local guy, moving in with him and his assorted family, bearing the requisite son, and then trotting back to her job held no appeal. Maybe like girls in ancient China who refused a husband, she'd chop her hair even shorter and retreat to the confines of her apartment. Was she destined to live her whole life just listening to stories of other people's adventures?

Considering the other women on the factory floor, who like her, were grateful for a job, never mind a skilled job that paid fairly well, she had little hope of advancement. Romance was but a dream, an elusive, golden thread she could only imagine. Perhaps Gwai Ha wasn't half as delicious as he sounded. But it didn't hurt to dream; and there was no need to feed bitter thoughts. How could she be sad with the choicest of projects right on her lap? The colors alone would lift anyone's spirits. Who cared about this Li Gwai Ha?

She grinned, suppressing a giggle, though she wanted to laugh aloud, fling her arms out and dance across the room in wild jubilation.

He was probably a spoiled playboy, a narrow-fingered aristocrat who had never done a hard day's work in his entire life. He'd probably never been shipped off to work at a farm.

She looked up to see the forewoman's pursed lips, and returned to her work. She scanned the whispy pattern on the silk, chose a starting point and then lowered the needle. Work was what she needed—steady, reliable, invigorating work. Taking a deep breath, she focused on the thread.

She hummed as she slipped into her usual trance, beginning with yellow—pure sunshine against crimson silk. Her hands flew as she daydreamed, her mind drifting to the beach, where tiny brown crabs skittered across fine amber sand. The sparkling sun glinted upon the surface of clear green water, its spray cool and inviting. The China Number One Beach was her favorite destination on her days off. Too bad the cost of a taxi ride relegated it to a once-a-month excursion.

Soon she would make her monthly pilgrimage. She'd stroll in the salty cool waters of the South China Sea, breath in the damp air and watch the tiny fishing boats bob against the horizon. A deep satisfaction washed over her as a silken yellow bird grew bold and curious beneath her hands.

She stopped her machine now and then, changing threads from green to aqua, and then to purple, while intricate flowers grew large and audacious for her treasured bird to admire. Over and over her hands moved with expert timing as a pile of finished backs grew on the small table beside her.

Then a shadow obscured her light. Startled, she looked up into the most exquisitely handsome face she had ever seen. The young man's black eyes glinted with laughter. They were mischievous demon eyes that held the promise of both danger and knowledge. His smooth cheeks bloomed roses, framing the broad, flat planes of his long sculpted face. She swallowed hard and looked at his hands. They were perfectly formed, with elegantly tapered fingers and well-manicured nails. Scholar's hands.

She could only look at him, her work forgotten.

Then he smiled shyly, like a naughty boy; and she giggled.

She gasped. In the shadow behind him was Manager Li.

Her hands fluttered over her work, yet she could barely think. What thread should she use? What picture had she been working on?

Manager Li's usually passive face wore an indulgent expression that quickly gave way to sick gloating. Confused, she hung her head and tried to return to work. He had caught her daydreaming. Was he a mindreader?

It came to her that the young man could be none other than Li Gwai Ha, the manager's infamous nephew. Of course, he would never be interested in a sturdy worker such as she. Chung would be more to his liking, or a Hong Kong fashion mode, or better yet, a dazzlingly beautiful actress whose looks would compare favorably to his.

Manager Li coughed loudly, causing her to look up.

"She's one of those we sent to Huazhou," he said softly, yet loud enough for her to hear. "A worthy investment."

An investment? Was that how he saw her? But it was true. Without her skill, she was nothing to him—nothing without the gift of training that he had so benevolently bestowed—for which she was grateful.

Her cheeks flamed, yet she dared peek once more at the marvelous young man. He stood beside his shorter uncle, nodding in response to his clipped remarks. There was unmistakable warmth between the two men.

Or was there?

She looked closely, noting the young man's rigid shoulders, the way he bowed slightly.

Her heart beat furiously as she opened the box of left sides that a harried stock girl had dropped beside her station some time ago. The men continued their conversation, their voices a low rumble against the whine and whir of the embroidery machines.

A strange, pleasurable glow warmed her belly, as she looked through lowered lashes at Gwai Ha's silky, black, short-cropped hair, reminded of his modest, half-apologetic smile. She blushed, imagining him sneaking a glance at her.

Were they talking about her? She didn't dare look up from her work.

Another stock girl came to remove the stack of finished backs; and she helped her heft the box over to the door, and smiled her thanks. When she'd returned to her seat, the men were gone.

Sighing deeply, she looked over at Baak-Hap, surprised by the avid speculation on her friend's lovely face. Blushing furiously, she grabbed a yellow skein and threaded her machine.

Chapter 2

As the morning progressed, Ying Fa half-expected the manager's nephew to reappear. But Manager Li must have assigned him to another floor or another factory. The manager came by once, but didn't linger, as was his habit. His gaze was cursory, albeit speculative, making it difficult to concentrate.

The lunch hour passed without the nephew in sight—just the usual scurry for tea and yum-cha at the lunch-vendor's stalls. She concentrated on the light meal of sausage and cabbage-filled steamed buns, ignoring the din of car horns, bicycle bells and the excited chatter of her over imaginative friends, unable to shake the vision of a pair of bright black eyes. Her friends teased her and she laughed along with them, certain that nothing would come of Li Gwai Ha's strange interest. What was a lowly machine embroiderer to a man of his prospects?

She buried herself in her work that afternoon, glorying in the vivid, delicate butterflies that grew bold beneath her needle. With a few pauses to exchange finished pieces for supplies, the afternoon passed quickly.

In contrast, the lingering final hour of her shift seemed interminable, though she managed to finish all three boxes of silk, earning the forewoman's pleased nod. The stock girls were already gathering stray threads, organizing baskets, straightening boxes and disinfecting the floor for the night shift.

She rubbed the ache at the small of her back as she filed out of the embroidery room with the other women and stretched her neck to ease its stiffness. With a slight tap of her pocket to ensure the safety of her embroidery case, she stepped through the door. Careful not to distract the next shift, now listening to Manager Li's speech, she and the other woman filed silently through the courtyard.

She could only glance at Manager Li's bland and frightening face, sensing his critical regard as she moved past him. Would his day end with this speech, or would he work late into the night, or attend a meeting. It was said that he rarely went home to his ugly wife. And where was his nephew? Would he go home to Mrs. Chan, or did he live with his uncle?

Outside the main door, she let her shoulders sag, and then chided herself. Li Gwai Ha was far above her. She'd never see him again except in passing. She smiled softly at Chung who patted her arm in consolation.

At least the day was over; and she could look forward a pleasant evening with her grandmother, Hsiao and Anji. Her parents had the following day off and were going out for the evening, while Yutang was driving Maoming's number-two Party official to a special meeting on park sanitation. He wouldn't be home until well past midnight.

"See you tomorrow!" she shouted to her friends; and waved to them as they walked hand-in-hand toward the market. Unlike her, they had no kind grandmother to do their shopping.

Her mouth watered, already tasting her grandmother's prawn patties in crabmeat sauce and spicy fried squid. Poh Poh liked to make her favorite foods when the others went out for the evening.

She waited at the corner to cross, spying a dark blue car parked on one of the less-busy side streets. Its engine was running, the back passenger window lowered.

She took a second glance and her jaw dropped.

Gwai Ha, looking boyish with a huge grin, stuck his head out the window. "Come on!" he shouted. "Come for a ride! I've got my uncle's car all evening!"

"Me?" she asked, looking around. Her heart pounded as she approached him. Such boldness so near a busy street was unspeakable. She could barely breathe. She looked around, hoping her friends had already slipped into the crowds.

"Of course, silly." His laugh was deliciously masculine. It sent chills up her spine. "Come along with me and get some fresh air?" His head was tipped slightly like an eager boy. "You're Wong Ying Fa, right?" he asked, smiling into her eyes, melting her heart.

"I can't," she said, picturing Poh Poh hurt and angry if she arrived late. "Go with you? How can I go with you?" she muttered under her breath. He'd probably had his pick of Beijing girls, and was looking for an easy conquest. His laughter was loud, brash and enchanting. Had he had learned such untenable behavior in Beijing?

She pictured her grandmother adding rice to the steamer; her movements slow in anticipation of her imminent arrival. Who'd carry the fragrant bowls of food from the kitchen up to their apartment? Not Hsiao. She'd just delivered Anji that morning.

"What about your uncle?" she asked, her curiosity getting the better of her as she leaned closer to the car, shouting so he could hear her above the passing traffic. "He has to go home sometime."

She blushed, seeing the driver glance back at her. He was a friend of Yutang's and sure to gossip.

"He doesn't need it," he said with a sly smile, glancing down at the car. "He's working late tonight. He's scheduled to attend a Park Sanitation meeting at the Maoming Building. Then, later, he'll be entertained."

As he uttered the last statement, his gaze slide away, and she realized he was referring to prostitutes, who were often in abundance at the Maoming Building for just such an event. Built by the Russians in the forties, the Maoming Building was tall and glitzy, a four-star hotel that offered the best entertainment in Maoming City. After dark, many lovely girls practiced the ancient pleasure arts within its solid walls.

Six days a week Zhaodi labored as a dim sum cook in the hotel's fancy breakfast room; and liked to poke fun at her hotel's entertainment customs, sometimes threatening Ying Fa with such a fate whenever she argued or complained. She spoke of gorgeous girls dancing to erotic music while patrons sipped tea and ate her tasty dumplings; and hinted at other bawdy things that went on, supposedly in secret.

"Please, Miss Wong, I'm all alone," Gwai Ha pouted "My mother's visiting a sick aunt in Guangzhou, and won't be back for a few weeks. I just got here, and I don't know anyone."

He caught her wrist with his elegant hand; and she backed away, shocked by his audacity.

"I can't," she repeated and pulled away, hoping he didn't think Maoming girls gave themselves away so cheaply. She was a nice girl from a good family. Though she knew about men and sex, she'd had no actual experience.

"My grandmother's expecting me any minute," she stammered, her cheeks aflame at the thought of sitting beside him in the back of his uncle's car.

"Some other time," he said, nodding in approval, his gaze boring into hers with a curiosity that matched her own. "Your next day off, perhaps," he said with a smile. "And that is . . . ?"

She smiled slyly. "Figure it out for yourself," she said, raising her chin. "After all, you're the one with the university education."

"Suit yourself," he said with a shrugged, and then gestured to the driver and waved at her as the car pulled away from the curb.

Chapter 3

In three quick days, the full moon came and the seventh month began. Ying Fa found that her laughter bubbled easily. Her gaze darted about each working hour in search of a pair of jet eyes. She spied him twice: at the start of the Monday morning ritual and on Tuesday, across a crowded rice-plate restaurant. Both times his gaze had caught and lingered. Hope had built within her until she'd lowered her eyes in pleased embarrassment.

According to Chen Ming, Manager Li kept Gwai Ha hopping, regulating even his visits to the bathroom. Just yesterday, the forewoman had joked that his uncle even had to wipe his bottom, causing all the women to titter. At the forewoman's scowl, the laughter had ceased abruptly. Ying Fa had returned to her work quickly, fearing yet another of the loyalty tests Chen Ming liked to inflict upon the gullible, demotion to stock girl her unvarying threat.

There would be no chance of seeing Gwai Ha today, however: it was her day off.

She rubbed her face and peered around the darkened room she shared with Grandmother, Yutang, Hsiao and

32

now Anjie. Yesterday's sticky heat had not abated with the setting of the sun or the rising of the soot-obscured moon.

She had tossed and turned all night, soaking her nightdress and sheets, in a futile attempt to avoid her grandmother's over-heated body.

She sighed, hoping that Zhaodi would spare her the questions. For three days now, she'd nagged her about getting married. She bit her lower lip, wondering what she should tell her about the manager's nephew. Perhaps she'd only imagined his interest. It was flattering to claim the notice of two decent men, yet at the same time, oddly disconcerting.

"I wish Mother would leave me alone," she whispered as she sat up.

"She just wants you to be happy," Poh Poh said, her voice pleasantly muffled in the dim space behind their privacy curtain. Her grandmother remained supine while she rose and stretched. Since childhood she'd shared her bed with her; and as she'd gotten older, a wardrobe; their love cemented by years of cooled fevers, whispered confidences, and comforted nightmares.

She peeked out at the other screened bed across the room, shared by Yutang and Hsiao, Anji's sturdy crib clearly outlined behind the heavy brocade curtain that hung around it. Another massive wardrobe stood at its foot.

She sighed as she looked down at her grandmother; honored to share space with her esteemed matriarch and beloved Poh Poh, the name she'd called her since infancy; though Zhaodi claimed it was disrespectful, coming from a grown woman. If she only knew that she called her Zhaodi—purely out of love.

While the Cultural Revolution had destroyed the system of family land ownership, it had failed to destroy family fealty where pure love reigned, as it did in her family. With soft words and gentle smiles, Poh Poh did all in her power to ensure that harmony reigned in the Wong family's home.

"Mother starts in on me and I can't even think," she whispered. "I wish she'd accept me as I am."

"She can be loud and abrupt," Poh Poh said with a slight nod, "but she runs this place with efficiency and pride. She's simply looking out for your best interests, my child."

"I know," she said and sighed.

Zhaodi kept the apartment spotless through sheer hard work and strict organization. Her stringent use of three wardrobes, unspoken symbols of the family's illustrious past, helped contain the clutter that was common in many apartments. The wardrobes, two in the main room and one in Zhaodi and Father's room, were cheap replicas of those that had once graced the Wong family compound on the outskirts of the city. Before the Cultural Revolution, the Wongs had been wealthy landowners, who had collected rent and produce from the countryside, as was common at the time.

Strangers now lived in their ancestral home; and the original wardrobes were gone, burned in a heap by the Red Guards, and blown to the four winds.

By the time Zhaodi had married Wong Weigo, Grandmother's only surviving child, life in the family compound had become a fond memory; and it was Grandmother's memory that had helped design the wardrobes' replicas, badly needed in the confines of their apartment.

Unlike most of her friends' apartment, there were no piles of clothes on the floor, no books or papers strewn about. Zhaodi was a stickler for cleanliness and order. Each item found its assigned place, or her stinging words would slice deep, encouraging immediate conformance.

Ying Fa swung open the wardrobe's top doors and inspected herself in its central beveled mirror.

Her face was oily and her hair stringy. She lifted a strand and grimaced.

"If you hurry, you can bathe and wash your hair at the same time," Poh Poh said.

"All right," she murmured, scanning the three pairs of trousers hung neatly beside two flowered dresses and four cotton blouses, a wealth she had purchased with her own allowance.

All were clean because Poh Poh washed their clothes six days a week, maintaining Sunday as her day off—her Christian holiday, kept in honor of the religion she'd secretly clung to since childhood, when the missionaries had offered basic schooling for both boys and girls.

Because the Party looked askance at religion, Poh Poh was secretive about her beliefs in an effort to protect the family from even the mildest threat of persecution.

Poh Poh claimed that one day she'd be rewarded in a place called Heaven, which was probably how she'd transcended the evil that had befallen her with both grace and dignity.

She thumbed through Poh Poh's few clothes that hung beside hers, all gray and black, as befit her age, selected her outfit for the day and set it on the bed. The closet to the left of the mirror contained cooking utensils, bowls, cups, platters, chopsticks and spoons, while the bottom chest of drawers served as the base of the wardrobe. The bottom two drawers were for Poh Poh's treasures.

She pulled out the top drawer, her own private space. "I know she means well," she whispered. She reached inside and found a bra, panties, a pair of dark blue shorts and her sandals. "Why is she so desperate to get rid of me? I don't take up much room. I try to be useful."

"You can't be a spinster," Poh Poh said, shaking her head. "You are ripe at your age, and time moves swiftly. What aren't you saying?"

Ying Fa looked at her shyly. "Won't you miss me?"

"Don't ask stupid questions when you know the answers." Poh Poh's eyes were bright with false anger. There was a hint of laughter in the slight curl of her mouth. "Must I constantly remind you that you are my sweetheart? You already have a swelled head from my endless compliments."

Ying Fa chuckled softly as she collected her toiletries. Between Poh Poh and Zhaodi, she was smothered by love, her every move and decision inspected and challenged. Yutang never attracted even half the attention. Her family was always talking behind her back, and had probably dissected every detail of what had occurred between her and Gwai Ha, and speculated on the rest.

"Who told you about Li Gwai Ha?" she asked, glancing at Poh Poh out of the corner of her eye as she piled her belongings on the bed.

"Both Mrs. Wen and Mrs. Huang told me how he looked at you at the factory and the boldness he showed from his uncle's car." Poh Poh tried to sit up, her hands scrabbling for purchase. "The neighbors knew before me," she moaned, clutching her head. "Such shame, such mortification to endure their gloating. Li Gwai Ha was a difficult boy and his mother's pet. How can you expect me to condone your meeting with him while she's away? How will I face her when she returns from Guangzhou? Her cat's eyes will spark evil that her precious one looked so low. And then there's Anwei's mother, Mrs. Fa." She peered up at Ying Fa. "How will I greet her in the kitchen? You know that she wants you."

Ying Fa smiled to herself, hearing the pride in her criticism.

"Then Mother knows?"

Poh Poh smiled, her chin lowered, her hands covering her mouth slightly as if caught in a lie.

Giggling, Ying Fa clasped her strong, gnarled hands, helping her sit up. Then with great care, she lifted her nightgown over her head and off. Humming softly, she dressed her, while carefully planning her precious afternoon.

Perhaps she'd take a taxi to the beach. She finally had the money for the fare. She saw herself running along the edge of the sand. The beach would be crowded, but not as crowded as the city's markets.

"Going to the beach this afternoon?" Poh Poh asked. She lifted her foot, allowing Ying Fa to slip on a stocking. Poh Poh tired easily these days, and she'd do anything to ease her.

"How did you guess?" she asked, sitting back on her heels.

"You're humming," Poh Poh said, her hand resting gently on her shoulder. "Whenever you think of the beach you hum. I just need you to help stock the refrigerator and food cupboard before you go." She nodded at the small white refrigerator, which stood beside their privacy curtain. It made soft whirring sounds as if it too were content. "I haven't been able to carry much from the market the past few days." She let out a long breath. "Too hot."

"All right, Poh Poh," Ying Fa murmured, and pushed back the heavy curtain. "Whatever you need."

She collected her things, and then helped her grandmother to the bathroom.

The tiny bathroom tucked in beside her parents' small bedroom was outfitted with a sink, toilet and bathtub. Though the white porcelain sparkled, the tight space reeked of night waste from the small basket beside the toilet now brimming with soiled tissue.

Within moments, she had washed and dressed. She selected a comb from the basket beside the tub and pulled it through her tangled hair, turning her back on her grandmother, affording her privacy while she cleaned her false teeth.

The Red Guards had smashed out her front teeth; neglect had taken care of the rest; and she was mortified by the loss. Ying Fa still trembled each time she saw her naked pink gums—stark evidence of her many sacrifices. By placing her needs below those of others, she had led the family through precarious times with her strength alone.

Though the apartment was small, the Wongs had experienced far worse. The past several apartments had been in similar buildings, beginning with a rat-infested tenement near the park. Zhaodi told of beating the rats off her babies the one time she neglected to wash their sticky hands. City planners had razed ir, replacing it with a modern hi-rise—another tree in the growing forest of such buildings.

When Yutang was born, the family had lived for a brief summer in a one-room shanty on the beach—after the Red Guards had burned down their first apartment, part of a dank, listing structure with no heat or running water in what had once been one of their storage barns.

Poh Poh whispered stories of growing up amidst great wealth in Guangzhou—against Zhaodi's stern disapproval, who complained that such tales only added fuel to Ying Fa's imagination, adding to her list of unattainable dreams.

Poh Poh had adored her handsome father, the second son of wealthy landowners. As the fifth daughter, she'd been relegated to serving her aunties delicately spiced dishes as they played mahjong well into the night. Thus began her lifelong love of the game, interrupted only by its ban during the Cultural Revolution.

Beautiful and intelligent, Poh Poh had been seventeen when she'd consummated an arranged marriage with the eldest son of the Wong family in far-off Maoming. In place of foot bindings, she and her sisters and female cousins had not been named, in hopes of making them marriageable. She'd been called Fifth Daughter, and later First Wife, Daughter-in-law, Mother, Mother-in-law and finally Grandmother. Ying Fa smiled down at the woman who sat dozing, swaying gently on the stool beside the tub.

Zhaodi adored her mother-in-law simply because she'd welcomed her, a frightened, clumsy young peasant girl, with kindness and patience. Used to a harsh life of lugging wood, planting rice and sleeping foot to head with her many siblings in an unheated one-room farmers hut, she had been overwhelmed by the petite, well-spoken lady. With a toughness earned from hard times, Poh Poh had married her prized and only child to a laborer's daughter, wisely sparing the family from certain persecution, warranted by their previous wealthy status.

It often gave Ying Fa pause, seeing Hsiao's elegant mother assisting her with clothing and makeup. Zhaodi had no such skills; and Poh Poh, in an effort to protect her daughter-in-law's tender feelings, simply refused to offer her advice.

Taking one last look in the mirror, Ying Fa helped Poh Poh stand. Zhaodi was already banging about the apartment, gathering pots and pans, collecting food to cook in the kitchen downstairs.

Zhaodi's words could be as sharp as lightning; yet her love bathed the household like a gentle rain. Crude and caustic, she was vociferously grateful that she had her own home and shared her own bedroom with her esteemed husband. Their spotless room was just big enough to hold a bed, a desk and a wardrobe. On one small corner table was the family's television—another miracle. Each day before she left for work, Zhaodi would arrange her bed so that her beloved mother-in-law could watch it in comfort.

Ying Fa pulled stray hairs from the comb and dropped them on top of the brimming wastebasket. Then she grabbed the wastebasket and left, carefully closing the door behind her.

Holding her nose, she tiptoed through the main room, seeing in an instant that Zhaodi had already pulled the table away from the wall, placed rice bowls, chopsticks and teacups on its center tile, and arranged six chairs around it—tasks that she was supposed to perform. Zhaodi was probably fuming.

On tiptoes, she sprinted through the apartment's open door, catching the sound of Yutang's murmurs, probably telling Hsiao which clothes to lay out and how to prepare his breakfast. As if she didn't have enough to do. Anji's thin wail sounded as she turned down the hallway. Was he hungry again? He'd been crying just a few hours ago.

At the end of the hallway, she placed the basket on the floor, and then used both hands to lift the lid off the large steel receptacle. Holding her breath, she emptied the basket and then closed the lid with a thunderous boom. It was her least favorite chore, but one assigned to the lowest status family member. Even little Anji commanded higher status now. Maybe it was time she chose a husband.

She caught her breath as she ran back to the apartment. Zhaodi would need her help with breakfast.

"Your father's in there," Poh Poh whispered, nodding toward the bathroom. She sat near the table with mending in her lap.

"Thanks," Ying Fa mouthed, then left the wastebasket outside the door and grabbed a heavy kitchen towel on her way out of the apartment.

"Slowly, slowly," Zhaodi hissed as Ying Fa burst into the kitchen. Hating a public debate, she quickly scanned the room. Aside from Zhaodi, it was empty.

She'd heard from chatter at the factory that all the new apartments being built these days had their own kitchens—a luxury she could hardly imagine. The communal kitchen was a shack tacked onto the building, as if in apology, its floor a cement slab. Running alongside

41

the building was a bench used for meal preparation. Below it were two scrap bins: one for fruits and vegetables, the other for meat. Only spoiled or rotten food was ever discarded. Nothing was ever wasted. The bins had been Zhaodi's idea; and as a member of the Apartment Committee, she'd made sure that they were installed, and also that they were emptied.

Across from the room's inner door, beside the door to the alley, stood an old-fashioned water pump and several buckets. Against the far wall were two industrial gas stoves.

Zhaodi stood in front of one of them, examining a pot of boing water, looking irritated. Rice steamed on another burner. On the bench beside her was a straw basket of eggs and a few smoked fish wrapped in brown paper.

Ying Fa picked up the eggs and dropped them gently into the water. "What do you know about the Li family?" she asked, ignoring her mother's downward curling lips. Smiling, Zhaodi was almost beautiful. She rarely smiled.

Zhaodi looked up sharply. "Courting on street corners? In heavy traffic, like a prostitute? You make us lose face. I thought you were too good for the uncle . . . and now the nephew. And while the mother is away." She shook her head in disgust.

Ying Fa hummed under her breath as she began scaling the two smoked fish, carefully avoiding her mother's disapproving glare.

"Be sure to give only that which is necessary in order to lure the fish," Zhaodi said, her eyes narrowing in speculation. "Don't take less than you deserve, my daughter, or you'll be sorry in the end. We all will."

Ying Fa started at the slight endearment. It wasn't like Zhaodi. But her mother was already lost in thought, her lips pressed tightly together. She took the fish from Ying Fa and with a few deft movements, arranged it attractively on a white glazed platter that was dotted with pickled vegetables.

"We've barely spoken," Ying Fa said, fighting to keep the annoyance from her voice as she dropped the fish skins into the proper bin. "Everyone keeps saying that he's interested, but I don't know . . .."

Zhaodi shot her a tight, knowing smile. "Ah, but looks have been exchanged and he has changed his day off."

"He has?" Barely, just barely, she suppressed a smile.

Zhaodi smirked as she lifted her hand, gesturing for her to check the rice.

Her hand was already on the pot. Exasperation rose like a crested wave at sea, warming her cheeks as it always did with Zhaodi's relentless instructions. Would she forever be the child, the woman in training, never a real woman, competent, worthy of respect?

Gwai Ha changed his day off? She looked at her mother sharply.

"Good morning." Anwei's mother startled them both. Her round face beamed as she stepped through the doorway. She set a large metal platter on the bench with a loud clatter.

"Hello." Zhaodi returned her greeting, her previously tense expression melting into careful friendliness.

Ying Fa smiled shyly, aware of the woman's confident perusal. Did she know of her son's rival? Everyone else in the building seemed to know all about it. Not that Anwei had ever had a chance.

43

"The kitchen is yours," Zhaodi said. She nodded sternly at Ying Fa, gesturing toward the finished meal with her open palm. Ying Fa was already scooping the eggs into the basket, and looping the basket onto her arm and lifting the steamer with the heavy towel. She smiled as Mrs. Fa held open the door.

Like an empress, Zhaodi sailed past, holding her plate of fish aloft as if it were a prized delicacy.

"Thank you, Mrs. Fa." Ying Fa smiled weakly as she followed her mother, and lowered her lashes under Zhaodi's backward glare.

"Next week Anwei begins taking Tuesdays off," Anwei's mother called out as the door closed on her glowing, hopeful face.

"You could do a whole lot worse for a mother-in-law," Zhaodi muttered.

Ying Fa flushed. Why did everyone want her married off? Was Chan Yanru truly the cold witch that everyone claimed, thus raising Mrs. Fa's appeal?

She smiled to herself and lifted her chin. Surely Mrs. Chan could be charmed by a smile. With a son like Gwai Ha, how could she not? Surely the son merely copied his mother's cheerful example.

Following Zhaodi into their apartment, she made quick inventory of the main room as she set the steamer on the table. The family was already seated, anxious to start their day.

She looked around, relishing the small gestures of love and quiet consideration, so ordinary and familiar. Hsiao took the morning paper from Father, then folded it and carried it into Zhaodi's room, leaving it on the bed for Poh Poh to look at later.

Yutang held Anji on his lap; and Hsiao hovered, adjusting a tiny nightdress, patting Yutang's arm. Father sat stiffly his best black suit, indicating an appointment with some high-level official. Would he have stories to tell them later?

"You're just a big kid yourself," Ying Fa said, nudging Yutang, who was making silly baby sounds, trying to engage the newborn.

She set the basket of eggs on the table and began distributing them, one to each bowl.

Poh Poh smiled at Zhaodi as she reached for the teapot, the gracious lady with her teeth now firmly in place. Zhaodi set the platter of fish on the table, then took the teapot from Poh Poh, and gently pushed her into her chair.

"Good morning," Ying Fa murmured, catching Father's eye, nodding first to him and then to Yutang, her daily show of respect. Acknowledging their nods, she moved to her chair across from Father; and winked at Hsiao, who lifted a dainty hand to her mouth, hiding a giggle.

Trying not to smile, Ying Fa peeled an egg, slipped it into Poh Poh's rice bowl, then added rice, fish and pickled vegetables, just the way she liked it. Poh Poh smiled up at her and smacked her lips in anticipatation as she handed her the bowl.

Zhaodi served Father, Hsiao served Yutang, while Ying Fa filled her mother's and Hsiao's bowls; and then served herself last, as was the family's custom.

For several minutes, there was only the sound of chopsticks against crockery, the slurping of tea and the munching of eggs. They passed cruets of soy sauce around and ate their fill in quiet contentment.

Ying Fa smiled across the table, watching her slight, silent father savor the last bite of his breakfast. Though he didn't return her smile, his gaze held a wealth of kindness and concern. Bent and gray, his happiness was her happiness. It didn't matter that he rarely spoke. When she was small, he had often taken her to a nearby bakery for puffy custard rolls or an almond cookie—trips kept secret from over-protective Zhaodi.

She was proud of him, though he was just a lower city official who stamped marriage certificates and similar documents. He was their leader, their patriarch. Even Zhaodi hung on his few words with the eagerness of a child.

Before the Cultural Revolution, a marriage such as her parents–between the eldest son of a wealthy family and a peasant girl–would have been impossible. But the Wong's prospects had been stripped away during that time of terror: with only Zhaodi's lowly family connections granting them peace.

Bright, ambitious Weigo had been in his second year at university in Beijing when he'd been shipped off to a farming commune. For two long painful years, Grandmother had not even known if he was alive. He was her only child, his two younger sisters having died during the great famine of the late fifties. The commune's manager had inflicted such horrors upon him that he did not speak the first six months upon his return. Blind determination had led him home; but sadly, he'd discovered strangers inhabiting his beloved family compound. An old servant had found him, skeletal and crawling with vermin, out of his mind with grief.

He was able to speak of his ordeal for short periods; but any mention of his deceased sisters brought a strange glazed expression to his face; and Poh Poh would begin to cry.

Their refusal to speak of what had happened only fueled her curiosity. She made up stories about her late aunts, imagining them as silk-clad ladies—slim, graceful and lovely. She sometimes caught Father staring at her as if she were a missing object now happily found—but only when Zhaodi wasn't looking. According to Zhaodi, affection toward a daughter was inappropriate and unwise.

Sometimes she'd catch an odd unreadable look on Father's face—dark and shadowed, hiding unspeakable secrets. For many of the men and women of his generation, China's road to Communism had been hard-won. Though he'd never seen a day of battle, the price of China's struggle had been gouged in the harsh lines on his face.

Most of the marriages around her were little more than prison sentences—especially for the women, who worked like a slave to meet their family's needs. Not so with her parents, who shared a rare love. She'd never been able to imagine Father sitting through a floorshow or attending an opera, but he often shared such evenings with Zhaodi.

Zhaodi's eyes sparkled each time she told how she'd brought him to life, with Poh Poh filling in the juicier parts of the story. Newly wed, Zhaodi had been terrified of Weigo's dead eyes, reminded of her three younger brothers, swept into the Red Guards through bloodlust and hate. Yet she'd accepted her marriage, determined to make the best of it.

Under Poh Poh's kind tutelage, she'd shattered Weigo's silence with her body, warming him back to life with her tender caress. According to Poh Poh, the love that had bloomed had been the couple's greatest surprise.

Father held his teacup out to Poh Poh with a nod; and then gestured for Yutang to hand Anji to Zhaodi. They all turned to look at the rosy, plump baby.

Zhaodi swiftly abandoned her teacup and reached for the child with eager hands. For once Anji was quiet, his bottomless stomach filled.

Ying Fa studied his shock of black hair and his round, smooth face, completely captivated. That such a small scrap of humanity could mean so much to her family—it was an unbelievable joy.

Yutang leaned back in his chair. Slim and lanky, he looked like a movie star in his dark blue chauffeur's uniform. Hsiao scurried about, asking soft questions about his preferences for dinner. She straightened his collar and smoothed his hair, while he casually accepted her ministrations.

Ying Fa looked away, embarrassed. Did they have to be so public?

The question in Yutang's eyes alerted her. Warily, she rose and took the teapot from Poh Poh and refilled her cup.

"I hear you've got a new boyfriend," Yutang said, his smile slanting as he dropped his chair onto four legs. "Won't settle for a simple boy like Anwei, eh, Mooi Mooi? Mrs. Fa will be sorely disappointed."

"Mooi Mooi? What am I . . . five?" she cried, detesting the childhood nickname, though she was his little sister. "I asked you to stop calling me that when you got back from school." It had been a simple request, considering that she'd helped pay for his education. She glanced at

Poh Poh, looking for support, but she was busy looking at her plate, her head turned slightly away.

"Which boyfriend?" Zhaodi asked, peering at Ying Fa sharply.

"Mother!" Ying Fa glared at her.

Father looked up from his tea, his eyelids crinkling in amusement.

It wasn't funny, especially with Zhaodi and Poh Poh taking Yutang's side. Again.

"Let your brother talk," Poh Poh said softly as she rose from her chair, her look imploring.

"Does everyone on earth know all about my supposed boyfriend?" Ying Fa flung her eggshells into the basket. "I only spoke to Li Gwai Ha once. Yes, it was in traffic. No, I didn't get in his car." She began gathering the other eggshells, keeping her lashes lowered, her face burning. "Any other questions about my supposed love life, now that you're all so busy making wedding plans?"

"Silence!" Zhaodi cried. Then she glanced at Father as if to solicit his approval. They all looked at him; but he was bent over his tea, as if in contemplation. His shoulders shook slightly. He was laughing.

Zhaodi smiled slightly as Hsiao placed a towel upon her shoulder and lifted Anji onto the towel. Zhaodi rubbed Anji's back absently.

"More is going on than you know," Father said softly, as he lowered his teacup and looked at Ying Fa.

She closed her eyes briefly, and took a deep breath, trying to regain her composure.

"Calm down, little sister," Yutang said, his gesture conciliatory. "I was only teasing. You know how guys talk. Yeah, so his driver got a good look at the two of you and

49

was asking me about it. Every day with the brother-in-law jibes. It's getting really irritating."

"I'm telling you," she said, looking around at her family, "that it's nothing; and I'm tired of your speculation and all too vivid imaginations. So what if the man asked me to go for a ride with him. He's probably on to some other girl by now, someone with more sophistication, more daring. So he asked me to go with him. I said no, and haven't spoken to him since. Why can't you just leave it at that?"

"That's enough," Father said, his expression cool.

Ying Fa looked down at her trembling hands, wishing she'd kept her mouth shut. Father need not concern himself with her petty annoyances. And it was all Yutang's fault. He liked to bait her, and knew just how to get her going.

"We all know what happened," Father said slowly, his tone willing her to lift her head and look at him.

She focused on the kindness and strength in his gaze, and told herself to ignore the ridicule in Yutang's eyes, the humor in Poh Poh's, the rebuke on Zhaodi's face and Hsiao's avid curiosity. If only Hsiao hadn't married Yutang. As best friends, they'd once shared secrets. Hsiao told Yutang everything now, and was his eager slave. Were they all against her, gossiping, creating a flood when there was no rain?

"Your virtue is a family matter," Father said softly. "You are of marrying age and we are aware that Tsang Anwei is less than you expect. The Li's are a good family. If this Gwai Ha interests you, tell us. We will have you married within six months. Marriage is a venerable state and not to be avoided. It is what we would like for both of you." He nodded at Hsaio, who blushed prettily.

Ying Fa dared not speak, honored as she was by his concern. Instead, she bowed slightly, indicating her obedience.

"His mother's away," Zhaodi said. "You have less than two weeks to win him if he's the one you want. She's a tough old bird—difficult and proud. Manager Li's looking for a wife for his nephew, with or without her approval. He has given us his approval."

"He has?" Ying Fa looked up, surprised. "But why the rush? Why two weeks? Why while she's away?"

"Chan Yanru is possessive to the point of obsession," Hsiao said, and then smiled, causing everyone in the family to gaze at her fondly.

Ying Fa wanted to throttle her. Why had she brough this pampered, sweet-mouthed friend into her family's home? She'd met Hsiao at lunch one day, soon after she'd begun her job as a lowly stock girl. Though Hsiao's father was a Party Boss at Manager Li's level, Hsiao had been assigned to the weaving looms; and she'd been assigned to help her. It still amazed her that the well-connected girl had condescended to speak to her at lunch one day. As their friendship had progressed, she'd noticed that Hsiao's modest ways and honey-soft voice pleased both Zhaodi and Yutang.

And now look what was happening? Baby Anji had turned her into an old auntie, the object of pity and ridicule. She'd become a trespasser, a thief whose hand still tumbled among the cabbages. Was marriage her only escape?

Out of the corner of her eye she caught the note of mischief on Yutang's expressive face. Hsiao, her slender hand resting like a pale flag upon his shoulder, mirrored his barely concealed laughter. Probably at her loss of face.

Then as sudden as a slap, her parents' dead seriousness and her own anger struck her as ridiculous. Manager Li approved of the relationship; and he always got what he wanted. Her nose began to twitch. Then her chest heaved as a giggle burst like a painful bubble of gas from her throat; and she laughed.

Then Yutang and Hsiao laughed; and Poh Poh started to laugh. Tears spilled down her wrinkled face, which she hastily wiped with a handkerchief pulled from a trouser pocket. Taking Poh Poh's cue, Zhaodi laughed, too. Then Father, his face shining with mirth, coughed and turned his head away in an effort to regain his dignity.

"I guess you all want what I want," Ying Fa said, grinning. "So why am I fighting you?" Impulsively, she threw her arms around Zhaodi, ignoring her shocked expression.

"All right, you silly girl." Zhaodi shoved her away. "All you want to do is laugh. One day soon, I guarantee you won't find much to laugh about. You'll see. You'll see."

"Aw, Mother," Yutang said. He patted Hsiao's shoulder and headed toward the door. "Why not laugh? It takes her forever to see what a joke she makes of herself."

"And you," Zhaodi said, shooting him a mock wounded look as she collected her purse and string bag of essentials, "always the charmer."

"Come along, husband. She spoke softly to Father who'd stepped back into his bedroom to grab his briefcase. It held a few papers, an extra tie, a pair of socks, a small folding umbrella and a pair of rubber boots, giving him an official look.

"Enjoy your day off," Father said over his shoulder as he followed Zhaodi out of the apartment. "Where are you headed this afternoon?" he asked, turning back, his stance overly casual, his eyes too bright.

"To the beach," she replied, uneasy. He'd never asked such a question. He nodded and was on his way, hurrying to catch up with Zhaodi.

Ying Fa shook her head as she closed the apartment door. The incessant talk about suitors was beyond annoying, especially when she hadn't even been asked out on a date. Maybe she was being overly sensitive. If only she could steer the conversation to other topics.

"Sometimes Yutang jokes too much," she said and moved to Hsiao and put her arm around her shoulder. "I suppose you know all about that. How are you feeling?"

"Better every day, little sister." Hsiao patted her cheek. "As strong as a dragon, as fit as a well-fed rat. I just hope you have that date soon, to wipe that pinched look off your beautiful face."

"Enough with the little sister bit," Ying Fa said, wrinkling her nose. "I'd savor such a date, when and if it should ever take place." She turned her back on Hsiao as she scraped the meal's remainder into a bowl, to be used later for soup. "All by myself. Me alone," she muttered under her breath.

With quick sure movements, she pulled the curtain from around her bed, smoothed the wrinkled sheets across the bed, then returned the condiments to their place in her wardrobe. She looked up and found Poh Poh and Hsiao laughing, shooting each other looks that excluded her. She shrugged her shoulders, refusing to be hurt.

"Don't expect a moment-by-moment description if I even have a date," she said loudly. "Good thing the days of arranged marriages are over."

Still seated in her chair, Poh Poh sent her a shrewd knowing look. Hsiao ducked her head as she straightened the chairs around the table.

"Of course, there's Manager Li . . .." Ying Fa drew a sharp breath. In essence, it was an arranged marriage; and all speculation about such arrangements would now be focused upon her.

She sat heavily on the bed, a little unnerved. Had Manager Li really chosen her?

"Does it bother you?" Poh Poh asked. She held a fragile shell of a teacup in her hand, one of the rare objects salvaged from her childhood.

"I'm not sure," she said, surprised by the quaver in her voice.

❀　❀　❀

They left with a stiff, hot breeze coming off the mountains; but by the time they'd filled their cart with chicken, pork, seafood, vegetables, fruit and two six-packs of orange juice, sweat was pouring down their backs. Poh Poh's breathing had become labored and uneven.

"Just a few steps more," Ying Fa murmured as they passed through the alley to their building. If only there was room for Poh Poh on the cart.

"Are you sure I can't help with that?" Poh Poh said through clenched teeth, her face crimson.

Ying Fa shook her head and kept moving; hoping Hsiao had boiled water for tea and that the window fan was blowing.

Inside the building, the hallway was blessedly cool. The stairs were torture, but they made it, step by painful step and then down the hall toward their apartment. It's door was propped open. Her shoulders still shaking from hefting the cart up the stairs, Ying Fa struggled inside, Poh Poh leaning heavily on one arm.

Hsiao hurried from the bathroom, her hands flapping. "Let me help you with that!" she cried, pushing Ying Fa aside as she took Poh Poh's arm and led her over to a chair in front of the fan. Arms and elbows flying, she unpacked the cart, while Ying Fa took plates and cups from her wardrobe and set them on the table.

She eyed Hsiao as she scurried about, a little out of sorts. As soon as she'd recovered from childbirth, she'd be the one accompanying Poh Poh to the market—just as she'd be performing most of the household tasks during her yearlong maternity leave. It was as Zhaodi said—a daughter was destined to leave, to live out her life with a husband and his family, making of them her own. Lucky Hsiao, to have found her place.

She pressed at the pain between her eyes. It just wasn't fair. With the addition of Hsiao and now Anji, her own role in the family had been rendered insignificant. Though the family loved her and gladly took the money from her job, she was merely temporary, as she had been all along.

She looked up sadly, seeing Hsiao's soft profile as she bent over the table, pouring the tea. It wasn't her fault that by marrying Yutang, she'd become essential.

"Let's eat," Hsiao said, pointing with open palm at the covered pot and small platter on the table. There was a large bowl of soup, too, a heavenly scented combination of clear stock, chunks of fresh and salted fish, and a sprinkling of green onions.

Poh Poh rose unsteadily from her chair.

"Sit. Sit," Hsiao murmured and helped her to the table.

Ying Fa lifted the pot lid to reveal fragrant, steaming dumplings. "What kind?" she asked, appreciating their uniform size, delicate golden color and savory aroma.

"Cabbage, shrimp and pork," Hsiao said proudly. "Zhaodi's been teaching me. I wanted to surprise you."

"And you did." Ying Fa patted her arm. She could never hurt this frail-looking girl, no matter how much she envied her.

"Such delicacies. Such good fortune," Poh Poh said. Leaning forward, she used her chopsticks to arrange the dumplings onto the platter; and then popped one into her mouth, and closed her eyes, chewing in delight.

Ying Fa giggled and patted her grandmother's arm.

"I guess I did okay," Hsiao said, smiling brightly. "Maybe Mother-in-law will think so, too. Maybe next week, she'll let me cook the family meal."

"When you get up the nerve," YingFa said with a tight laugh.

"That's for sure," Hsiao replied, her eyes widening. "I'm sure she'll find some fault."

"That's her job," Ying Fa said, rolling her eyes.

They were chewing contentedly when Anji wailed. "I should call him little pig," Hsiao said as she rose to fetch him.

"Let me?" Ying Fa asked, following her to his crib. With Hsiao's nod, she scooped him up, kissed his red, bawling face, and then crooned to him as she bounced him gently.

His rosebud lips closed in an instant; his steady black eyes trained on her in stern disapproval.

"So young to be such a fierce little tiger," she whispered and handed him to Hsiao.

Hsiao took him with her to bed, opened her blouse and let him nurse.

"But he's so skinny," Hsiao said, oblivious to her startling beauty and the bright love that shone in her eyes as she gazed at her son.

Embarrassed, Ying Fa retreated to her chair, scooped another dumpling onto her plate and took a swallow of tea.

"I know you don't want to talk about it," Hsiao said from the depths of her bed, "but I —"

"But you'll say it anyway," Ying Fa said with a laugh.

"Just listen, girl," Poh Poh said behind her teacup. "You might learn something useful." She shifted in her chair, her cheeks now returned to their normal pale color.

"What is it?" Ying Fa looked from one woman to the other. Obviously, they'd spoken behind her back. "It's about Gwai Hi, I'm sure; and I won't sleep nights until I have heard your detailed opinion."

Hsiao cleared her throat, looking hurt as she smoothed down Anji's nightdress. "Li Gwai Ha will crumble in the presence of his mother; though it is said that he dreams of his uncles's approval."

"Chan Yanru has great plans for her son," Poh Poh added. "She'll get down on her knees to scrub Manager Li's toilet if it spelled advancement for him. She has gobbled up every available committee position, no matter how trivial or time consuming. In her son's absence, she is driven by power—for him alone. His strength, however, is an unknown quality. Can he fight her? Can he make his own way in the world? It remains to be seen."

Ying Fa inspected her hands as she searched for the right words. There'd been much talk about this prospective mother-in-law. In the few seconds she'd been with the son, she'd seen laughter and an exuberance that matched her own. "Surely Mrs. Chan has a heart?" she asked. "With a son like that—"

"She wants to ensure that what happened to her husband doesn't happen to her son," Hsiao said, looking concerned. "She sees Manager Li's ability to skip through hard times as her only salvation. She wants her son not only to survive, but to prosper, to be somebody." She stroked Anji's silky head.

"What's wrong with that?" Ying Fa asked, shaking her head. "We're alive today because our parents survived." She glanced at Poh Poh. "Why the lecture? Why the concern? Isn't Mrs. Chan just another tough soldier? And do you really know that much about Gwai Ha, with him being away all these years?"

Hsiao and Poh Poh exchanged glances as if dealing with a child.

"Maybe I should consider Tsang Anwei after all," Ying Fa said heatedly. "If the Lis are so problematic, why would I want to join them?" She shuddered at the image of Anwei's doglike expression. "Anwei's already exceeded his mother's meager aspirations."

"No! No!" both women exclaimed, shaking their heads, laughing lightly.

"That's not what we mean," Poh Poh said.

"We just want you to be happy," Hsiao added, which was what Poh Poh had said about Zhaodi that morning. "We just want you to know what to expect, so you won't be surprised."

"Yes, Granddaughter," Poh Poh said, reaching for her hand across the table, looking into her eyes. "These days, you have a choice. You shouldn't even consider a boy who disgusts you."

"We'll have to see what happens," Ying Fa said with a shrug. She rested a forearm on the table. "I just hope it's a home as caring as this one."

Poh Poh patted her hand and nodded, accepting the tribute.

Ying Fa rose to clear the table, her thoughts churning. Though Mrs. Chan was supposedly a trial, wasn't the son's charm worth taking her on? Too bad Anwei, with his kind, soft-spoken mother, was so revolting.

She glanced at Poh Poh, who was nodding in her chair. She'd probably mutter something about the equation being out of balance—that she should look higher for a mate. Anwei's father had been stodgy and steady, much like his mother; while Li Gwai Ha's parents had come from money and were powerful and arrogant. Wealthy people were not usually the nicest people, unless blessed with a healthy dose of humility somewhere along the line. Was that where she came in?

She chuckled. Poh Poh had always praised her intelligence, saying that one day she'd find an outlet for it—and not with silk embroidery. But was she ready for it?

She laughed again, this time louder, carefully avoiding Hsiao's curious gaze.

Of course, this was all mere speculation. It had yet to be proven that the young man in question was truly interested. Was he pursuing her only because his uncle had ordered him to?

Manager Li was a legend, a tyrant and not to be refused. Even so, did she really have a choice in the matter, especially considering Gwai Ha's handsome face and his flashing dark eyes? In the end, all that mattered was that both Manager Li and his nephew had set their unwavering sights upon her.

Chapter 4

Ying Fa glanced at her watch and flew down the steps of the apartment building, her flower-printed dress swishing against bare legs. It was nearly noon. Her feet, shod in her best white sandals, skimmed along the dusty pavement, reminding her of the sun, the wind and the sea. It was wonderful to be dressed so prettily: perhaps Hsiao was right. 'Dress pretty, feel pretty,' she'd said, an echo of her sophisticated mother.

She hummed as she slipped between her apartment building and the one beside it. Crossing a small side street, she noticed a long, dark limousine parked and running in front of the taxi stand that was her destination. Was that Yutang behind the wheel?

Someone bumped into her, distracting her, knocking the bag from her shoulder. She clutched it tightly as the crowd swarmed about her.

She approached the taxi stand, hoping for a glimpse of the car's occupants, her curiosity rising. A hot breeze ruffled the hem of her dress, and she quickened her pace. Honking car horns and jingling bicycle bells faded to background noise as she pondered her small cache of Yuan. Would the taxi driver try to overcharge her? Perhaps another beach-goer would split the fare, as often happened. Could she convince the driver to return for her at the end of the day? Mentally, she tallied her funds, hoping she had enough.

Traffic cleared and she stepped out onto the street with the rest of the crowd, and looked down, trying to avoid the pounding feet and scattered rubbish. Someone poked her in the back with an elbow, but she kept moving. The smell of oily skin, bad breath, over-ripe melons, petroleum and rotten meat mingled in the heat. She stepped up onto the curb and, thankfully, the people around her moved on.

Her jaw dropped at she took in the limousine.

"Yutang," she gasped. He sat in the front seat, smiling at her with that goofy grin of his and waving like an idiot.

Crossing her arms about her waist, she sauntered over to him. "Well, what are you doing here?" She looked the limo up and down. It wasn't his boss's car.

"Hurry up," he said. "Get in. We've been waiting for half an hour. Did shopping take longer than usual?"

"Who is we? And why are you here?" She looked down her nose at him, and tapped her foot on the ground.

The limo's back door swung open and Li Gwai Ha stepped out grinning. She could only gape at him as he walked toward her. Numbly, she let him take her by the hand, holding her breath, unable to speak.

"Sorry about the driver," he said, making her cheeks tingle. She looked around him at her brother, who was shaking with silent laughter. So that was why Hsiao had insisted she wear a dress.

"Uncle needed his car today, so he arranged for another." Gwai Ha crossed his arms over his chest, the picture of confidence. "For us, really, for you and me. Somehow everyone wants to help smooth our, uh . . . friendship. So I get this guy for a driver." He cocked a thumb in Yutang's direction.

She sighed and then looked at him slyly, seeing the twinkle of mischief in his eyes. He didn't seem to be protesting; and he was just a man after all. But could he hold an intelligent conversation?

She pushed his hand away, refusing to be intimidated by his relationship to Manager Li, or thrown by the fact that he might mean something to her. Her mind teemed with questions and possibilities; but first she had to set the proper tone.

"How long have you been planning this?" she asked, placing her hands on her hips.

"What do you mean?" he asked, looking taken aback.

"Just where do you plan to take me?" She peered at him through half-closed lids, scowling as if he were Yutang. "I'm not sure I like being tricked like this. All you had to do was ask me."

"No tricks," he said and snorted. "Yutang said you'd take offence. But I didn't think . . . .." He held his hand out and she looked at it, savoring the moment. "Please. Just come with me for the afternoon, Miss Wong. Let's forget our scheming families and have some fun. Please?"

She studied him, pretending to decide.

Slowly, he dropped his hand, looking like a treasured son in black pants and red and black Ameri-Cola T-shirt. "You look very pretty today," he said softly, with a heart-stopping smile.

"Flattery?" She giggled and placed a hand over her mouth. Then she dropped her hand and looked him in the eye. "And you look like a cola advertisement." She smiled brightly as she took a long, leisurely look, from his clean handsome face to his bright white sneakers, as if searching for flaws. "You sure clean up nice."

His eyes widened and he laughed.

She screwed up her lips and narrowed her eyes as if measuring him. "I was going to the beach today, if that's what you had in mind. I was thinking of wading at the water's edge, buying some fish, maybe even some shrimp. I was even thinking of going swimming. However, if that doesn't suit you, perhaps we can do something else another time. I really need to catch a taxi before it's too late."

He threw back his head and laughed, heedless of the stares of passerbys. "I can't believe you," he said, shaking his head. "Of course we're going to the beach. Yutang told me all about your plans." He held out his hand and she took it.

Out of the corner of her eye, she looked her fill, recognizing in him exhilarating, brash and all too dangerous man of her dreams. She giggled as she slipped into the back of the limo beside him.

"The beach?" asked Yutang.

They fell against each other laughing.

"What's so funny?" Yutang demanded, pretending to be hurt by their exclusion.

"Such a nosy brother," Ying Fa said, shaking a finger at him. She pulled away from Gwai Ha and slapped at an eager hand that had crept up her thigh.

"None of that," she scolded, her cheeks aflame. "You're far too free with what's not yours, Mr. Li." Her stomach clenched as she imagined what else he might do with those long-fingered hands. But he was going too far, too fast.

"Sorry. Sorry," he murmured, and moved away. "Yes, we must behave properly in front of our exceedingly proper driver." He sat up straight, folded his hands in his lap and cleared his throat. "Driver," he said, nodding sternly, imitating his uncle in both tone and voice, "to the beach." He pointed ahead.

Ying Fa caught her brother's eye in the rearview mirror and they both laughed; and then the car pulled out into the traffic.

For the next few miles, Gwai Ha entertained them with a running commentary on the houses and families they passed: the sun-weathered farmers on bicycles, the rickety trucks laden with chickens, the modern dump trucks, brimming with pipes.

They were speeding toward the coast when he reached under the seat and pulled out a beautifully illustrated book, written in what looked like English.

"Did someone forget this?" he asked, leaning over the front seat to show Yutang. He flipped through pages that were embellished with tender drawings of baby animals in pastoral settings. "They're nursery rhymes, children's stories," he said softly. "Uncle hired me primarily because of my fluency in English, but I've never seen anything like this."

She looked at the book, mildly curious. Rumor had it that he spoke Russian and German, too.

"Oh, it must have been left by one of the American couples from yesterday," Yutang said with a dismissive shrug. "It must have been another driver," he added quickly, his expression clouding, his lips tightening. "I don't recall which."

Ying Fa's gaze slid away from Gwai Ha. She tried to melt into the seat, to become invisible. Like most government drivers, Yutang took side jobs when his boss was in meetings or otherwise occupied. Often, money was exchanged. But it was stupid, if not suicidal, to admit such a misuse of government property in front of the Party Boss's nephew.

"Americans?" Gwai Ha asked, curiosity lighting his face. "Did the driver say why they were here?"

Ying Fa released her breath as Gwai Ha looked from her to Yutang, his eyes widened in studied innocence. He'd let it pass.

"There were two couples," Yutang said tightly. By his glance in the mirror, Ying Fa could tell he'd regretted his candor. "An interpreter took them the beach for the day so they wouldn't be left to themselves. Can't have foreigners loose in the city, you know." He laughed nervously.

"Were they tourists?" Gwai Ha asked.

"No." Yutang shook his head. "They're adopting baby girls who'll be arriving today from Huazhou. They're returning to Guangzhou tomorrow by train, with the babies."

"I've heard of such things," Gwai Ha said, his expression thoughtful. "I've heard that's where the girls end up . . . you know, to make room for brothers and all of that. One of my friends at school has a sister who couldn't keep her girl. It's sad, really." He turned to look out the window.

Ying Fa's stomach clenched. She dug her hands beneath her dress. Such subjects were indelicate, especially on a first date: even someone as naïve as she knew that. She fumed, thinking of Baak-Hap's sister and other girls' families who made them wait for sons. Few of the young mothers she knew had baby girls.

"Let's not dwell on this," she said brightly. She smiled at Gwai Ha when he took her hand. It was a bold gesture, but he seemed as unable to keep himself from touching her, as she was from stopping him.

The car's air conditioner sputtered its last gasping chug; and Ying Fa quickly rolled down her window, gasping.

"It happens all the time," Yutang said with a shrug as he leaned across the front seat to roll down the passenger window, one hand gripping the steering wheel.

"Parts must be scarce," Gwai Ha said, yelling over the roar of onrushing air as Yutang stepped on the gas.

They were flying down the road, weaving around rickety trucks, swarms of bicycles, and tense commuters perched on droning motor scooters. Ying Fa's pulse raced as it always did when she rode with her brother. He drove fast and smooth, his foot heavy on the accelerator, one hand on the horn. Despite his many faults, he knew how to drive.

"Black market cars like this one take months to fix," Yutang said, looking like a pirate with his shaggy black hair and crafty eyes.

"This one's British made," Gwai Ha said, leaning over the front seat. "What's the horsepower?"

"Two fifty, I think."

Primitive highway stores, shacks really, zoomed past as Ying Fa half-listened to their desultory talk about Western cars. A grimy family—two parents and a boy—

heading into the city, their faces alight with the promise of adventure, shared a single motor scooter. Then there was a young man, pedaling a tired blue bicycle, toting behind him a tiny girl, perfectly dressed, her ankles crossed.

Tumbledown villages flew past, as did new three-story blockhouses, fields of snowy ducks and pens of spotted pigs. Papaya groves and rice paddies rose from terraced land. Placid water buffalo grazed in fields of green beside stooped farmers dressed in black.

The scenery ended as the marsh began, and then came the smell of the sea's salt spray. She clasped her hands on her lap, trying to hide her excitement. Was it merely the beach, or was it the presence of Gwai Ha? She couldn't decide.

Yutang sped down the long, paved road, a strip of dark gray that ran like an asphalt river from the edge of the marsh to the beach. Their destination, China's Number One Beach, was a popular vacation spot for hard-working local families and retirees from all over China.

Ying Fa's heart raced as the castle-like pavilion blazed white against the horizon. Its saw-toothed towers gleamed proudly against the hazy summer sky. Before and to the left of the pavilion was a jumble of buildings: small open-air markets, maze-like restaurants and sandy, musty hotel rooms. Golden sand beckoned, like a soft doorstep before the green-tinged sea.

She turned from Gwai Ha, suddenly embarrassed. He was a traveled man, an educated man. Such simple pleasures would probably seem countrified, and even boring.

Yutang pulled the car to a stop in the bustling parking lot. The lot was filled with cars. There were six tour buses, too, and several rows of bicycles and motor scooters.

"Thanks, elder brother," she said to Yutang as she grabbed her bag. "See you at six?" She scurried out of the car after Gwai Ha.

Yutang turned and nodded, his arm hanging out of the window. "Take care of her," he called after Gwai Ha; then shot Ying Fa a worried look as he drove away.

It was too late for worry. Father must have already spoken to Manager Li. Or had it been the other way around? Either way, some sort of message had been exchanged and a bargain struck. Now it was up to her and Gwai Ha to build a relationship.

She turned to him and saw a stranger—a man with a purpose. Was that purpose to marry her?

"Feeling odd?" he asked as he took her hand.

His hand enveloped hers completely, making her stomach ache in a strange, fluttery way. A pair of seabirds approached squawking, while others circled above, waiting for crumbs.

She nodded; the warmth in his eyes causing the corners of her mouth to turn up. "I don't know," she murmured, feeling her face burn, feeling suddenly tongue-tied, like a child on the first day of school. "Maybe this isn't such a good idea."

"We'll just start by enjoying the day," he said with a slight nod, tilting his head so that a strand of shiny black hair fell over his left eye. "Did you bring a bathing suit?"

"You like to swim?" she asked shyly. She'd been gripping the handle of her bag so tightly that it cut into her palm. A bead of sweat trickled down her back. She licked her lips as the smell of the sea filled her nostrils.

"Of course I do," he said, scowling; and then stepped back. "Now don't go modest on me, Miss Wong. You're a dragon lady, not a timid mouse with a tiny voice." He took her bag and dropped it on the ground. Then he took her other hand and faced her.

"Look, you and I both know that this has been arranged by our families. But you must also understand that I made the choice. You have the ability to decline, if you wish."

"Choice? Your uncle's a powerful man," she said, shaking her head. "What choice do I have?"

"Your eager smile prompted my decision," he said, pulling her to him. He touched her face and she moved closer, drawn to him.

"It seems like every moment of my life has been carefully planned," she said, her face tingling where his fingers traced. She stared up at him, mesmerized by the black depths of his eyes.

"Your expression gives you away no matter how you protest, Miss Wong," he said; and ran one finger across her lips, making her shiver.

She backed away with a nervous laugh. "Well, Mr. Li, you obviously have some experience with women." Her face on fire, she looked down at her coral-painted toenails. Was the color too provocative? "Why me?" she asked, looking up at his chin, unable to look higher.

"Beauty and intelligence are a rare combination, Miss Wong. Even in Beijing I could find no one I like as much as I like you."

"Again with the flattery," she said with a nervous laugh. "Is it my family, then?"

"Ah, no," he said, with the glint of mischief in his eyes, "It was your unaffected innocence, my dear."

A cloud passed overhead taking a chunk of polluted haze with it, leaving a patch of blue.

"You're teasing!" she cried, placing a hand on his arm. "What do you know about me, anyway?"

"I know you're inexperienced," he said softly. She looked up into his eyes and giggled, unable to disagree.

"Look, Miss Wong—"

"Please, call me Ying Fa," she said, releasing his arm. A smile brightened his face and he leaned closer, making her blush even more.

"Ying Fa," he said softly, caressing her arm with a long finger. "That's cherry blossem?" She nodded. "So apt," he said. She couldn't look away. "We're not children, my blossem, so let's not waste this precious time with useless posturing. Please, just be my playmate for the day." He rested a hand on her shoulder. "We'll be serious tomorrow. Okay?"

"All right," she said, a little stunned that he'd admitted he wanted her, more stunned by his use of her name as an endearment. "It's just that there are plenty of pretty girls from good families to choose from," she said, her insecurities overriding her common sense.

"Did you bring your bathing suit?" he asked, shaking his head in exasperation. He looked at her out of the corner of his eye. "I can't stand looking at that water for another blasted second. Lounging in this hot parking lot isn't exactly what I'd call fun."

She looked around and erupted into giggles.

"I know. I know," she said when she'd finally caught her breath. "Yes, I brought my suit and will need to change." She picked up her bag and they headed toward the pavilion.

"You don't have to wait for me," she said, looking up at him, practically running to match his long stride. "I'll change quickly and then join you."

When he didn't veer off toward the beach, she stopped abruptly. "Have you been here before?" He bumped into her, almost knocking her down.

"Of course," he said, laughing as he steadied her with both hands. "I practically lived here when I was small. That's why my mother called me Gwai Ha."

"Turtle mist?" She smiled.

He smiled as he nodded. "She couldn't get me out of the water without me flailing my legs and arms in protest, spraying urine everywhere, so that she had to rinse me off again, just before we left."

She flushed at his reference to urine. "Another story?" she asked, attempting to be sophisticated; and then chuckled, trying to cover her embarrassment, as she moved slightly away from him toward the pavilion. "She must have been furious."

"She certainly was," he said, his eyes sparkling as he strode beside her. "But only for a while. She can't stay mad at me for long."

When they reached the pavilion steps, she turned to him, her mind flooding with questions.

"Don't be long," he whispered, his full lips capturing her gaze.

They looked smooth and soft. What would it be like to kiss him? She ducked her head and ran through the pavilion's door.

The castle pavilion housed a game room, a restaurant, hotel rooms and public changing areas, one for each gender.

She breathed deeply of the old, weathered building's familiar smells: rotten wood, dirty socks and salty brine. After her family's apartment, it was her second home. What she wouldn't give to live here all of the time.

She peered into the gloom of the women's changing area. Booths were sectioned off beside the door with a row of toilets stalls opposite. In the summer, the room was packed with women in various stages of undress; and crying babies and children of all sizes. Today, the place reeked of human waste, the wastebasket overflowing with soiled paper. Below a row of windows were five sticky puddling sinks.

She moved closer to the sinks, unable to tear her gaze from the open windows, mesmerized by the roiling, heaving motion and the white-capped waves of the blue-green South China Sea.

She brushed against a sink, and then backed away quickly. It was stopped-up and overflowing onto the floor. She turned at a slight sound and realized she wasn't alone.

Against the right wall, two matronly room monitors chatted on rickety wooden chairs beside a single rusty shower stall. Between them on the floor was a basket, piled high with toilet paper, soap and various products for female needs.

"Hello there," she said, smiling and nodding, imagining theirs a boring job, where conversation was far more important than tending to business.

They looked up briefly, returned her nod, and then continued their conversation.

She slipped into a changing booth and changed quickly into a one-piece navy maillot with a thick white stripe across its square top, wide shoulder straps and slightly high-cut sides—perfect for swimming.

"Keep him waiting," she said to herself and raised each arm to check her freshly shaven armpits. She took a bottle of suntan lotion from her bag and with quick, sure movements, applied it to her skin. When she'd finished, she inspected her coral-painted toenails as she slid her feet back into her sandals. Then she folded her dress and underclothes and placed them in her bag.

A small noise indicated that someone else had entered the room. She gathered her things and left the booth.

"Hello," she said to a stout young woman who stood in front of the sinks.

"Lovely day," the woman replied, turning slightly to look at her, her face flushing with embarassment. She was holding a baby boy, his feet held apart over one of the sinks while he urinated. He was close to a year old, a sturdy child with bright, curious eyes and a thick shock of black hair that stood straight up, making her want to laugh.

"What a little sweetheart," she said, patting the woman's shoulder. She stroked the boy's head, marveling at his hair's stiffness. Though blue-black, Anji's hair was soft and fine. The little boy waved a sturdy fist, then stuffed it into his mouth.

"His father's hair was like that, too," the mother said shyly. Holding the baby with one arm, she made a big show of rinsing the sink and wiping it with a paper towel "His hair will flatten eventually, or so his grandmother says," she murmured.

"He's beautiful," Ying Fa said, smiling dreamily into the mother's bashful eyes, imagining similar good fortune for herself one day. "Lucky you." She caressed the baby's rosy face and then made her way out the door and down the steps to the sand.

Across the beach, she saw elderly vacationers tossing balls and practicing tai chi, office workers with jackets piled carefully off to the side, small families lounging on towels and folding chairs, and naked toddlers cavorting under the watchful eye of doting grandparents. Everyone seemed to be smiling on this beautiful day.

She trudged across the sun-bleached sand, her sandals sinking in, sending tiny crabs scurrying for safety. She crunched past a group of aged, gap-toothed men who chatted eagerly amongst themselves. Agents of the past, repositories of vast knowledge, they were like children on a well-deserved holiday.

"Where are they from?" she asked in Mandarin of a youngish-looking man who appeared to be their guide.

"Chongqing, in the Sichuan Province!" he shouted, trying to be heard above the elderly men who competed with each other to answer her question. She could only smile and nod, not able to understand a word they said. She spoke native Cantonese and the Mandarin she'd learned in school; but they might as well have been speaking Japanese, for all that she could tell.

She waved as she turned from the elderly men, tripped on a piece of driftwood, and caught herself before she went sprawling. She raised her head to look around, grateful she hadn't fallen flat on her face; and then saw before her a true sea god, a water-spun figure of incredible beauty and strength.

Gwai Ha was poised at the water's edge, water dripping from his smooth, golden torso, his swimsuit clinging to his groin, clearly outlining his masculinity. His legs, twin pillars, stood sturdily apart.

"How's the water?" she asked, then groaned softly at her lack of sophistication. He was gloriously fit, a figure to be worshipped from afar. The women at the Silk Factory claimed he had placed third in China's Ping-Pong championship last year. What could she possibly offer him?

She clamped her lips tight, trying hard not to gape, and trailed her bag on the sand, lulled by the stifling heat and the sparkling sea. She peered at him, confused, and then slowed her pace. He was staring at her?

"Fine, Miss Wong, fine," he stammered, the noble god now morphed into a mortal man, one with ordinary needs. He was eyeing her from head to toe, causing shivers to run up her spine despite the heat.

"Please. Call me Ying Fa. Is something wrong?" She stopped a few meters from him, wondering if she could possibly sound more inept.

He reached out a hand. "You have no idea how lovely you are, do you?"

A glow filled her as she moved toward him. "Flattery again?" she asked, thinking she was truly on fire. She took his hand, relishing his cool, wet touch, and then dropped her bag as his other hand clasped her waist. Elated, she fell into his arms and let him pull her, laughing, to the sea.

Cold, refreshing waves rose up and engulfed her as she plunged in after him. Free and light, she reveled in the weightless realm as her arms and legs flailed tirelessly. Then a hand grazed her breast beneath the waves and a jolt shot through her.

"Who do you think you are?" she cried, sputtering as she rose from the water, hair streaming, pulling her suit away from her chest, seeing too much of taut round breasts and alert nipples. With both hands, she gripped the front of her suit and strode from the water with measured steps. He'd pay for that.

He burst from the water and flung his hair aside. "Ying Fa?"

"Mr. Li, you assume too much," she said, coming to a halt, seeing the confusion in his eyes. "You are an eager pig for my bounteous feast." She slapped him playfully on the shoulder.

"Are you a tease?" he asked, his look questioning. She lowered her lashes.

"Alright. Alright," he said at last. His lips curled into a wicked smirk. "Then take some of this!" he cried and pushed the water at her with both arms.

She shrieked and splashed back; and then leaped away, slowed by the weight of the waves, laughing over her shoulder.

"I'll get you yet!" he cried, running toward her with his hands outstretched, attracting stares from two small families at the water's edge.

Ying Fa giggled and ran for the shore, nearly tripping over a small, naked boy who was shoveling sand into a red bucket.

"I'm sorry. I'm sorry," she apologized, frantically righting his bucket and patting him on the head. She ducked her head, mortified by the child's howls and his grandmother's scolding.

What a hopeless sow she was. If only she were slim and graceful like Hsiao. "I'm so sorry," she pleaded, begging for a smile from the old woman as she retrieved the boy's shovel, imagining Zhaodi with Anji under similar circumstances.

Gwai Ha was almost upon her. Laughing, she ran, veering away from him, one eye trained on his advancing form. He was too fast. He was closing in on her, making silly chopping sounds with his mouth, his arms scissoring out to catch her.

She shrieked and turned, swatting him in mock anger as he pulled her close. She wanted to melt against his sea-cooled skin; but he was handling her more carefully this time, holding her arms, touching just the top of her head with his chin.

"Come on," she said.

He grinned, his eyes expectant.

She took his hand and pulled him along the shore, splashing in the shallows, around to the back of the pavilion, away from prying eyes.

"You little monkey," he said, and pulled her to him, pressing her against the building, his skin against hers. In flashes, she saw into the women's changing area, thankfully empty. She could hardly breathe, crushed as she was against lean muscles, loving the feel of warm hands as they roved her naked back. Skin to skin she breathed his breath, oblivious to the South China Sea lying green and fluid before her, the rickety boats bobbing on white-capped waves, and the delicate trace of clouds languishing in the clear, blue sky.

Silken lips touched hers, and she gazed into black demon eyes that held the secrets of time. She closed her eyes and moaned as his soft tongue met hers, her lips tingling, as a wondrous need filled her loins.

Embarrassed laughter erupted all around them. She opened her eyes to find that they made a tall island amidst a sea of gaping children.

"Why aren't you in school?" she shouted and shoved Gwai Ha away. The children scattered like sand crabs, laughing as they ran.

She giggled nervously, then covered her mouth with a hand.

He prized her hand away, his face pinched with suppressed mirth. She looked up at him breathless, disturbed and suddenly shy.

"I'm sorry," he said.

"Sure you are." She whacked him on the shoulder. "You're fast and smart, but I will not succumb to your all too obvious charms. Whatever happens between us, we will start by becoming friends."

He scowled.

"Don't be so serious," she said, wrinkling her nose. "You have too many stories to tell me about Guangzhou, the city of my grandmother's childhood, and don't have time for these foolish little stunts. So tell me about Shanghai and Beijing." She took his hand and pulled him back to the water's edge. "Is it true that in Beijing, lakes freeze solid, and you can walk across them?"

She looked down at the foam on the edge of the sand and then at him.

"Yes it is," he replied, his expression a mixture of confusion and delight.

"What do you like to eat?" she asked, desperate to know every little thing.

His mouth opened, but before he could reply, she asked, "How did you live in Beijing? What was your apartment like? With whom did you live? I need to know all these things." She spread an arm out expansively.

"Slow down," he said, smiling into her eyes, warming her all the way to her toes. Lightly, he touched her face. "We've lots of time and not just today. I think . . .."

She swayed toward him, thinking him positively ravishing. "Yes?" It was all she could do to keep from tracing a finger down his muscular chest. She stuck her hands behind her back and blushed, seeing his gaze upon her breasts and then lower.

"I think, maybe years," he said, returning to her eyes, looking far too scholarly on such a glorious day. "Maybe a lifetime."

"How do you know?" she asked, tipping her head to one side and looking up at him, wanting to laugh. She flashed him a huge grin. "Maybe you're a little too sure of yourself, Mr. Li."

He laughed aloud, that boisterous, uncontrolled eruption of sound that he must have learned to make in Beijing.

"You're a strange girl," he said when he'd finally caught his breath. He slung and arm over her shoulder as they walked. "Very different from the rest." His eyes shone with appreciation as he pulled her slightly closer. "And it's Gwai Ha to you, not Mr. Li."

"Alright, Gwai Ha." She shook her head and lowered her gaze, smelling his sweat, which only heightened her longing. Maybe she was strange; but what was truly strange and wonderful, was that in a few short hours, this man, who continued to make her pulse race, was becoming her special someone. It was sheer good luck, really. Never in a hundred years would she have ever imagined Li Gwai Ha, the Party Boss's nephew, a prospective mate. Never in a hundred years would she have imagined relaxing at her favorite place on earth with this glorious creature. She hugged herself. The best time of her life had begun.

The next week flew past, with Ying Fa now the focus of delighted gossip, causing her confidence to grow. Even Manager Li seemed a little less fearsome. Like a bullfrog that had found the source of all insects, there was no mistaking his happy gloat whenever his glance should fall upon her. She lowered her gaze in his presence and maintained a carefully modest smile as she went about her work, ensuring his continued approval.

Gwai Ha was absent for most of the week, sent on the night train to Guangzhou to correct a supply problem; and ordered to stay away from his mother. She worried that he'd forget all about her, or find some excuse to delay his return.

Forewoman Chen kept passing her the most intricate projects. Silks and bright colors poured through her skilled fingers. She was gloriously, deliciously happy, humming to herself constantly, replaying in her mind each precious moment she'd spent with Gwai Ha.

On Monday, the women said he was home; which was confirmed in a brief note from him, handed to her by Chen Ming upon her return from lunch.

A day had never passed so slowly. She ran home from the factory that night, darting around harried pedestrians, sprinting across treacherous intersections, bravely avoiding honking cars and angry bicyclists. Finally, she rushed, gasping, into the apartment.

"Hello. Hello," she cried, stopping in front of Poh Poh and Hsiao, who sat companionably in the main room, mending clothes. The baby lay on a blanket on the floor between them, waving his arms and legs.

"Hurry. Hurry," Hsiao said with a laugh. She grabbed Ying Fa's embroidery case while Poh Poh pushed her toward the bathroom.

A fresh towel lay beside the already drawn tub. Freshly pressed clothing hung from a hanger on the back of the door. Was that a green evening dress?

She touched the slippery fabric in wonder. There were black high-heels on the floor, and a new bar of floral-scented soap in the soap dish. Steam rose invitingly from the tub.

"You have ten minutes!" Poh Poh shouted through the door.

Ying Fa smiled at the sound of their giggles. Like two eager young girls, they had gone to a great deal of trouble to help prepare her for the evening. Within a half-hour, she stood before them clean, combed and dressed.

"Where did you get these?" she asked, admiring the shiny black patent leather heels on her feet and the slim green dress that showed all of her curves to best advantage. Cut just above the knee, its short-sleeved jacket provided a modicum of modesty.

She shot Hsiao and Poh Poh a stern look. "Well, where?" she repeated, seeing the mischief in their eyes, their self-important gloating. "You're like two hens that just laid a nest of eggs. Tell me! Now!"

"They're mine, actually" Hsiao stuck out her chin. "I'm no longer as trim as you. Even my feet have grown two sizes."

"Nonsense," Ying Fa spat, eyeing her friend's slim figure. "I'll never be as thin as you, my friend. You'll wear them again. You'll go out with Yutang. Of course you will."

"Whatever you say," Hsiao muttered as she rolled her eyes and picked Anji up off the floor. Deftly she whisked away his urine-soaked blanket and replaced it with a fresh one, and laid him in his crib.

"It doesn't matter, girls," Poh Poh said, waving a hand dismissively as she rose, setting her mending down in her chair. "You must wear them tonight." She tugged on the front of Ying Fa's dress, pulling it down slightly, revealing and accentuating her cleavage.

"What are you doing?" Ying Fa cried, stepping back, gripping the front of her dress. "Gwai Ha does not—"

"Gwai Ha does," Poh Poh said smiling, batting away her hand. "Don't be foolish, child. He's a young man like any other."

Ying Fa bowed her head slightly. Who was this fire-breathing dragon in Poh Poh's tired old body?

"He's a man, isn't he?" Poh Poh asked again, mollifying her slightly with her soft tone. With a gnarled hand, she brushed a strand of hair from Ying Fa's face. Ying Fa's lips twitched as she peeked at her through lowered lashes.

"A fine prize should be shown fine bait," Poh Poh said with a chuckle. "Today's the seventh day of the seventh month, when the Spinster Maid reunites with the Cowherd, her long-lost love. It's a night for romance."

"That's an old fable," Ying Fa said, and crossed her arms beneath her breasts.

"Let the full moon spell true love," Hsiao said, her eyes dreamy as she turned to her. "This may be your only chance, Ying Fa, while Mrs. Chan's away." She handed her a small black purse that matched the shoes. "Li Gwai Ha's a fine catch," she said. "Just follow your heart and everyone will be happy. Perhaps even you."

"I'll try," Ying Fa said, smiling wryly. Gwai Ha was indeed the catch of the year, perhaps the decade. That he happened to make her pulse race, challenge her intellect and liked to play like a younger brother added a great deal of spice to the situation.

Anji let out a little snort and a thin cry. Hsiao moved swiftly to pick him up. "Unless of course you'd reconsider Tsang Anwei." She laughed over her shoulder as she patted Anji's back, soothing him. "His mother would be ecstatic."

Ying Fa groaned. No mother-in-law could ever make up for that face and those pudgy fingers. She shuddered, picturing Anwei stuffing food into his face like a gorging pig, crumbs and spittle flying everywhere. "Yes, and I told you what happened in grade school. If I didn't know any better, I'd swear you were trying to get rid of me."

"But we are," Poh Poh said with a light laugh, her face beaming with love and pride.

Ying Fa giggled as she pulled her into a warm embrace. "I don't know what I'd do without you," she said, resting her chin on her grandmother's ancient head. "No matter how loudly I protest, you always take care of me."

There was a knock at the door.

Hsiao moved quickly to stow Anji in his crib.

Ying Fa scanned the immaculate apartment, hoping Gwai Ha wouldn't find it too ordinary. As of yet, no one had been invited into his mother's new apartment; and so much was unknown about him—his years away at school, his travels. She clenched her teeth and turned, desperate to hide in the bathroom.

"Stay," Poh Poh ordered, pointing to the floor.

Ying Fa froze.

"And you." Poh Poh looked at Hsiao sternly. "Answer the door." She shook her head as if dealing with dimwits, then sat majestically in a chair facing the door, her expression serene, her merry black eyes sparkling with excitement.

"Mr. Li," Hsiao said as she opened the door. "Welcome to our humble apartment." She bowed her head slightly and gestured for him to enter.

He paused at the threshold.

Ying Fa couldn't help but stare. His gold watch gleamed in the hallway's dim light. In black pants and a crisp white shirt, carelessly open at the neck, he looked the picture of success—the young urban professional.

Yet there was a slight tic at the side of his handsome face—evidence that he was nervous. He stood frozen, as if afraid to enter.

She started to tremble. Of all people, he was nervous?

The sharp tang of frying shrimp wafted in from the hallway—probably food in transit from the kitchen. It mingled with the aromas of pungent cabbage, slightly burned peanut oil and delicate steamed rice. Her stomach growled in anticipation of the evening ahead. No matter what transpired, at least she'd have a good meal.

"Good evening, Mrs. Soong," Gwai Ha said, nodding at Hsiao. "Mrs. Tsao." He bowed at Poh Poh like a string puppet, and then stuck his hands in his pants pockets and anxiously jingled some coins.

His gaze snagged Ying Fa's.

Slowly he scanned her, from head to toe. "Miss Wong?" he whispered, his eyes aglow.

She took a deep breath and stepped forward. "Please come inside, Mr. Li."

She gestured for him to enter, and when he stepped forward, she closed the door.

"Would you like some tea, a snack perhaps, before we go?" she asked, feeling Poh Poh and Hsiao's amused gazes upon her. She dared not look at them. Her face was starting to twitch.

"No. No, thank you," he said. Then he made a slight bow to both matrons, and looked about the apartment as if searching for someone.

"The others won't be home for a while," Poh Poh said, answering his unspoken question. "Yutang's driving late, Mrs. Go's shopping and Mr. Wong has cross-town business to which he must attend." She smiled sweetly. "Perhaps you can meet them at a later time, though I understand you've already met Yutang."

"Yes, a later time," Gwai Ha repeated, his eyes forming dark lines against his smooth, impassive face.

Ying Fa went to him. "Thank you," she mouthed to Poh Poh, grateful for her coaching, her unwavering love and the way she'd taken control.

She took his arm, relishing the crisp feel of his shirt beneath her hands, barely able to breathe, anticipating the night ahead.

"I have a car waiting," he said, his lips curling into a smile as he looked down at her.

Her heart sang as she imagined his mouth closing in on hers. She looked away shyly, hoping her thoughts weren't revealed by her expression. A wave of heat spread up her neck as she spied the slight curl on Poh Poh's lips, indicating her approval.

"So pleasant to meet you both," he murmured to the two women, and then followed Ying Fa out the door. It closed behind them softly.

"I've missed you," he whispered, his voice a throaty hum, its vibration filling her head. He put an arm about her waist as if to steer her in the right direction.

"Have you really?" she giggled, vowing to laugh with him and enjoy herself. It was time to emerge from her protective cocoon. She smiled up at him with eyes half-closed, as they moved together down the hallway, the heat from his body searing through her dress. Suppressing the urge to hug him, she slid past him into the stairwell, his soap-clean scent tickling her nose.

She walked beside him to the car, a non-descript dark blue model that seemed to melt into the backdrop. A scruffy driver ran to open the door. Averting her eyes from the man's fervent gaze, she stepped in the car and then gasped as she slid across a remarkably cool smooth seat that smelled of leather. There were other smells, too: cigarette smoke and damp, used stockings. The windows were open, affording some relief.

She looked down, seeing that her skirt's hem had ridden halfway up her thighs, and tugged at it furiously, carefully pressing her knees together.

Gwai Ha flung himself onto the seat beside her, as if he did it all the time. The driver turned slightly, flipped the greasy hair out of his eyes and cast a hungry look in her direction. He lifted a hand and took a long drag on his cigarette, his eyes narrowing.

She looked down at her knees, bared immodestly, and took a deep breath. Should she have dressed so provocatively? Being an unwitting magnet for men's improper attentions was the last thing she wanted. She folded her hands in her lap demurely and looked out the window.

Who cared what the driver thought. Why let an oaf spoil her fun?

Gwai Ha barked directions at the driver, making her jump.

As the car pulled out, a stream of acrid cigarette smoke made its way into her mouth, and she coughed slightly behind one hand.

"Relax," Gwai Ha said and pressed a knee against her thigh. "You're mine tonight, my precious cherry blossom." He traced a long finger across her exposed thigh.

"None of that," she said, laughing as she grabbed his hand and clasped it on the seat between them, feeling his hot, racing pulse that was at odds with his stony expression.

"I can't help myself," he said in a throaty whisper that turned her stomach to quivering custard. He stared straight ahead, his lips barely moving. "You are beyond lovely, my little Ying Fa."

"I missed you, too," she said, wondering how it would feel to sit on his lap. "I've been meaning to ask you a political question," she said, waving a hand to fan her blazing cheeks.

The car swerved wildly, nearly missing a turn. The driver laid on the horn and he swore under his breath. Two motorcycles veered away, almost crashing into a row of worried-looking bicyclists. Gwai Ha's body shadowed hers as she leaned into him.

"Politics?" he asked with mild surprised.

He barked something at the driver and the car came to a halt outside a torch-lit restaurant, with a large goldfish above the door. Surprised by their destination, she could only peer out the window at the tall new buildings that crowded the narrow street, blocking out the summer's hazy light. She watched the people strolling by wearing curious, absent gazes, past shops where neon signs flashed the names of Western products, past rickety dumpling stands that sent plumes of steam into the hot night air. The scene was surreal, not Maoming at all—more like a movie set, a romantic back street community somewhere in Guangzhou or Shanghai.

An old man crouched in an alley across the street, relieving himself. She turned away, her stomach knotting. A clutch of bicycles sped past, weaving around the car, vying for pavement space, snapping her out of her mood.

A giggle bubbled from her throat and elation filled her as she turned to Gwai Ha. The delicious aromas of good food wafted from the restaurant's open door, and she smiled in anticipation.

"Ready," he asked, taking her hand.

The Golden Fish was Maoming's finest restaurant. A date within its hallowed walls was sure to signify a marriage proposal. It was Poh Poh's favorite eatery, reserved for special family occasions. Though expensive, it offered the freshest seafood and delicacies otherwise unknown in places outside of Guangzhou.

Gwai Ha stepped from the car.

"We'll talk about politics and anything else you want during dinner," he whispered, leaning into the car, holding out a hand to help her. She tried to sit forward and swing her legs out onto the street; but her skirt rode up, exposing more of her thighs. She giggled behind her hand as she stepped out.

"Lovely girl," he whispered and planted a kiss on top of her head. His eyes danced merrily, though his expression turned grave as he paid their repulsive driver.

As the car sped off, he smiled broadly and took her hand, and placed it on his bent arm, as she'd seen in movies.

"Mr. Li," she protested, laughing as she stepped toward him, sending him a teasing look guaranteed to spell her true feelings. He held the restaurant door and she preceded him inside.

She scanned the restaurant's lobby, eyeing the tanks of live fish and eel, the crates of snakes and bins of other rare aquatic delicacies. A selection of vegetables, wilted from the heat, was set out on shelves to the left of the dining room door. While some patrons preferred to order from the menu, the more knowledgeable could personally select their ingredients and order the methods of preparation.

Gwai Ha's hand settled on her waist as a greasy seafood vendor eagerly stepped forward, wiping his hands on his pants. His grayed shirt had drooped hours ago in the stifling heat. His chipped front tooth defined him as a man of little means and limited prospects. Hopefully, the food would outshine his personal habits.

She suppressed a laugh, seeing the disdain on Gwai Ha's face.

"Three dishes?" she asked him shyly, pretending to be the meek little mate, causing him to smirk. Then his expression became impassive, becoming the man about town—his curt nod making her want to laugh.

In fast clipped tones, she bartered with the vendor, blushing under his admiring gaze as she chose plump, pink seaworms, extra-jumbo shrimp and the freshest of seasnails. She glanced at Gwai Hi from time to time, hoping that the finesse with which she chose the sauces, vegetables and cooking methods would not only please him, but make him proud. She couldn't help but gloat; considering that his mother was supposedly a lousy cook and a marginal housekeeper, at best.

When she'd finished, he took her arm, directing her into the dimly lit restaurant, a large and lavish banquet hall, containing several round tables of various sizes. The tables to the back were empty, while those closer to the entrance were well filled. There were lit sconces along the dark-paneled walls, placed at regular intervals. Waitresses scurried about, arms laden with fragrant food on silver platters and pots of aromatic tea. Soft pleasant music played in the background. She listened closely, detecting traditional Chinese instruments and a pleasantly reedy soprano.

She preened as she walked with Gwai Ha between the tables. Nothing could compare to the glamor of holding a man's arm—especially when he belonged to her. The smiling hostess nodded at his clipped instructions; and then turned down a row, assuming they'd follow.

Patrons glanced up as they passed: smiling couples sharing tables; business-suited men, beers before them; several solemn Japanese executives sipping tea; and a large family that spanned several tables.

Gwai Ha hand pressed against the small of her back, firmly in command.

Her heart raced in anticipation of the intelligent conversation they would share along with their meal. Having never dined alone with a man, she hoped she would acted properly, that she'd make her family proud. They were counting on this match; and she didn't want to disappoint them.

Gwai Ha squeezed her waist and she looked up at him anxiously. His eyes held both warmth and passion, turning her worries to air. There was much that he could teach her; and she could teach him a thing or too as well. She smiled at him sweetly.

Soon they approached their table, a linen-covered square, tucked into a lamplit alcove. Gwai Ha nodded his approval as the hostess pointed at the table, her palm out. Then smiling, she bustled away.

Ying Fa sat gracefully with her back to the wall; while he sat facing her, his eyes like bright, black beads strung together with joy. Her breath caught as he took her hand across the table.

"Bring steamed rice with the meal and wine for now," he murmured to their waitress, a woman in her late twenties who'd appeard silently, wearing a crisp white apron over a starched blue uniform. Her artful smile seemed to promise much, but her lined face spoke of hard struggle and early depravation. Gwai Ha winked at her and her face lit up; displaying the beauty she must have once posessed.

Ying Fa watched her curvaceous retreating figure through narrowed eyes. Would he seek the smile of every female, even in the company of his prospective wife? He would find out fast enough that she wouldn't tolerate such treatment.

But he was looking at her as if he wanted to jump over the table to reach her; and she gazed into his eyes, her heart melting. Tingles shot up her arm and across her lips as he rubbed the top of her hand with one long gentle finger.

"Relax," he whispered. "You'll enjoy this."

She swallowed. Unable to speak or look away, she simply nodded.

When the waitress returned with a bottle of wine and two glasses, she released his hand. In smooth, practiced movements he took the bottle from the waitress, who was about to pour, and motioned her away. He poured the wine and handed Ying Fa a glass.

"To a rich future," he said and lifted his glass and scanned her face and her neck. When his gaze touched her cleavage, she shot him a stern look, daring him to stare. Her breasts felt tight and heavy. Her nipples scraped against the fabric as she breathed. She raised her glass to her lips, her mouth drying under his greedy scrutiny.

"You wanted to discuss politics?" he asked, a smile pulling at the corner of his mouth.

"Yes." She cleared her throat and lowered her glass, determined to keep pace with him, to spar with him whenever she could. "What's the correct way to behave with you dancing in and out of the factory all the time?" she asked, her eyes narrowing. "The women all smile at me in their knowing ways; as if they know every detail of what goes on between you and I. Of course they don't; and it's very difficult to work like that." She looked around to ensure no one was listening. "I'm like a princess to them somehow—the happy ending of their favorite fairy tale. What can I say to make them stop without hurting their feelings?"

A muscle worked at the side of his face. Was he about to laugh? There was a tickle in her throat; but she managed to keep a straight face.

Then he was laughing aloud, and looking up at the ceiling, probably thinking of a rejoinder. He took a sip of wine and eyed her speculatively. "You seem like an eager student of such things." His lips looked silky in the muted light.

"And I value your opinion, Mr. Li." She bowed slightly.

"Do you indeed," he said, with an abrupt laugh. Longing filled his eyes. "You're a lovely young woman," he said softly, meeting her gaze, making her blush, creating moisture beneath her arms. He hadn't answered her question.

"So, tell me about Guangzhou," she said, squirming in her seat, looking at him out of the corner of her eye as she toyed with her wineglass.

"The trip was fairly uneventful," he replied with a tender look. When he spread the linen napkin on his lap, she did the same, eager to match him grace for grace.

"The train was packed," he said, then set his glass down and sat back. "But I got a good night's sleep in my compartment, and plently of time to prepare for my meetings. The food was even passible. The hotel in Guangzhou was dingy, though the staff tried hard to please. I happened upon a few good dim sum restaurants and a noodle shop that made me weep with pleasure." He rolled his eyes.

"Did you see the river?" she asked, then raised her glass and took a sip. She'd cut her teeth on Poh Poh's tales of the meandering Peal River.

"Indeed I did, little one," he replied, smiling at her like an indulgent elder brother, soliciting her smile in return. "By night it looked lonely and haunting, the boats chugging up and down, laden with goods. In the early morning, the mist hung like a magic cloud, shrouding the muddy gray water." He poured more wine into both glasses.

"Did you take the ferry?" she asked, imagining a round-ended boat sounding its horn through the gloom.

"As a matter of fact I did," he replied, then held his glass beneath his nose and inhaled its fragrance.

She did the same, marveling at the luxury. On her eighteenth birthday, Father had allowed her a single glass And now, at the ripe old age of twenty-six, she was finally enjoying it as an adult.

"I must tell you a secret, though," he whispered. She leaned closer and he licked his lips as he stared at hers, his eyes narrowing with desire. She sent him a warning glance as the waitress arrived with their food.

His face transformed into smiling stone. He nodded his approval as each sizzling dish was uncovered: sea worms with chunks of green peppers glistening in a light broth; four steamed shrimp, each at least twelve centimeters long, nicely sliced; a delightful plate of snails, like fat little soldiers in their own sweet sauce. To round out the meal, there was also a bowl of spicy mixed vegetables and another of hot steamed rice. Then, like a ghost, the waitress disappeared.

Her mouth watering as she surveyed the food. She reached for the rice bowl and chopsticks just as he did; and giggled as their hands collided.

He smiled broadly and signaled the waitress for more wine. They each took rice into their cups and began to eat.

"What a delightful feast," he said, thanking her with his eyes as if she had cooked each bite.

"I'm just learning," she said, inordinately pleased.

"That's not what I heard," he said with a tight laugh. "My uncle claims you're an excellent cook, taught by your mother, a professional. A meal like this would have been simple for you to prepare, given similar ingredients."

"Is that why you like me?" she asked, then giggled and covered her mouth.

He lowered his chin. "Of course," he said, with a teasing smile. "And rumor has it that while my mother's away; my uncle will have a chance at his fondest wish."

"Which is?" she dared to ask. Her heart pounded. Had she said too much?

His expression darkened. He toyed with his wineglass and stared at the wall to the left of her, looking pensive all of a sudden . . . and a little angry.

It didn't surprise her. His uncle had ignored him for years. And now, after the demise of his two ugly sons, he wanted Gwai Ha to carry on the family name. By most people's estimation, Gwai Ha had everything. In reality, he was like a child's rag doll once tossed away, now the revived and dressed in finery.

"I remember your cousins from a brief encounter at the factory," she said softly. He looked wary, but she continued. "They were teasing one of your uncle's foremen, imitating him, throwing his toolkit back and forth. Some people laughed, but I didn't think it was funny. Your uncle, of course, did nothing to stop them. It was a sad day when he received news of their deaths—sad for him at least."

"What else do you recall of my cousins?" he asked through clenched teeth. He hunched over his wine, his knuckles white around the glass.

She would not placate him so early in their relationship. Poh Poh had once said that dishonesty between husband and wife was the surest way to kill passion. And she'd have passion.

"I remember two big boys with thick, starchy black hair," she said, raising her chin slightly. "Smart boys with great promise, if you like bullies. All of us at the Silk Factory knew that your uncle's fondest wish was to beget a new generation through them. For a while, I thought he had singled out my friends and me as potential wives. I wasn't sorry to see them go to Beijing; but I never wished them dead." She looked down at her rice bowl, her cheeks flaming. Had she gone too far? Zhaodi always said that one day she would let her mouth get the better of her.

"So, how does it feel to be the object of a powerful man's dream?" he asked. There was a cruel glint in his eyes.

Her hand froze in place, chopsticks halfway to her mouth, rice falling back into her bowl. She'd done it this time. He would never ask her for another date, much less marry her. There was a strange, questioning look in his eyes. Was he playing games with her? And who had made him judge?

"Your uncle's very powerful," she said coldly. "I have no choice, now do I."

He looked stricken; and she softened her gaze. What a prickly pear he was—and she wasn't much different.

"So tell me about your cousins?" she asked softly. She scooped vegetables into her rice bowl, and took a delicious bite.

He glared at her, looking about as happy as a snake whose stone had just been turned. If he would only talk it out, he would feel much better. He seemed to be an expert at holding things inside—things everyone knew all about anyway. Yet this was no embroiderer's gossip session. This was the man himself, needing to pour his heart out. He seemed to study her face, as if looking for guile.

"Can't you please tell me?" she asked, trying to hide her exasperation. "I really want to know," she said, reaching a hand across the table. "You're smart and handsome. You've been many places. What tales you can tell me. I want to know everything about you, including this."

His expression softened. He patted her hand and then pulled back.

"Wherever my cousins went, I tried to run in the opposite direction." He spoke slowly, as if testing his voice. "But we went to the same school for a while, and sometimes they'd get something stuck in their heads, and wouldn't leave me alone. My mother and theirs shared mutual friends; and they would backstab at each other, refusing to attend the same events. My aunt liked to use me as bait to hurt my mother and provoke her boys at the same time. She thrives on turmoil. My uncle didn't even acknowledge my existence until they were lost to him." He took a sip of wine.

"So painful to live outside the circle." She shook her head. "Rumor has it that his boys played tricks on you and even hurt you a few times."

"Yes," he said, nodding. "They broke my arm, causing my mother to plead with Uncle on her knees in the kowtow fashion of ancient times, losing much face. He backed his boys, of course, saying that they were just being playful. My mother kept me home from school after that until my arm healed and they had moved into a better apartment, my cousins going to a different school. Uncle never even looked in my direction—not even once—though he . . . ah . . . still came around to visit my mother."

She looked down at her plate; her face in flames, horrified that she had even broached the subject. What had she been thinking? Honesty was one thing, but talking behind Manager Li's back would land her a job at the work farm.

"You continually amaze me," he said, and lifted her chin with his hand. "I take no offence, my blossem." He held his breath until she smiled. "Are you afraid of my uncle?"

She nodded. The Party Boss's approval was a matter of survival for both her and her family.

There was a flickering of passion in his eye, and then it was gone. He dangled a delicate seaworm aloft, and then took the bite into his mouth, closing his eyes and smiling as he chewed.

She narrowed her eyes, trying to imagine what it would be like to sit beside him in their own apartment, watching him eat the food she had prepared.

"How do I surprise you?" she asked. She sucked on a snail shell and extracted its tiny occupant.

"You have such depth of understanding, considering how sheltered you've been." He nodded at the waitress as she set another bottle of wine on the table, and then hurried away.

"I'm just a simple girl," she said, her hair sliding across her face as she bowed her head.

"Unlikely, my brave actress," he said with a short laugh, then reached to brush aside her hair.

"You still haven't answered my political question," she said, grinning. She took a slice of shrimp with her chopsticks and popped it into her mouth.

"Ah that." He chewed thoughtfully for a few seconds. Then he poured wine into their glasses and took a sip from his own. Drawing out the easy silence between them, he filled his rice bowl with crispy vegetables, as did she. They chewed in companionable silence.

"Pay no attention to those gossip-loving women," he said, giving her a sharp look over his bowl. "There are plenty who are jealous and few who are not. Follow my example and seek your own happiness above all else. Their lives are simple, while yours is changing in ways you can't even imagine."

She nodded in agreement, and then brought her chopsticks to her mouth. A few grains of rice fell down into the front of her dress; and he teased her by imitating a diver going after pearls until she was helpless with laughter.

❁   ❁   ❁

The rich meal ended all too soon. After Gwai Ha paid the bill, he led her stumbling from the restaurant with his arm around her waist. They wandered for several dreamy minutes, caught in each other's scent in the steamy twilight, searching for a taxi. The moon was full and hazy, its outline blurred by thick, choking smog.

"Please, Moon Maiden, be my guide," she whispered, helpless against the pull of Gwai Ha's allure.

In the taxi, she fell into his arms, her lips hungry for him. He kissed her soundly, caressing her face, her neck, his fingers searching lower. She didn't care that the driver saw. She didn't care that her dress rode up and Gwai Ha's hand brushed against her buttocks.

When the taxi dropped them off, it took her a moment to realize where she was. She couldn't help but gape at the fourteen-story Maoming Building—her mother's employer—a stark gleaming tower against the dark night sky. She had always entered through the back door, toting her mother's provisions. But not tonight. Like in a dream, she rode the elevator with Gwai Ha to the eighth floor.

He took her trembling hand at the carved front entrance to a popular disco, not quite tempering her fear and excitement. Her parents had never permitted her inside such a place. Chin down, eyes lowered lest someone recognized her, she followed him into the smoke-filled room, through the maze of couples and small groups perched around tiny tables, laughing and talking all at once, their faces blurry amidst a sea of black hair.

He led her to a small table in a dark corner, where they sat with their thighs touching. She coughed, covering her mouth with the back of her hand. Smoke whirled and eddied all the way up to the lofty ceiling; and there was the unmistakable odor of unwashed bodies and sour oil wafting from somewhere to her left. A waitress hurried over and took their order, while Ying Fa strained to hear what Gwai Ha said. Glasses clinked. Murmured conversation roared in competition with Western rock music that blared from several speakers. As her eyes adjusted to the dark, she turned and gasped.

Six young women, brazenly beautiful in low-cut evening gowns, gyrated to the music on a small stage. With each hip thrust, long, sleek legs were revealed. Their breasts bounced like golden balls. It was just as Zhaodi had described. She gaped, never having seen such a sensuous display.

Though Gwai Ha's face lay in shadow, she could see that his eyes were narrowed with lust, like twin lines catching at her heart. Her palms began to sweat. She took a sip from the glass he offered, and then coughed, her throat on fire. She downed the rest in one long draught, while he faced her and did the same.

Her stomach ached in the strange heavy way that only he could evoke. She looked at him, puzzled, and then understood.

"Please?" he asked, his gaze burning. He caressed her neck, begging her kiss; and she lifted her lips as his soft mouth brushed against hers. It seemed fated as deft fingers stroked her chest, pulling aside her jacket, trailing heat and delight. Acts she'd only seen illustrated in books began to make sense.

He pressed a hand to her breast and she leaned toward him. The music's wild tempo matched her racing pulse, as she watched the wild girls dance. He took his hand away, leaving her cold and wanting.

"Gwai Ha?" she asked. "What shall we do?"

"Do you trust me?" he asked. "To know what's best for us?" His eyes were unfathomable, his tone firm.

She nodded quickly. He was older and wiser and more experienced.

He took her hand and kissed it reverently. Then he stood, pulling her to her feet beside him, and threw money down on the table.

"Where are we going?" she asked, and didn't quite hear his mumbled reply.

The answer came to her as she followed him out of the club and toward the elevator. There was no mistaking the wetness between her legs. Suddenly afraid, she stopped.

"We can't," she whispered. "Can we?"

He held out a hand, his honest face pure and beautiful; his eyes filled with desire. And love? "Our families want this," he said, kissing her hand at the elevator door. "Please say that you want it, too."

"You've booked a room," she said dully, watching him as if from a great distance as he pressed the elevator button.

"My uncle booked it." He looked away, his shoulders slumping. "Please, don't take offense. He just wants to speed things along. He doesn't want a huge war with my mother. She's lost too much. She'll never be satisfied with any woman I chose." He took a deep breath. "She'll try to postpone our marriage as it is; while he's eager for it. Either way, it matters little, dear Ying Fa. I'll have you no matter what they decide."

Marriage? She stared at him, at a loss for words; and then the elevator door slid open.

The surprised elevator girl's expression changed from curious to cautious. Unlike the girl on their ascent, this one was a friend of Zhaodi's. By tomorrow morning, everyone would know what she had done.

Her face burned as she entered the elevator. She stared at her shoes as it rose. When it stopped and the door opened, she stepped out quickly, unable to look at the girl.

"There is nothing to fear," Gwai Ha told her sternly at the door to the hotel room. He kissed her hard on the mouth, leaving her breathless and weak. Then he turned the key and pulled her inside.

Even as she stood before the bed trembling, she couldn't help but look about her in wonder at the space afforded a traveler. A quick inventory would help in the telling later. Surely, Poh Poh would want to know every detail. Well, maybe not every detail.

She chuckled as she twirled in place, making note of the massive bed, dual dressers and nightstands, the tiny refrigerator, the table and chairs by the window. There was even a small bathroom.

"Look at this!" she cried as she lifted the lid of a strange looking toilet and peered inside at the basin of water. "How do you use it?" she asked, turning to Gwai Ha in amazement.

"It's a Western toilet," he said, chuckling as he slung an arm around her. "You sit on it like a chair and do your business. Then you push this." He grasped the little chrome handle and pushed. The water swirled loudly as the basin emptied and refilled, in a manner similar to what she was accustomed.

"It must be easy on the legs," she said, shaking her head, struggling for words. "A boon for the elderly and sick."

"My sweet, little duck," he said, shaking with laughter. "You are the perfect, curious student and I have so much to teach you. So much joy to share with you."

He took her hand, intertwining his fingers with hers, and pulled her toward the bed. She giggled nervously as he removed her jacket. Her hands shook as she slid down the straps of her dress.

Was this a test? She licked her lips nervously.

"Don't be afraid," he whispered. He nibbled her neck just below her ear lobe, sending shockwaves of pleasure across her chest, making her forget that she had just met him, that this was their first evening date, and that he did not have to make her his wife. He was maddeningly, heartbreakingly delicious and her lips tingled in a curious way that made her want more.

His lips trailed down her chest as he unzipped her dress.

"Kiss me," she whispered and slipped off her dress, craving his instruction. No matter the cost, she wanted to do all the magical things that his eyes so clearly promised. She moaned as his hands slid around her backsides.

As time and place melted into liquid pleasure, he gently taught her how to move, where to touch and how to give. Grateful for his instruction, she worshipped his muscular leanness, reveled in his obvious delight of her own lush form, and bent her pleasure to his will. Later, she would recall his tender wooing, his unselfish restraint as he led her beyond his fulfillment to her own.

"This was not the way of most Chinese men," he told her proudly afterward; though she had no way of knowing whether it was true. "I will cherish you and protect you always," he said, as they lay moist and breathless in each other's arms.

"Gwai Ha, my love," she whispered as she clung to him. "When will we marry?"

He lay silent for a long dreadful moment, his breath even.

Had she been too brash? Had she assumed too much? Perhaps, like Yutang, he would quickly move on to another eager prospect.

Then he rolled over and caressed her hair, his skin warm against hers.

"As soon as the astrologers can be consulted," he said firmly. "This week, Uncle will announce our engagement. Then Mother's friends will doubtless write to her; and all hell will break loose."

She breathed a sigh of relief, and he smiled warmly, his gaze resting upon her swollen lips. "Leave everything to me, my soft rabbit. You are mine now and always will be."

Ying Fa's family made no protest of her early morning return as they rose quietly and prepared for their day. When Poh Poh awoke her later, however, just before lunch, she treated her to a terse lecture on the responsibilities of becoming a woman.

Ying Fa fumed as she ran to the bathroom, trying to escape her knowing looks, trying to ignore the soreness netween her legs, for which Poh Poh, of course, had handy remedy.

After a quick shower, several cups of tea, and a bowl of sweet and sour soup she ran outside to Gwai Ha, who was waiting for her in a government car.

Yutang grinned from the driver's seat; and Gwai Ha moved over to let her in, ready for another glorious day at the beach.

Two weeks passed and then three, yet another sick relative in Guangzhou stalled Chan Yanru's return. Meanwhile, Ying Fa's joy bloomed like a rare flower, opening to the sunshine of Gwai Ha's adoration. At work, silk flew through her hands. The forewoman claimed she had never seen such high-quality production. At home, she was the honored daughter, bringing her family much face as Gwai Ha's chosen one.

All fear of Gwai Ha's abandonment left as she met him each day for lunch, when he would good-naturedly endure the giggling scrutiny of her friends. There was always a car at his disposal at the end of most workdays, when she would meet him outside the Silk Factory and join him for dinner at some trendy new restaurant, followed by a few hours in a fancy hotel room, courtesy of his indulgent uncle.

On her days off, he took her to the beach, or out to the country for fresh produce or a goose for her grandmother. She found herself laughing more, hugging her family more, eating more, and looking forward to those startling black eyes that gazed so lovingly into hers.

Then there were the nights when she would bring him home for dinner. He fit right in, laughing and arguing with Yutang, flattering Zhaodi, pampering Poh Poh, and even making Father smile. At the end of each meal, Father would shake his hand at the door and wish him prosperity.

Finally, on the eve of Mrs. Chan's return, Manager Li announced their engagement during the Silk Factory's opening exercises. Ying Fa glowed with happiness as she stood between Gwai Ha and Manager Li in the courtyard, accepting the warm wishes of her co-workers. That

Manager Li blessed their union was indeed auspicious. Now anything was possible.

If only she knew how Chan Yanru would react. Dare she hope that her new mother-in-law would share Gwai Ha's intelligence, honesty and his great love for her?

With Gwai Ha's arm around her, she put aside such gloomy thoughts. Tomorrow would take care of itself.

Chapter 5 – February 1996

A cold, damp wind blew hard as Ying Fa stumbled down the steps of the family court building, clutching Gwai Ha's arm in a desperate attempt at balance. It must have rained buckets in the last half-hour, clearing only for a moment. Bicycles splashed through standing puddles, bestowing muddy stripes upon their riders' backs.

She swallowed the lump in her throat and turned her face slightly to stem her rising nausea, counting the nondescript brick buildings that stood like a row of soldiers on either side of the street. Small plaques above each door indicated the offices of Maoming's government agencies, courts and officials.

"Father's office is in one of these buildings," she said, glancing up at her new husband. "I can't remember which one." Blaring traffic obliterated the sound of her voice. She was sure that Gwai Ha hadn't heard her.

He smiled down at her, looking happier than she had ever seen him. He clasped her arm possessively, taking some of the sting out of his mother's recent accusations. Though the words had been spoken through him and not directly to her, they'd bitten bone-deep.

Mrs. Chan hung on to his other arm, looking like a wounded bird, fooling no one. Her face still burned from the brutal perusal she had given her burgeoning figure. As of yet, her mother-in-law had not directly addressed her, preferring instead to speak through Gwai Ha. It seemed she could hold a powerful grudge.

Yes, she was pregnant. What did the woman expect?

She took in her mother-in-law's rail thin figure. Her forehead was furrowed in a thoughtful way that banished laughter as well as any questions. Her delicate head was inclined toward Zhaodi, and her lips pursed in a manner that said she could barely tolerate her existence.

Gwai Ha claimed that his mother had screeched for well over an hour upon learning of Manager Li's orchestrations. Consequently, what should have been a quick trip to the marriage registry had turned into a monumental effort to track down the proper astrologer. Mrs. Chan's expert stall tactics had dragged on for months what should have taken place right away—and now her pregnancy was painfully obvious.

Her lace demi-veil tickled her forehead, but she suppressed the urge to scratch. She glanced down at the red dress that had look magnificent a few months ago, seeing a stuffed red cow; its seams ready to split. For the hundredth time, she wished she had smaller hips, slender legs; and of course, her face had decided to swell today, making her look like an old toad.

She chuckled—the image of a toad's head on a cow's body too much on such an auspicious day.

"Are you alright?" Gwai Ha asked. He halted, and looked at her with a tenderness that made her want to cry.

"Yes," she mouthed, wishing the day were over; wishing he'd step out of his role for once and put his arms around her. Was a hug too much to ask for?

However, such an immodest display was forbidden in public, especially in front of their elders. She couldn't remember the last time he'd held her close. They had met in secret upon Mrs. Chan's return from Guangzhou, though little escaped that woman's notice when it came to her son's activities.

She turned to look for her parents, caught Mrs. Chan's malevolent glare, and nodded in mute acceptance, unable to bame her. Though this was supposed to be a happy day, an auspicious day, her wedding day, their relationship had been forced upon them.

She straightened her spine, refusing to succumb to shame or sadness. She was a nice girl from a good family, with nothing to hide. She had gloried in her role as the sought-after bride, and would now cherish her role as beloved wife and fruitful, productive partner. For today, she would tolerate Mrs. Chan's resentment and ignore her rancor. Her family had gained much face by her marriage to Li Gwai Ha; and she would treasure their love and support for as long as she lived.

She looked up to see Manager Li gesturing for Gwai Ha to hurry. He was Uncle Li now, and even more important to her than before.

There were two black sedans parked at the curb, forcing the traffic to swerve around them. Each driver stood at attention, cap in hand, awaiting instruction. Father stood stiffly beside Uncle Li, his face a mask of worry.

Father's long white hands hung from the sleeves of his new black suit. His wary smile reminded her of the sinking feeling she had often felt in the Party Boss's presence. Uncle Li was a powerful man—a dangerous man. Beside him, Father looked like a sleepy, long-legged spider examining a fat wasp.

She moved swiftly to her father. He looked at her briefly, then turned to Gwai Ha and mumbled what sounded like congratulations. In the depths of his eyes was the hint of panic and sadness. If only he would acknowledge her. Pride had bloomed in his usually somber eyes over the past few months. Soon after Uncle Li had announced her engagement, he had been granted an impossible promotion. Now, much to his colleagues' surprise, he stood two levels above his former boss.

She stepped away from him, realizing that he would not acknowledge her—not here anyway, not in front of Uncle Li.

She took in Uncle Li's rotund shape as he spoke with one of the drivers in harsh, clipped tones. He was Party Boss to thousands of people, with the power to rectify all failures and humiliations—such as the destruction of Father's youthful promise.

She smiled at him gratefully, though he too, paid her no heed. After all, she was just an obviously fertile female, good only to be bargained with and used.

With a sigh, she turned to observe the rest of the wedding party, seeing Hsiao extend her hand first to Mrs. Chan and then to the Mrs. Li, Uncle Li's dowdy wife, both acquaintances of Hsiao's mother and mahjong aficionados. Standing meters apart, they expressed warm congratulations over her new son, with Zhaodi hovering protectively, smiling in appreciation, her face bright with humor.

Hsiao's eyes were flatteringly downcast, as befit a young woman. Yet there was an air of maturity about her, an unconcealed pride in her new role of mother. Dazzling in smoky pink, she reeked of such sophistication that it poured over Ying Fa like vinegar on a wound. Even Zhaodi looked smart in a new tan suit; her gray-streaked hair perfectly styled to frame her swarthy peasant's face. And there was Yutang, preening like an awkward teen under the women's teasing scrutiny.

Hsiao and Zhaodi touched often, a love built through their sons. They were kindred spirits—a relationship she would probably never share with Gwai Ha's mother. She rubbed her swollen belly, sending loving thoughts to the tiny traveler inside, hoping that one day, she, too would be appreciated in such a manner.

Her breath came quickly as her perspective changed. Hsiao would always be her sister. She would laugh with her as they watched their little sons grow. She chuckled, earning a sharp glance from her mother-in-law, and then quickly covered her mouth with her hand.

Zhaodi must have sensed her mood, for she was smirking as the two old women moved past, ignoring her completely. Zhaodi dared to laugh? And was that an avid curiosity on her face, an eager watchfulness—as if she were at some lively show?

Ying Fa glanced at the limos, seeing Mrs. Chan pause beside the first car and wait, seemingly patient, for Uncle Li's plump wife to enter first.

"Let's go!" Uncle Li shouted over the traffic's din. Ying Fa started to move with Gwai Ha, but Uncle Li nodded in her direction, indicating that she should speak with Zhaodi first.

113

"I won't be long," she said to Gwai Ha, who was clasping her arm as if she would bolt at any moment. She nearly melted under the sweetness of his gaze. Was he really hers? She forced her eyes away and inclined her head at Uncle Li in acquiescence. Then she pushed Gwai Ha lightly, sending him toward the limo; and watched as he helped his mother into the car, sitting across from his aunt.

Uncle Li followed stiffly and sat beside his wife, her deep respect for him measured by the tilt of her slightly bowed head.

"That ought to be interesting," Zhaodi whispered as she took Ying Fa's arm. "Those two haven't been in the same room for decades. Like cats in a rice bag if you ask me."

"Later," Ying Fa said, shifting her eyes nervously, keeping her expression carefully neutral.

She pulled away from Zhaodi and hugged Hsiao, accepting her congratulations.

"It's all working out for you," Hsiao said as she patted her abdomen.

"I hope so," she said, her gaze sliding in the direction of the lead car.

"His mother will come around," Hsiao whispered. "She has to. With a grandchild on the way, she'll be tripping over herself to help you, you'll see. Babies change everything."

Ying Fa nodded, as Hsiao took Yutang's arm. "Best of luck, little sister," he said, patting her shoulder, looking jaunty in his black suit, a man of prospects. Perhaps Uncle Li would see to his future as well.

"Thank you," she whispered and watched him pull Hsiao toward the second limo where Father was waiting.

The three got into the car, Father facing forward, as was his due.

Ying Fa's eyes filled as she faced Zhaodi. She held herself stiffly, though she longed to fling herself into her mother's arms and sob like a child. They had argued, fought and scratched like rats after the same territory; but she would miss her sorely. She would miss Poh Poh too, who was waiting with Anji at the banquet that Uncle Li had so generously arranged. Already, there was a sad distance in Zhaodi's eyes.

"Go," she said sternly. "They are your family now." She pushed Ying Fa arms-length away to look at her. "We can give you nothing more. You are her daughter now."

"Can't I visit?" Ying Fa asked, stung by the finality of her words. "Can't I come home to have my baby?" Tears rose easily now, and she cried, hoping Zhaodi would understand.

"Have I not prepared you for this moment?" Zhaodi asked, her eyes blazing with scorn.

"Please, Mother," She held out a hand.

"It is as she allows," Zhaodi said, ignoring her hand as she nodded in the direction of Uncle Li's limo. "You belong to her now and you must strive to please her. No theatrics, you hear? Not today. Not ever. You give honor to our family with your compliance."

"Yes, Mother," she said, bowing her head. "I'll do my best. You know I will." She wiped the back of her hand across her eyes.

Zhaodi, her expression warming slightly, handed her a lacy handkerchief.

Ying Fa blew her nose and then stuffed the scrap of fabric into her purse. It was a gift of passage that she would wash and press and show to her grandchildren.

"Learn to bend, my stubborn daughter," Zhaodi said softly, her harsh smile lines deepening. "Hold your tongue or surely that bitter old woman will eat you alive."

Then, without warning, Zhaodi shoved her toward the first limo, causing her to skip once before regaining her balance. Then, with as much dignity as she could muster, she climbed into the car.

Silence roared in her ears as she slid onto the fragrant leather seat. The door closed with a smooth clunk. Soft and luxurious, the seat's upholstery warmed to her touch. Though she was the lowest member in her new family, just as she had been in the old, her new life held much promise.

She scanned each face under lowered lashes; seeing black unreadable eyes stare back. She trembled slightly. Gwai Ha, her precious lover, was a stranger now.

Surprising her, Uncle Li flashed a quick smile of approval before turning to Gwai Ha.

"You have chosen well, nephew," he said gruffly as the limo began to move.

Ying Fa blushed and stared at her hands, squirming under the attention now focused upon her. The two women were busily scrutinizing every inch of her pregnant body, their scorn like a slap of heat across both sides of her face.

But, Uncle Li approved; and for that she was grateful. Would Gwai Ha have wanted her otherwise? He had said he did, but had he meant it? Would he have bowed to his uncle's pressure, if circumstances had been different?

"Thank you, sir," Gwai Ha replied happily, as he laid his hand upon her knee. The car rounded a curve and she leaned against him.

She started at his touch, not daring to look up, her cheeks aflame. Then she told herself to relax. The women were merely curious. She was an object to them—a novelty. They were her elders now—each in her own way worthy of emulation, making the biting comebacks she had conjured over the past few months seemed trite and disrespectful.

Her stomach churned as the baby kicked, and she couldn't suppress a grimace. She clenched her fists, resisting the urge to rub the spot; and breathed slowly in and out in, striving for calm. She glanced around; gratified that no one seemed to have noticed her distress.

"I want you to check on our supplier in Zhanjiang next week," Uncle Li said. "Check the dye process for flaws. Some bleeding has been reported with the purple fabric."

Gwai Ha nodded furiously, and gazed at his uncle with open adoration, his eyes alive with excitement, his eagerness making her feel shut out, an accessory. The limo paused at an intersection, and then lurched forward, causing their necks to jerk.

"Soon, you will be joining him on his trips," Uncle Li added kindly, as if reading her mind. She blinked in surprise and caught his brief proprietary glance at her swollen midsection.

All eyes were upon her once again.

"Thank you, sir," she mumbled, and tried not to twitch, though her right leg had fallen asleep.

"After your absence, you'll be trained in silk purchasing," he added, his beady gaze forcing her to look downward at his puffy hands. "You'll learn about quality and geographic tendencies, as well as the dyeing process.

That way, Gwai Ha won't have to hire an untrustworthy assistant. We'll keep it in the family, eh?"

She nodded eagerly, making imperceptible eye contact; stunned that he had even considered her. Then she shrank back into herself wondering if Gwai Ha's mother would make her pay for his kind acknowledgement.

"She's a fast learner," he said to Gwai Ha, ignoring her. "She's the best of the three I sent to Huazhou, so I'm pleased you selected her. Smart mothers produce smart sons."

Gwai Ha nodded, his smile too bright.

"There are many things that I can teach her as well," his wife said, her thin mouth twisting into a wry smile. Her voice was discordant and high-pitched, making Ying Fa wonder if it was her natural speaking voice, or if she spoke that way with the intent to annoy.

"Best wishes, little niece," Mrs. Li continued as she scanned her, her tone slightly belittling, as if proximity to anything connected with her rival would contaminate her. "Please call me Auntie Li."

"Yes, Auntie Li," Ying Fa said carefully, remembering the countless tales she had heard about this powerful woman. She was a distant cousin of Uncle Li, many times removed. Her flat puffy face wore a mask of practiced modesty. It was said that living with Uncle Li had sharpened her political skills to the extreme. Her malicious gaze informed all who dared that they risked being put swiftly and effortlessly into their sorry place.

The flicker of kindness in Auntie Li's eyes, an obvious attempt to draw her out, made all of her senses go on alert. It was merely bait and a dangerous illusion. Auntie Li could never be an ally. Befriending her would be an act of suicide and outright stupidity, for which Mrs. Chan would never forgive her.

She returned Auntie Li's smile coolly, her expression carefully bland. She noticed the tiniest sliver of a scar on her cheek, as if a fingernail had punctured its smooth, dry surface.

So it was true.

She could barely restrain herself from leaning closer to look. Rumor had it that the two women had fought over Gwai Ha's crib. Mrs. Li, seeing her rival's beautiful child, had wanted to claim him for her own. But was Gwai Ha Uncle Li's son, as the rumor alleged? It seemed unlikely.

Auntie Li's eyes were both watchful and hateful as she conversed with Mrs. Chan about the weather, the banquet preparations and the invitation list. Their rivalry was to be honored and feared, as one wisely feared the benevolent, black sky that was shaded with billowing gray. While the ghost of Chan Yanru's youthful beauty hovered over her face like gossamer silk, Auntie Li's middle-aged visage bore the evidence of a harsh, jaundiced life that could no longer be hidden by unguents and creams. Spiteful glances, lips twisted by sarcasm, pale unhealthy skin and a fingernail scar now burning red, lay naked the raw emotions that swelled and eddied around her.

Like a winter's downpour, Auntie Li suddenly broke into non-stop chatter about her third cousin's nephew who lived on a duck farm on the road to Zhanjiang. He had done something important related to genetics or composting or was it ecology? Ying Fa wasn't quite sure.

She slipped into a daydream, imagining the two women as caricatures of wind-up crows: Mrs. Li's lips ever moving while Mrs. Chan nodded repeatedly in detached, unhappy agreement, her pasted-on smile matching her glazed-over eyes.

For a few tense moments, Auntie Li held absolute control of the horrible one-sided conversation, patting Gwai Ha's knee every so often to emphasize a point.

Finally, Uncle Li placed a firm hand on his wife's fleshy arm and she stopped in mid-sentence, her mouth open.

An oppressive silence then filled the limo and Ying Fa leaned toward the window seeking even the smallest breath of fresh air, desperate for the ride to end.

Unwittingly, her gaze kept returning to Auntie Li. Then she quickly looked away. Uncle Li's reprimand had had no effect upon her chilly hauteur. Her evil eyes glinted above a slight half-smile, her gloating satisfaction unmistakable as she eyed her beautiful, though less fortunate sister-in-law and rival. She shifted her body a mere fraction toward her husband in symbolic submission—or was it possession?

Out of the corner of her eye, Ying Fa noticed that Gwai Ha's mother held her back straight, refusing to melt into her seat like a scolded child, drawing her deepest respect.

It struck her that Auntie Li's practiced cruelty actually highlighted her mother-in-law's rare strenght..

What would it take to bring a smile to her beautiful face? Would it crack into a thousand pieces or melt and soften, crumbling into tears, washing away her grief? What courage she must have pulled from her heart, to have live amidst the countless spiteful rumors—and yet she had survived. She had faced her enemy and rival, admitting defeat, when in fact by her dignity alone she had clearly won.

For months, she had feared this tiny woman. Now, sitting in her presence, she found it easy to imagine her forbidding expression transformed—pasty skin turned dewy, angry eyes converted to sparkling jet, and tense lips softened by love. Gwai Ha had such a face, yet unspoiled by savage disappointment.

She glanced down at his hand beside her, longing to cling to his strength. Such cravings were folly, for a bitter reprimand would follow if she dared. How carelessly he sat, his other hand open in his lap; while beside him his mother folded hers together, tense and white.

She folded hers gently in her lap, imitating her new aunt; and then studied Gwai Ha, who was too busy emulating his uncle's indifference to notice his mother's small victory.

She smiled to herself, grateful for having observed these few things. It would take years of studying these people to fully understand them.

The limo made another turn, and Gwai Ha leaned into her, his hand grazing her thigh. She looked up, caught his smile and smiled back. Then quickly, surreptitiously, she scanned the limo's other occupants.

Uncle Li's expression softened as he glanced at Chan Yanru; who grimaced slightly, and looked out the window, her face obscured. They were lovers still. She was sure of it. And who could miss Gwai Ha's profile—a younger shadow of his uncle's?

Tense lines crossed Gwai Ha's face. Perhaps he had sensed each measured nuance in the closed car, felt his mother's humiliation and cringed under his aunt's false kindness. Mrs. Li's claim to the future had been bankrupted on her sturdy sons; and now Gwai Ha, her rival's child, commanded her husband's complete attention. No matter how thick Auntie Li poured on the syrup, Chan Yanru was the honored matron of the day.

Ying Fa straightened in her seat, proud of her passionate and courageous new family, content to produce their next generation.

Then, like a tumbling avalanche, her need for a bathroom rumbled and grew. With each bump, turn, stop and start of the quiet, well-tuned limo, pain and need swelled to the point of desperation.

❀   ❀   ❀

She stumbled from the car clinging to Gwai Ha's arm. Through a haze of pain, she spied the red banners posted above the doorway to the Silk Factory's courtyard. Flowering potted plants of all colors filled the courtyard: they must have cost a small fortune. Another larger red silk banner hung above the far doorway, emblazoned in gold with their family names.

She crossed her legs tightly. Any second she would explode.

Chin lowered and eyes downcast in practiced meekness, she allowed Gwai Ha to lead her through the far door and up the stairs to the banquet room. She had never set foot inside and its enormity stunned her; as did the number of red linen covered tables, around which sat her friends, relatives and beaming colleagues. Servants scurried about with tea pitchers and baskets of chopsticks and napkins. The scent of delicious food provoked her immediate craving for a plate of salty shrimp.

Her face now pinched with pain, she permitted Gwai Ha and his mother to lead her in like a prized buffalo through the first wave of well-wishers.

"Are you alright?" Gwai Ha asked; his brow furrowed with concern.

She mouthed the word "bathroom," whereupon he whispered a terse explanation to his mother and pointed her in the proper direction.

"It was so sudden," she explained to him, mortified that his mother need know of her bodily functions. Pain overruled shame as she lumbered to the bathroom and, once inside, began to undress, her panic rising. Squatting was impossible now without help. She looked around wildly, her heart pounding, her stomach lurching from the incredible stench. It seemed that everything offended her nose these days.

"There you are," Hsiao said, poking her head in the door. "Anji's asleep with Grandmother and I was getting worried about you."

"Come quickly," Ying Fa begged, knowing Hsiao would understand her dilemma. She grimaced as Hsiao held her elbows for support; and sighed as relief quickly followed.

"Western toilets must have been designed for pregnant women," she said with a tight laugh when she had finally caught her breath.

"What's that?" Hsiao asked, helping her to stand. "Western toilets? What are you talking about?"

"Western toilets have seats. Have you seen them?" Ying Fa turned to her with a brilliant smile, then pulled up her underwear and hose and pulled down her dress.

"You talk about toilets at a time like this?" Hsiao shook her head.

"Why not?" Ying Fa asked, giggling. "What could be more basic or useful than a toilet?"

Hsiao laughed and then clasped her arm warmly. "I'll miss you, my dear friend," she said, smiling. "Always a joke with you, Wong Ying Fa. Life won't be the same without you at home."

"I'll miss you, too." Ying Fa moved away. "It's kind of scary, yet exciting all at once."

Still breathless, she began to smooth down her dress; though there wasn't much she could do about the wrinkles and the way her abdomen puffed out. Hsiao held out a hairbrush, which she promptly put to use.

"Those two women in the car," Hsiao whispered, glancing at the door. "What sharp daggers you must have seen, what evil looks and practiced smiles. What happened? What did they talk about? Did they even speak to each other?"

Ying Fa handed her the brush, then shook her head as she moved to the sink, her steps heavy.

"Those two practice harsh lessons," she said with a smirk. She turned on the water and measured her words as she washed her hands, her gaze locked with Hsiao's in the mirror. "They talked alright—about nothing. Hate runs deep between them; and I cannot condemn Mrs. Chan for much of it. She is a brave one and so dignified. Not much gets past her. Auntie Li though—she is pathetic, and very dangerous." She shot Hsiao a significant look.

"They are your family now," Hsiao warned. "You must accept the good with the bad." She handed her a brown paper towel from an extravagant stack, stocked for the occasion. Normally, they dried their hands by shaking them in the air.

Averting her eyes from Hsiao's questioning gaze, Ying Fa dried her hands quickly and dropped the wadded paper into a small wastebasket.

Hsiao then took her by the hand and led her to the door. "You did well, Ying Fa. Gwai Ha is every girl's dream. He is handsome and devoted. He won't stray like your elder brother."

Ying Fa looked at her sharply, reading in her eyes the mute acceptance of all that she had longed to say about Yutang, but could not. He was still her brother, her elder.

"Gwai Ha's not perfect," she said and looked away, embarrassed, unable to think of a single flaw.

"Zhaodi's love more than makes up for Yutang's lack," Hsiao said softly, her expression earnest, her firm, narrow chin showing grim determination. "In his own wild way, Yutang loves me best."

"Are you sure?" Ying Fa asked, stroking her soft cheek.

Hsiao smiled faintly. "In time, Gwai Ha's mother will learn to love you as she loves him. A great deal of time, I expect."

"I'll just make her laugh," Ying Fa said with a grin, determined to make the best of it, as Hsiao had. She clasped her hand, wondering what she'd done to deserve such a friend.

"Ah, Ying Fa, you are obedient, hard-working, lovely—"

"Please." Ying Fa held up a hand. "I'm no one special. I'm just me."

Hsiao's voice dropped to a whisper. "You were always the most highly skilled worker, Boss Li's number one choice. And now you'll give him his heart's desire—a healthy great-nephew." Hsiao touched her belly.

"Yes, he's an active one," Ying Fa said, and rubbed the spot where an arm or a foot poked sharply. She pressed the spot, love pouring from her to the tiny, precious babe.

"You know I'll do my best," she said softly "I'll regret his mother's losses along with her, and make her joy my delight."

"Like your brother, ever the braggart," Hsiao said, and laughed as Ying Fa hugged her.

"I'll adore whatever Gwai Ha loves," Ying Fa said brightly, like a student reciting from a book. "Whatever he craves will become my obsession."

"As it should be," Hsiao said giggling. She checked her watch.

"We've got to go," she said, her expression melting to cool modesty as she pushed the door open and pulled Ying Fa behind her.

Ying Fa studied the cavernous hall, the banners hanging on its far side, the round tables, around which her friends and family sat, the row of banquet tables laden with steaming food, behind which stood cooks in tall white chef's hats, intent upon their work. She saw hands shaken, nods and smiles all around. She took in the excited faces: some flushed from wine, some alive with sprightly debates, some laughing over jokes. This was a rare day for the Maoming Silk Factory, a fine day despite the rain.

She spied Chan Yanru, still clinging to Gwai Ha's arm. They were talking with a large group at the far end of the room.

"Good luck," Hsiao whispered, patting her arm.

Ying Fa squeezed her hand one last time, then pushed her in the direction of Anji and Poh Poh—two pairs of loving eyes, eager for the sunshine that only she could give.

A soft silence settled in her heart as she pondered the true meaning of this celebration, which marked a crowning success far greater than acceptance into the Pioneer League or the completion of silk embroidery training. By marrying Gwai Ha, she had stepped from childhood into a future of assured success. Many guests shot her looks of seasoned envy, but most glances wished her good luck.

She moved deliberately across the room to her new family. It was now time to take her rightful, well-deserved place in the Li family as their honored daughter-in-law, wife and mother-to-be. She kept her face carefully neutral and her eyes downcast as she accepted the heartfelt congratulations of those she passed.

She saw traces of both fear and sadness on Mrs. Chan's perfect oval face as she approached. Then anger appeared, and disdain. It was an ugly veneer.

Ying Fa smiled, her confidence building. She would break through her mother-in-law's icy reserve and create a joy-filled home. From now on, she would do everything in her power to love and care for this tiny, hardened woman.

Chapter 6 – March

The afternoon light cast dull shadows against the piles of linen, clothing and household goods perched precariously against each other along the main room's far wall. Ying Fa sighed as she pressed the iron down hard onto the neatly embroidered pillowcase, turning her face to escape the rising steam. Mrs. Chan didn't own an ironing board; so she'd had to make do with towels on her bed and an ancient iron that snagged if she wasn't careful.

How she longed for her own sturdy bed in Zhaodi's efficient home—a bed that was no longer hers. She looked down the bed she shared with Gwai Ha, and sighed again. In the apartment's main room, it afforded no privacy; because of course, it didn't have a curtain around it. Supposedly, they couldn't afford one.

Two weeks had passed since the wedding, and she was ready to explode.

Mrs. Chan had yet to speak to her directly; and now she had run after Gwai Ha, leaving her choking on suppressed rage and mounting frustration. Today was supposed to have been her day off. She was supposed to have gone home to visit her family. Nevertheless, here she was, faced with yet another day of grueling drudgery, and no one with whom she could talk.

There had been some accomplishments, hadn't there? The place had been a disaster when she'd arrived: clothes and household goods everywhere, dishes piled and food-encrusted in the kitchen and on the dining table, layers of grime and mold in the bathroom.

She gazed in appreciation at the large dining table, gleaming and round, the room's only furniture, aside from her bed and four sturdy chairs. Its polished surface spoke of honey wax and tender care; but it didn't hide those awful piles stacked against the walls.

She shook her head as she scanned the piles, each merging onto the next like some distorted, open-air market. According to Gwai Ha, his mother wouldn't hear of having another stick of furniture; and she'd have no pictures on the walls, or drapes on the windows or a dividing curtain around their marital bed. Too much money was always her excuse.

She shuddered, thinking of the sounds she and Gwai Ha made when they pleasured each other in that bed.

Another tired sigh escaped her lips as she glanced toward the tiny, spotless bathroom. Had she remembered to hang the family's stockings up to dry? She visualized the pile of stockings in the tub lying next to the string she had yet to hang. Many things escaped her memory these days as she struggled to adjust to the demands of her new family.

Pants and shirts were soaking in the kitchen sink, yet another demand on her dwindling energy. She glanced tiredly at the closed door against the main room's far wall, wondering when she would have a chance to clean the room behind it. It was Mrs. Chan's bedroom, her exclusive domain; yet she was as determined to clean and organize it as she had the rest of the apartment.

She added the last pressed pillowcase to the pile before her, then carried the iron to the kitchen, deep exhaustion slowing her pace. Tears filled her eyes. How could she possibly go to work the next day without falling asleep?

She set the iron down on a trivet, than turned to the clothes in the sink, wrung them out, rinsed them, and carried them to the bathroom in a large pot, lest they drip across the floor. She hung the string, and on it, the stockings; then hung the pants and shirts on metal hangers, her movements slow.

"Mother," she whispered in the gloomy silence, wishing she were home, wishing she had some help. Two other grown women eased Zhaodi's burdens. She shook her head in bewilderment, thinking of Mrs. Chan, who seemed to delight in laziness, her disapproval quick, harsh and yet hurtfully silent. What was worse, she liked to topple the piles every chance she got, creating chaos in the apartment's limited space, creating more work. Though retired, she was always busy with her numerous committees, and claimed she had no time for chores— that such menial pursuits were beneath her.

She didn't dare ask how she and Gwai Ha had fared before she'd joined them; and hated to complain— especially when Gwai Ha insisted that his mother truly appreciated her efforts.

But what did he know about houskeeping or his mother's cruelty, for that matter? He had lived on his own in Beijing for the past several years; and now was hardly ever home.

She rubbed her aching back, gasping as the baby kicked and sent her off balance. She grabbed the sink, catching herself in time.

"My sweet baby," she crooned, rubbing her swollen abdomen, sending loving thoughts to her child. "You'll be just like your father," she said, trying to ignore the niggling fear that it was a girl. A daughter was useless, futureless; and it was no secret that Uncle Li wanted a grandnephew, and Gwai Ha a son.

Zhaodi once told her that in the early days of the one-child law, illegal second children were routinely aborted, even late-term. Poh Poh claimed that it still happened, though it was more common for women to let miscarriages and stillbirths deal with the problem.

She clutched her abdomen, suddenly and painfully sick to her stomach. What glib words people used to hide their mountains of pain? Just yesterday, Mrs. Chan had calmly suggested through Gwai Ha that she have an ultrasound. Of course, she had rejected the idea. She would never abort her child. She rubbed her eyes and moved tiredly to the main room, to one of the chairs. She sat down heavily.

A knock at the door startled her.

Quickly, she pulled herself together, then went to the door and opened it.

"Poh Poh!" she cried, and flung herself sobbing into her grandmother's arms. "I can't take it anymore! I'm soo tired and so worried. Mrs. Chan doesn't like me. She never—"

"Quiet!" the old woman spat. She staggered on spindly legs, held upright by whipcord strength alone. She patted Ying Fa's back a little too hard. "Get a hold of yourself," she said sternly, taking her firmly by the hand. Then she pulled her into the apartment and shut the door.

"Making a scene in the hallway so that everyone can hear?" she scolded. "What are you—stupid?"

Unable to speak through her sobs, Ying Fa stumbled to a chair and sat, pressing her hands to her face. "I know. I know," she said at last. All the neighbors will come running to Mrs. Chan . . . and . . .." She took a big gulp. "I shouldn't be bothering you with my problems, anyway." Her voice dropped to a whisper as she looked up at Poh Poh through her tears.

"Self pity is a waste of time," Poh Poh said, turning her back on her as she hefted her bag onto the table. She looked around the apartment and waved expansively. "And with such luxuries abounding." She shook her head and the headed to the kitchen. "Your own kitchen," she said over her shoulder. "Now this I must see."

Ying Fa sniffed loudly, and then took one of the plainest handkerchiefs from a pile on the floor and dried her eyes and blew her nose. Considering that it was the first visit from a member of her own family, she was utterly ashamed of her wild display. She retreated to the bathroom to wash her face.

Later, with eyes downcast and expecting a well-earned lecture, she found her grandmother poking about the kitchen, satisfying her curiosity while she brewed a pot of tea.

Ying Fa piled an assortment of pork dumplings, shrimp toast and dried noodles onto her best porcelain plate; then balanced the plate, teapot, two teacups and two sets of chopsticks onto a tray, and carried it out to the table. Poh Poh limped behind her.

"I'm really sorry," she said, as she waited for Poh Poh to arrange a lace cloth, pulled from a pile of tablecloths, over the gleaming table. She set the tray down carefully, then placed the food and tableware out attractively, as she had been taught. She poured the tea and handed Poh Poh a cup. They ate in silence for several minutes.

Poh Poh looked at her over her teacup, her eyes soft with compassion. "I'm ready to listen," she said softly.

Ying Fa's eyes stung, but she looked her in the eye. There was no one on earth she trusted more than her grandmother.

"My fears grow in this lonely place," she said at last. "I've no one to argue with, no one to share the work. Gwai Ha's always at work or at a meeting or on a business trip and Mrs. Chan doesn't—"

Poh Poh held up a hand. "Now, before you start telling tales about Chan Yanru, just answer this." She leaned toward her, her eyes bright with curiosity. "Is married life all that you expected?"

Ying Fa raised her teacup to inhale its steaming fragrance. "That and more," she replied with a nod, her lips curling into a smile. "Sleeping in Gwai Ha's arms is wonderful. I've gained much face with my coworkers; and Uncle Li has become moderately respectful." She slid her chair closer to Poh Poh, craving her warmth. "It is difficult to be sad around you," she murmured, patting her arm. "And you make the most delicious tea." She took a sip.

Poh Poh smiled at her warmly and clasped her hand. "You'll tell of these times with your children and their children, as Zhaodi and I do." Poh Poh looked deep into her eyes, as if seeing into her soul. "Perhaps someday

Chan Yanru will tell you her stories. She's certainly had her share." She set her teacup down and pressed Ying Fa's belly.

"I fear it's a girl," she said, frowning.

Ying Fa closed her eyes. They burned against the swelling tide of tears ready to burst. "I think so, too," she whispered. A single tear trailed down her face. She made no effort to brush it away.

"Chan Yanru will tell you what to do when the time comes," Poh Poh whispered. She rocked slightly in her chair, a gloomy, ancient figure that Ying Fa barely recognized. She clung to her hand, struggling to focus on the soft, singsong words that fell from her trembling old mouth.

"If you bear a girl and keep her, prepare for divorce. Prepare to suffer the Li's scorn, to lose your job, to live in some wretched hovel far from your husband. Prepare to give up every last thing you've accomplished for a child who can be easily replaced."

"No," Ying Fa moaned, covering her middle with both hands. "It's my baby. How can I live without this child?"

"Chan Yanru is on the Family Planning committee," Poh Poh hissed. She gripped Ying Fa's arm, her nails digging in. Ying Fa cried out, but didn't pull away. "You know how they punish parents of illegal second children."

Ying Fa sobbed quietly.

"She owes Manager Li her life," Poh Poh continued, laying a hand on her shoulder. "With him at the top level of polical power, those two are desperately afraid of taking the wrong step, backing the wrong policy. Because of their illicit relationship, they'll observe the law, no matter the cost." She leaned closer. "It's a well-kept secret that Yanru's favorite daughter produced two untimely girls before finally producing a son."

Ying Fa closed her eyes. That Yanru condoned such behavior was like a sharp pin beneath her nail, dissolving all hope.

"You must do as you are told," Poh Poh said, caressing her face. "Please do as you are told, my sweet granddaughter." She shook her head. "I fear for you, my headstrong dragon."

"I've never felt so alone," Ying Fa whispered.

"Yanru is a hard woman," Poh Poh said, gripping her hand with both of hers. "She watches you, trying to understand your motivation. Will you steal her son away? Will you push her aside, stripping her of her rightful authority? She is a complex woman driven by fear. Her grief and shame blind her; even cripple her. But deep inside she is as soft as five-day-old fish, a child trapped in a woman's body. Someday she will love you. It is in her heart to do so; as it is in yours to love her first."

"I try to please her," Ying Fa said, hearing the whine in her voice.

Poh Poh cocked her head as if puzzled. "It's only been two weeks. Give her time."

"But—"

"Listen to me, girl. Yanru was once a haughty, cherished daughter who gave her life to a doomed man. She chose the eldest brother out of pride, when it was the second son who loved her the most. Life has a way of spinning out of control sometimes." She reached out her gnarled hand as if to snatch something. "Yet we must cling to survival. The only way to ensure the future is through our children."

Ying Fa sipped her tea, comforted by its warmth and by Poh Poh's soothing voice that rose and fell in musical cadence.

"My mother-in-law had the heart of a rotted cabbage," Poh Poh said with a sage smile that invited Ying Fa's grin. "I was naive, just seventeen when I married her precious son. She ruled our household with such cruelty that I was unable to lean toward my husband, as a wife should. She berated me in front of the servants and humiliated me in front of her arrogant friends. She made me out to be a confused young wife, who was too stupid to understand the ways of her new family; and liked to hit me with a willow branch for each so called infraction. How I cried during those years—secret tears shed without witness, lest I be reported." She pressed her lips together for a long moment.

Ying Fa nodded slightly in encouragement, now understanding the oft-told tale. While she had been lonely at the work farm, she had known that eventually, she could go home. Now like Poh Poh and countless generations of Chinese women before her, she had been pushed out of the nest, given to her husband's family, unable to return. Yet unlike Poh Poh, who had been bound to a stranger and sent to a far away place, she at least had stayed in Maoming.

"I was twenty when the Long March began," Poh Poh continued. "By then I was too busy with my new son to pay much attention. Mother-in-law adored Weigo, your father; and with his birth, she finally granted me some semblance of respect." Poh Poh frowned. "I should have known she'd try to take him from me, as she had my husband. But at the time, I was still too trusting and didn't recognize her intent."

Ying Fa sipped her tea quietly, seeing Mrs. Chan in the same light, monopolizing Gwai Ha's time. Would she take away her child?

Poh Poh grimaced and turned away as if in pain.

Ying Fa leapt up. "What is it?" she cried. Spying the small bit of crust on Poh Poh's lap, she realized that it was her teeth bothering her again. "That dumpling was too hard!" she cried, and swept up the piece and picked up her grandmother's teacup and urged her to drink.

After a few sips, Poh Poh motioned for her to sit. "I'm fine, just fine," she said, her eyes averted in embarrassment.

Ying Fa patted her arm, not wanting to cause her further distress. Then she poured more tea, and resumed her seat.

"Fourteen years later, Chairman Mao declared the People's Republic of China," Poh Poh said softly. "I was oblivious to the turmoil around me. Sheltered as I was, I didn't hear the rumors and paid no attention to the loss of this servant and that, as our financial situation became increasingly dire. By that time, I had had my two beautiful girls. Graceful and strong, their laughter was my greatest joy. They walked and spoke early, easily outdistancing their steadfast older brother. They were my shining lights, my reason for living." She paused, gazing as if into the far distance of her memory.

Captivated, Ying Fa leaned closer. She had fantasized about her aunts for as long as she could remember. Simply mentioning them brought shadows to Father's face and caused Poh Poh to run crying from the room. At last, she would hear the awful tale.

"I was forty-three during the late fifties, the time of the Great Famine," Poh Poh said, her tone resigned. "Mother-in-law was counting each mouthful of food. She slowly decreased my daughters' allotment, unbeknownst to either Weigo or my husband. For you see, they adored my laughing sweethearts as much I did. They would never have harmed them."

"She was jealous?" Ying Fa asked, holding back the other fifteen questions she longed to ask.

"Perhaps," Poh Poh said, tipping her head slightly to the side, pondering her question. "Or maybe she was just making an honorable choice under horrible circumstances. Time changes ones' perspective. Like with all of us, my girls were destined to become the daughters of other families. Like you, they laughed away sorrow and found happy amusement even during the darkest of times. We don't often know how we'll react until such choices are presented." She bowed her head slightly. "I can say that now, but at the time . . .." She shook her head sadly.

"What happened to them?" Ying Fa whispered; then held her breath. This was the question she had always wanted to ask. Tales of expendable girls always snagged her attention; but this was about her father's sisters—Wong girls just like her. Looking around at the table, she made a mental note to send the untouched food home with her grandmother. It was the least she could do, considering the distance she had walked, the comfort she had brought.

"Food became scarce," Poh Poh said with a grimace.

Ying Fa watched her closely. As much as she longed to hear the tale, if it caused her pain, she would make her stop.

"The remaining servants were let go," Poh Poh continued. "The house rattled with emptiness. My husband buried himself in ancient studies, while his father tried, without much success, to earn money bartering some of our belongings." Poh Poh's expression darkened. "My husband didn't even try to stop his mother from moving me and my daughters into a dingy room, far from the rest of the family. She had decided that since I had already produced an heir, I was expendable, as were my girls. My husband didn't care what happened to me."

Tears rolled down her cheeks.

"Please stop," Ying Fa said softly, her hand going to her wrist.

Poh Poh shook her head and waved her hand, warding her off.

"After she sent your father to school, she cut our food supply even further. Then I became sick. Weak and fevered, I could do nothing when first one girl and then the other stopped eating in order to save the food for me. By the time I had recovered, they were gone. Cholera moves fast."

Cholera! Even the sound of it was frightening, evoking images of mass graves and huge bonfires. She had read about such things in school. Even now, in the aftermath of monsoon floods, the threat persisted.

"What were their names?" she whispered, wanting to cry.

"Xian was my bossy dragon girl, and YeTo, my giggling dumpling glutton." Poh Poh covered her mouth, stifling a sob.

"How old were they?" She had always wanted to know.

"Xian was twelve, almost a woman, and YeTo was ten. You are the image of YeTo, I am afraid. Your father recognized it first."

Poh Poh rose with tight lips and gestured for her to stay, as she limped to the bathroom, then closed the door softly behind her.

Ying Fa refilled the teacups with slow movements, as if in a dream, tears rolling down her cheeks. How could anyone have survived such pain? How could an old woman have made such a desperate choice?

Poh Poh emerged a few moments later, her expression closed. Ying Fa averted her eyes, granting her gift of silence as she returned to her seat; and pushed her teacup closer.

"I remember Mother-in-law standing over my bed a few days after my girls' bodies had been carted away to a burn pile by some wretched laborer," Poh Poh said softly, her face ageless with its lined ridges, her obsidian eyes as cold as January.

Ying Fa could only stare at her, praying she would stop.

"It didn't matter that tears streaked down that old woman's face, or that she wrung her hands in desperation." Poh Poh laughed harshly. "It was too late. I had no sympathy left to give. 'I had to save Weigo,' she told me. I could barely make out her whine through the layers of my confusion and grief. 'We must sacrifice our daughters for our sons,' she insisted, as if my acceptance of what she had done could somehow disperse the blame and ease her guilt." She shook her head. "Nothing can alter what she did. I turned from her and was sick to my stomach."

"But you still lived with her," Ying Fa said, recalling the stories of Poh Poh shuffling her feeble in-laws and incoherent husband out of the family compound just ahead of the Red Guards. She took her hand gently, wondering at her strength, ashamed that she had complained about a few overturned piles of household goods.

Poh Poh grimaced, her eyelids stretching into two taut lines. "Your father returned by the end of the week and revealed her treachery. His scathing denunciation of what she had done pushed her into a complete mental collapse. Then, as suddenly as he had arrived, he left again for Beijing, leaving me with the scattered remnants of our household. I had no servants, two senile in-laws, and a husband who hid from all responsibility." Poh Poh rocked as she spoke, her face a calm mask. "It was so long ago," she whispered.

She turned to Ying Fa and patted her belly. "I pray it's a boy," she said sadly, "though with your high, round shape . . . I know different."

Ying Fa choked back tears and shook her head. "Perhaps Uncle Li will allow it."

"Wishing won't make it so," Poh Poh said with a soft laugh. "You can abort now, though I know you won't. If it makes you feel any better, think of those foreigners your brother took to the beach that day."

"What do you mean?" Ying Fa asked. "What foreigners?"

"The ones who adopted those babies. Remember?"

Ying Fa gazed at her, now recalling the incident. It had been her first date—such a magical time, so long ago—as if it had happened to somebody else. Absently she lifted a chopstick then dropped it on her plate. "Where did those babies come from? I've forgotten."

"Don't ask foolish questions," Poh Poh warned. "Or borrow trouble. Fate will bring what it will." She leaned forward "Now, let's discuss what we can correct." She smiled softly and lifted her teacup with both hands. "Tell me what else is bothering you, child."

She took in Poh Poh's red-rimmed eyes and her soft, wrinkled face. It was difficult to look her in the eye, now that she was fully aware of her capacity for grief.

She sighed as she pressed a hand on her abdomen. Like the flip of a coin—a boy or a girl—each would offer a fateful choice. Meanwhile, she had to contend with this hurtful longing, this dreadful suspense. Was her body merely a vessel for Uncle Li's dreams?

She began to smile. Men could be such desperate creatures. There had to be a way to placate Uncle Li. Hadn't Chan Yanru done it for years?

"Tell me everything," Poh Poh said, forcing a laugh. "Lest you grow bitter roots in your heart to harvest later upon your own unsuspecting daughter-in-law."

Ying Fa giggled nervously and hid her hands in her lap. Though she feared for her future, her piddling tale of woe was nothing compared to Poh Poh's heartbreaking sacrifices. She looked around at her spotless home, grateful to be its caretaker, then settled into her chair, taking the time to choose her words carefully, aware of Poh Poh's keen observation.

"I don't mind the work," she said, waving a hand to indicate her surroundings. "What bothers me most is that Mrs. Chan ignores me. She talks through Gwai Ha, and everything is no, no and no. He and I have to whisper when she's home." Ying Fa shook her head. "And look at those piles." She pointed to the stacks against the walls. "We need a wardrobe; but will she listen? And I've yet to see the clutter in her precious room."

Both women turned at a sound.

Mrs. Chan, her face a mask of rage, stood in the doorway, her arms laden with bags.

Ying Fa gasped, wanting to melt into a puddle beneath her chair.

"Mrs. Chan?" Poh Poh said with a tight nod, her smile half-practiced, half-honest amusement. "What an honor to see you, my dear." She held out a hand.

Mrs. Chan looked down her nose at the profured hand and then at her bags. "Wardrobes!" she spat. "All she talks about are her mother's rediculous wardrobes." She dropped her bags and threw her hands up, causing Ying Fa to shrink back. "As if a blasted piece of furniture could solve every little problem!" She slammed the door with a backward kick, then grabbed her bags and stomped past them to her room.

"Mrs. Tsao," she said, nodding with a backward glance. "I'll be right out." She slammed the door, causing a nearby pile of shoes to topple.

Ying Fa turned to see Poh Poh clutching her thin chest and barking with laughter. She stared at her. Then her lips began to twitch and her throat started to tickle. Stifling an erupting giggle, she ran to the kitchen.

She filled the teapot with shaking hands, then splashed her burning face with cold water, hoping to douse the flame. Then she gasped, remembering the plate of food she left on the table. Mrs. Chan was fussy about food, continually complaining to Gwai Ha that her dumplings were too salty, her pancakes too flat, her eggs too tough and her vegetables overcooked. Nothing pleased that self-righteous crone. What would she say about serving leftovers to an honored guest?

She was arranging teacups on a clean lace tablecloth when Mrs. Chan emerged from her room.

"Didn't your daughter-in-law ever teach her about housekeeping?" she asked, her color high. She deliberately avoided Ying Fa's gaze. "And her sense of order . . . terrible, terrible—as if she was raised on the streets."

With shaking hands, Ying Fa handed her a brimming teacup. Mrs. Chan accepted it without comment; then sipped noisily as she paced the room. Exhausted, Ying Fa sat on the nearest chair.

"In what way is she lacking?" Poh Poh asked softly.

"Those piles, for one," Mrs. Chan replied, sloshing tea all over the freshly washed floor. "They are common and unsightly."

Ying Fa's breath caught as Mrs. Chan held out a slender foot and kicked over a pile of freshly pressed sheets. "What a mess she leaves," Mrs. Chan muttered, her eyes alight with such mischief that Ying Fa almost burst out laughing. Chan Yanru was but a naughty child, delightful and precocious.

She watched her, now boldly curious, a smile threatening her lips as she shared the laughter in her grandmother's eyes. "Wouldn't a wardrobe look nice against that wall?" she asked, trying to keep the smile from her voice. She picked up her teacup and took a sip, and glanced at Mrs. Chan out of the corner of her eye. "She could probably use one in her room, as well." She lifted her chin slightly in Mrs. Chan's direction. "It would straighten this mess right up."

"You see what I mean about those wardrobes, Mrs. Tsao?" Mrs. Chan glared at Poh Poh in mock injury.

Poh Poh chuckled. "You create such chaos, Yanru, such wounded-duck energy. Make your own misery as you will, but please, spare my poor granddaughter. She deserves better than that, and you know it."

"In my day, only servants cleaned," Mrs. Chan replied as she tipped over a pile of newspapers with her toe. They slid forward, covering the toppled sheets.

Ying Fa covered her mouth in a desperate attempt to stifle her giggles. Then, using her best imitation of Uncle Li during one of his tiresome morning lectures, she began to speak.

"The use of servants is a concept of the past, a failed concept that went out with property ownership," she began. "To quote Chairman Mao, 'we must remain modest, prudent and free from arrogance and rashness in our style of work. We must help preserve the style of plain living and hard struggle—'"

"I know Mao's words better than you!" Mrs. Chan shrieked. She lunged at Ying Fa, spilling tea all over the lace tablecloth. Poh Poh took Ying Fa's arm as if to protect her, but Ying Fa brushed her aside. She rose from her chair and crossed the distance to her quaking mother-in-law.

"Well, at last you speak to me," she said, looking her in the eye. It was like yelling at Zhaodi. Why had she ever held back? "Imagine that, dear Mother-in-law, I actually exist. And I have feelings, too, as you well know."

"Ying Fa?" Poh Poh exclaimed, pressing a hand to her heaving chest. "She is your elder."

"See! See!" Mrs. Chan shouted, backing away from Ying Fa. "She's trying to take over. She's trying to steal what is mine."

"I am not!" Ying Fa shrieked back. "Until now, you haven't even looked at me! Can't you see that I am pregnant with your grandchild? Can't you see how hard I have tried to please you? But nothing I ever do is ever good enough for you, now is it?"

Poh Poh rose stiffly. "I see that you have much to discuss." She smiled wryly. "Though I'd love to stay, this should remain between the two of you."

Ying Fa hurried to the kitchen, her pulse humming, ready for a fight, and returned with a sheet of brown paper.

She didn't care that Mrs. Chan watched, tapping her foot disapprovingly, her arms across her chest; as she wrapped the dumplings, shrimp toast and dried noodles for Poh Poh to take home. The gift was but a small token in exchange for Poh Poh's kindness. How she dreaded her departure.

"Please take this," she urged at the door. She hugged Poh Poh as she pressed the package into her hands. "Come again soon," she whispered, dreading the imminent confrontation with Mrs. Chan. "And bring Mother and Hsiao and Anji. Please, Poh Poh."

Poh Poh nodded stiffly, the love in her eyes granting her both strength and compassion as she shuffled away.

She closed the door quickly and turned.

"Now you're giving our food away?" Mrs. Chan asked. She stood in the middle of the room, furious.

"She's my grandmother," Ying Fa said as she pressed a lump on the side of her swollen belly. "You said you hated my dumplings. You said they were too salty and bland."

"I didn't say you could give them away." Mrs. Chan shook her fist.

"To my grandmother? I thought you liked her. You said she was the only decent member of my family."

"You should have given her something better." Mrs. Chan's lips curled in satisfaction. One of the overhead light bulbs popped and the room darkened considerably.

"But you said . . .." Ying Fa looked at her. "Are you trying to torture me?"

Suddenly, Mrs. Chan smiled. It was the smile of victory, the silliest smile she had ever seen. Ying Fa burst out laughing.

Mrs. Chan bit down on her trembling lip and her face grew crimson. Her left eye and the muscle along her right cheek began to twitch. Then she was laughing, too.

Shyly at first, Ying Fa moved toward her.

Mrs. Chan's eyes finally spoke of a welcome that she had longed to receive. But, as they were about to touch, the door swung open.

Laughing, they turned to see Gwai Ha striding into the room. "What is going on here?" he demanded grimly.

"We were discussing a wardrobe," Ying Fa said, trying to compose herself.

"Two wardrobes," Mrs. Chan added with a curt nod; and then she fell giggling into Ying Fa's outstretched arms.

Chapter 7

It was pitch dark and warm beneath the covers. Ying Fa moved a toe and then a foot, relishing the rasp of smooth, soap-scented cotton against her skin. Thankfully, it was Tuesday, her day off. The sun would soon creep over the horizon, warming the cool spring morning with its rosy glow. Languidly, she reached for Gwai Ha only to find a cold, empty spot where his warm body should have been. Was he already up and out the door to his first committee meeting? The nights passed all too swiftly, with barely enough time for simple pleasures and open conversation between husband and wife. If only Mrs. Chan would leave them alone for a few hours.

She felt a soft fluttering on her nose and brushed it aside, then burrowed deeper into her soft cocoon. The fluttering reached her lips, prompting her to open one eye.

Gwai Ha stood beside the bed grinning. In his hand was a speckled goose feather.

"What are you doing?" she cried, rising too quickly, batting at air as he sprang away. Her mound of a stomach caught her short and she gasped. Her bladder suddenly screamed for relief.

"Time to get up, my cherry blossem," Gwai Ha sang as leaped back with the feather; a swath of glossy bangs covering one devilish eye.

She gasped as she looked down at her nakedness, then hastily pulled up a sheet. "Gwai Ha!"

"What a shame to hide such a feast," he said, chuckling.

"Your mother," she said, looking about wildly.

"Back at any minute." He grinned wickedly.

She hadn't heard the usual clanging of pots and pans, or the clipped obscenities or angry complaints coming from the kitchen. The only sounds were Gwai Ha's voice, morning traffic and the neighbors thumping about overhead as they prepared for their workday. There were no aromas of cooking food—just cool moist air from last night's rain.

"You!" She shook a fist at him, then threw back her head and laughed. He leaped to her side making monkey noises, and pulled her into his arms and kissed her, all the while massaging her aching back, making her moan.

"How do you know these things?" she asked, and offered her lips for another kiss. The previous night, he had caressed her body until she had gasped with pleasure; and she was eager to do the same for him. At his urging they had slept naked, the heavy curtain around their bed a dark shield.

He held her away from him, his gaze adoring. The perfection of his smooth, strong face, bright with love, brough tears to her eyes. No man had ever even hinted at the things he so lavishly provided. Sometimes it was hard to believe he was real.

"Why are you still here?" she asked, pushing him away in embarrassment. "And where is your mother?"

"So many questions from such a beautiful young woman." He pressed his fingers to her lips. "I reward silence, you know." He cuped her breasts, making her tender nipples rise in happy greeting.

"Oh, really?" She rose awkwardly and peered down her nose at him. "Do you have to joke at this time of day?" One wrong move and her bladder would explode. "Did you cancel your meeting or get someone to cover for you?"

"Such a fresh ripe melon," he said, then took her face in both hands and stared into her eyes, imitating his uncle's scowl. "You are a very crabby lady." Then he grinned as he yanked away the sheet.

Her cheeks started to tickle. How dare he look so delicious in the morning light while her tired body looked like a puffy beach ball someone had lost behind the concessions? Then her face began to twitch.

"You will be pleasant," he intoned and hoisted her to her feet. "You will join me for fun and games." He held her in his arms, his captive of love, and peppered her with kisses as she squirmed, chest heaving with suppressed glee, desperate for the bathroom.

"Let me go!" she cried, and finally broke away.

Twenty minutes later, she emerged from the bathroom, relaxed, bathed and ready for the day.

"Feeling better?" he asked, looking up from the morning newspaper. He lounged on the new red sofa he had insisted on purchasing to go with the wardrobes—much to his mother's chagrin. The wardrobes had yet to arrive.

"I am," she said, eying the shopping cart he had parked by the door. "So you have plans, do you?"

"You know it," he said with a smile as he set the paper aside and came toward her. He pulled her close for lingering kiss.

The baby kicked and she muffled a moan. "It won't be long," he said, running a gentle hand over her belly, a soft smile on his face.

"It can't be too soon," she agreed, and ran both hands along the lapels of his leather jacket.

He was a gorgeous creature; but telling him so would only give him a swelled head. She closed her eyes and relished his strong arms as they went around her, feeling safe and treasured.

"I can't believe I have you all to myself today," she said, caressing his lips with her gaze. "It's been such a long time."

"Too long," he agreed. "And so much has happened. Soon your focus will be on our son and I'll miss your personal attention." He smiled wryly. "Especially now, we need this time alone."

"I haven't had a chance to think beyond the next few months," she whispered, wanting to pull him back to bed. "Tell me your dreams and I'll make them mine."

"We'll talk over dim sum," he said, looking pleased. "You choose the place, since you're the culinary expert. I trust your choice will be excellent."

She laughed as they strode out of the door side by side. Never in her wildest dreams had she imagined she would experience such miraculous bonding, such pleasantly painful yearning for a man who was her own.

Something caused her to look back as they rounded the corner of the building. She caught a glimpse of her mother-in-law running alongside Uncle Li. Mrs. Chan's expression was excited and gleeful, while Uncle Li looked hot, uncomfortable and angry. On his head was a grizzled wig and on his face, a huge pair of sunglasses.

A disguise?

She stifled a giggle. There was no mistaking his flushed face and haughty stride.

Like guilty teenagers, the two ran up the steps of the apartment building and disappeared inside.

"Did you see that?" she asked and accidentally pulled Gwai Ha around in a wide circle. He stepped off the sidewalk, directly into the oncoming path of two unwieldy bicycles piled high with tree branches. She watched in horror as the bicycles veered around him, seemingly in slow motion, forcing cars and trucks to merge, almost crashing. Drivers shouted and sounded their bells and horns; and then Gwai Ha stepped back onto the safety of the sidewalk.

"Are you trying to kill me?" he shouted, his face suffused with rage. She cringed and pulled back, seeing on his face the image of his uncle. He stood with his arms stiffly at his sides, his fingers stretched like twigs, glaring at her.

"Sorry," she said, and batted her eyelashes, trying to mollify him. It wasn't her fault he didn't watch where he was going, though it would probably do no good to point it out to him. She wasn't about to cry, though tears filled her eyes. She wrung her hands, a habit she thought she had broken under the hot summer sun of the farming commune.

How could he be charming one minute and overbearing the next? He was just like Yutang or Father, thinking he could rule with a glance. She sighed, wishing she could erase what had happened. Admittedly, she was no prize at times with her bossy tone and rigid rules of order; but she had never been mean—not to anyone. Perhaps this was the way marriage worked, the man always censuring the woman. It didn't seem fair; but what was ever fair?

"Ying Fa?" His expression softened. He took her hand, her dejection lifting as he placed his other hand against her belly.

Smiling tremulously, she pulled him close, needing to reclaim him, needing his forgiveness. "I'm sorry," she whispered into his ear.

Pedestrians streamed around them making her dizzy. She hesitated before she spoke, afraid she would spoil their time alone. But, there should be no secrets between them—no lies to trip them up at later, less fortunate times.

"I just saw your mother and Uncle Li sneaking into the apartment," she whispered, her heart pounding. "It surprised me, that's all. I thought maybe I was seeing things, you know . . .."

"You saw what you saw," he said, looking away briefly, clearly annoyed. "They probably waited in the alley for us to leave." He shrugged. "Since Mother's returned from Guangzhou, I've made a point of being out at certain times. Like right about now."

"Why?" she asked, and then blushed and looked at her feet. Why indeed? Where else were longtime lovers supposed to meet? What an idiot she was.

"It's okay," Gwai Ha said with a sharp laugh. "Ever the innocent, my little Ying Fa."

He pulled her out of the flow of foot traffic to stand beside him against an old stone building.

"I thought you already knew what was going on," he said kindly, his finger brushing her cheek, acceptance shining in his eyes. "Surely, you've heard the rumors. Your grandmother must have told you about it." He put a hand on her waist and she leaned toward him. "Come, my little naïve chicken," he whispered. "Let's go for that dim sum and we'll talk."

"Over by the park?" she asked, recalling a place Baak-Hap had mentioned. Though the Maoming Building was closer and offered more variety, Zhaodi would be there.

Gwai Ha nodded and she smiled up at him, grateful for his understanding. When would she learn to think before she spoke?

Probably never.

Grinning, ignoring the curious stares of passersby, she took Gwai Ha's hand and strode with him in the direction of the park.

The Rice Pot was one of those new upstart restaurants, claimed to be fly-by-night, yet destined to become the decade's most popular establishment, especially with young couples looking for an intimate rendezvous away from prying families. It was a dimly lit warren of rooms, with small battered tables, the menu tacked on each wall, and servers floating about, pushing gleaming metal carts, passing fragrant teapots, and handing out chopsticks and teacups.

They sat across from each other at a table in the back. Between them were two fragrant cups of tea, a fat teapot and a platter of glistening dumplings. There were only a few other couples present; all speaking in muted tones.

Little Sister

She scanned the room, pleased with her choice. How wonderful to be married, to be a part of a couple, a love match. Though husbands could be troublesome creatures, and Gwai Ha was no exception, they were fascinating, unpredictable and vastly entertaining; making her past life seemed dull and ordinary by comparison.

She smiled as she popped a dumpling into her mouth and closed her eyes briefly, savoring the exquisite flavors. They surpassed even Zhaodi's wondrous creations. She would have to ask how they were prepared.

"These are delicious," she said, reaching for another.

"I see that," Gwai Ha said with a laugh, then leaned over and wiped a spot of grease from her mouth with his napkin. He tipped his head back and opened his mouth like a baby bird and she dropped a dumpling in.

Imitating her, he closed his eyes, moaned and rubbed his stomach.

"Gwai Ha!" She whacked his shoulder playfully.

His eyelids formed mirth lines and his shoulders shook. He downed another dumpling and then took her hand, looking anxious.

"Do you mind about their affair?" he asked, speaking softly. She leaned closer, straining to hear. Would she ever get used to his mercurial moods?

"I mean, do you think less of us? Of me?" His look was earnest.

Thinking fast, she laid her chopsticks on her plate while he gazed at her with a worried frown. He had become dear very fast. She wanted to touch his strong chin and rub the side of his face where he clenched his jaw, to alleviate his fears.

"As if I could judge you," she said and took a sip of tea. "We're all helpless against what our ancestors did before us. People make choices that their children must live with. But if you want to talk about it, I'll be glad to listen." She scanned the room. "I've always wanted to know what really happened."

"Alright. I'll tell you," he said, looking resigned. "But it's only my mother's truth. I'm sure Uncle Li has his own version."

She nodded, seeing the sorrow in his eyes, the shame. She reached for his hand across the table and he met her half way, taking her hand with both of his. "If anything, Gwai Ha, you're my friend. It wouldn't be right for you to keep this from me—for yourself or for our future as a couple.

"Alright." Warmth filled his gaze.

"It's true," she said. "I've heard a lot of rumors." She toyed with her teacup, savoring its warm smooth, delicately painted surface. "But I'd like to hear the truth from you." She looked up at him, cocking her head to one side, trying to read his expression.

He reached for another dumpling and popped it into his mouth. "These are nowhere near as good as yours." He chewed thoughtfully.

"Of course they are," she said, smiling as she rolled her eyes. He was obviously stalling—gathering his thoughts more than likely.

He took a gulp of tea, and then gestured for her to pour him some more.

Lowering her lashes, she obliged, wanting to be a good wife to him, to take pleasure in her role, even with the smallest of gestures.

"My mother was the only daughter of Boss Chan, one of Guangzhou's most powerful men," he began softly. Ying Fa nodded in encouragement. "She was allowed to choose between the Li brothers, a decided achievement for a girl. It was because her father adored her. As a Party Boss, he was far more powerful than the landlord who had once counted the district as a minor part of his family's holdings. Boss Chan appeared as a god to the two sons of a third-rate city's ranking clan."

Ying Fa smiled faintly, impressed with his comportment. It was how his business associates must see him: articulate, intelligent and wondrously charming. She dropped her hands to her lap, all tension gone as she listened.

"It was 1959," he continued. "The time of the Hundred Flowers policy. Travel restrictions were eased and trade flourished. Grandfather Li took his two sons, An and Zuomin, to Guangzhou on silk business. They wanted to reestablish contacts, and move toward a new prosperity. Both families had suffered during the famine, having lost many relatives. Both families craved an auspicious future and had already begun discreet marriage negotiations by mail at the urging of a distant common relative."

He sat back in his chair, holding his teacup, his eyes taking on a faraway look.

"The Chans, once skilled servants, had taken on the management of their former master's property. Control had come gradually, inevitably, as each member of the once illustrious clan had been killed, either by the Red Guards or by starvation."

It was China's story, and yet intimately hers: like with her little aunts and her father's long walk to their ancestral

157

home. She pictured the peasants who had squatted at her family's compound, fighting amongst themselves over a few battered household items.

"The Lis, however, had always been involved in the silk trade," Gwai Ha said, his mouth twisting in a grimace. "Prior to the Cultural Revolution, they'd been mere spectators with minor feudal claims on the revenue. Afterward, however, they managed the factories and shipped the silk, performing all of the duties except the actual spinning and weaving, which they relegated to low-wage workers eager for a job." He paused. "At least my uncle did."

"And your father?" she asked, already knowing the answer.

"He was a professor," Gwai Ha said proudly. "'Insurance against the future,' my grandfather claimed. My father was a brilliant man, who taught mathematics and economics to the country's top students. He was articulate and sophisticated, admired by his peers and venerated by his students."

"Was that why your mother chose him?" she asked, imagining a man much like Gwai Ha—tall, handsome and bright—warming his way into Yanru's fickle heart.

Gwai Ha flashed an indulgent smile. "Let me tell it, my rabbit?"

She giggled and then took a sip of tea, reminded of Yutang's teasing. The image quickly faded as Gwai Ha continued.

"That evening, after the Li's brief audience with Boss Chan, Uncle excused himself from his family's temporary apartment to water the peonies."

"Water the what?" she asked.

Gwai Ha rolled his eyes. "He had to go to the bathroom."

"Oh." She giggled and with her chopsticks grasped another dumpling and ate it slowly. She nodded for him to continue.

"Well, Uncle slipped into a back alley and, once relieved, looked up into my mother's face, totally surprised."

"Your mother caught him? Saw his . . .."

Gwai Ha nodded, grinning. "For a moment, Uncle couldn't even breathe."

"He told you this?"

"Many times, over and over, for the past several months." Something in his eyes hardened.

"Uncle Li must have been mortified," she said softly, hoping he would finish his story, hoping he wouldn't go off into one of his odd silences.

"Yeah, that's for sure," Gwai Ha said harshly. "Uncle covered himself and then bowed and bowed. He couldn't get his head low enough. He practically banged it on the ground." He gazed over Ying Fa's head as if he saw something through the window. "Even in army green, he told me, the uniform of Mao, the sight of Mother had taken his breath away." His lips thinned into a sneer as his gaze returned to her. "Supposedly she reached out her hand, touched his face and then raised his chin. When their gazes met they fell in love, and have been ever since."

"So why didn't she choose him?" she asked, though she already knew that answer, too. How could one compare an aspiring elder son, a professor, to a lowly silk manufacturer and second son?

"She told him to keep their meeting a secret," Gwai Ha said harshly. He gripped the edge of the table, his knuckles white.

"What's wrong?" she asked, and reached across the table to rub his arm. "Gwai Ha, tell me."

"My uncle has a way of twisting the truth," he said, his eyes bright with fury. "I can believe that he saw my mother first. I can even believe that he imagined she was infatuated. But . . .."

"But what?"

"He claims my father bragged that night that about his impending marriage to my mother, while he kept his secret to himself. He claims that my father was just tagging along at their mother's insistence, that she didn't want him impregnating any more of the local girls. He implies that my father cared little for family honor, that once he'd seduced a woman, he'd carelessly discard her in favor of his next pursuit, that my mother was just another skirt to him, a conquest easily taken."

"Do you believe it?"

"From that pig's stomach, absolutely not." He raked a hand through his hair. "You should have seen his disgusting manners when he came for me in Beijing. Spitting in public, blowing his nose in his hand, chomping food like an old sow."

She had seen Uncle Li's behavior firsthand: Many men of his generation lacked good manners; but it wasn't their fault. In hard times, the niceties were quickly discarded in favor of survival. Yet she shook her head in commiseration. "What happened next?"

"In the morning, Yanru only had eyes for my father. Of course, she saw right through Uncle's deceptive innocense and accepted my father as her husband. Uncle was crushed, but he made the best of it."

"What about now?" Ying Fa asked, seeing a ripple of pain cross his face.

He looked down at his lap. "I don't remember a time when Uncle wasn't sweet-talking her, buying her things, kissing her. Always as if I wasn't there." He shook his head, looking so forlorn that Ying Fa wanted to cradle him in her arms. "As if my father had never existed."

He looked up at her. "That is, of course, unless we're with his family. Then he always makes a big deal of my mother's role as his elder brother's widow."

He looked away and crossed his arms over his chest. "It's like in ancient China, with my mother as his concubine, when she should be treated as the honored matriarch."

"It that why your cousins were so nasty?" she pressed.

"Let's talk about something else," he said, his expression flat.

She nodded quickly, wanting to appease him, then picked up the teapot; grateful he'd told her as much as he had.

They would have years to become acquainted, a lifetime of changing moods and heartfelt glances, of smiles, hugs and angry silences. It would be up to her to listen, learn and love him unconditionally. After all, he wasn't a dream. He was a real, thinking, feeling man who would soon be the father of her child.

Chapter 8 – Early April

"You are doing too much," Mrs. Chan scolded from the kitchen doorway.

Had a week passed since the shopping excursion with Gwai Ha? How she missed him today, the day of her success. She wiped the sweat from her forehead with the back of her wrist before dipping her red puckered hands back into the dishwater.

"I'm almost finished," she said, smiling wearily at her mother-in-law. Her back ached and her ankles were swollen— not that she could see them. She could barely bend over now. Gone were the days when she could pull up her stockings or tie her own shoes. Not that anyone noticed.

Mrs. Chan remained in the doorway, her lips moving, struggling to say something. Her eyes shone with rare kindness.

"Are they all gone?" she asked; and Mrs. Chan nodded. She had worked hard for her mother-in-law's first mahjong party, scrubbing and cooking each night for the past week in excited anticipation. The apartment had sparkled. Thankfully, the two wardrobes had arrived in time. Every household item was out of sight and a newfound sense of space and light brightened the modest rooms. Delicate pictures of the Chinese countryside that Gwai Ha had purchased in Beijing from some obscure sidewalk artist graced the walls. If only Poh Poh could have witnessed her achievement. Sadly, she was home in bed, nursing a stubborn cold.

Ying Fa gasped as Mrs. Chan took the last dish from her. She scrubbed it hard, belying her weeks of laziness, and then rinsed it and placed it on the counter. Too tired to protest the resulting puddle, she backed against the counter and released a long sigh.

"You will rest now," Mrs. Chan said. She took her by the arm and guided her through the main room to her bed.

A picture needed straightening, stacks of teacups balanced precariously beside a plate of congealed gravy, chairs were askew and bits of food were stuck to the floor. Ying Fa gravitated toward the table, not knowing where to begin.

"I will tend to what remains," Mrs. Chan said sternly, surprising her. "You have proven yourself more than worthy and have shown our family well."

Her words filled Ying Fa with immeasurable joy as she felt herself being pushed into bed and covered with a soft blanket. Mrs. Chan then pulled the privacy curtain halfway across, leaving a gap to permit a meager breeze.

"Your dumplings were amazing," Mrs. Chan whispered, "as were your spicy shrimp."

Ying Fa could only nod. Tears pricked at her eyes from such kindness.

"It is time for you to sleep," Mrs. Chan said. "Tomorrow will come soon enough. Will you be alright if I leave you for a few minutes?"

Too weary to speak, she nodded once more. Though she and Mrs. Chan had come to an understanding of sorts, she still did the bulk, if not all of the housework. Over the past six weeks, she had learned that Mrs. Chan was incapable of performing even the most basic household task. Had it been six weeks? It seemed a lifetime.

"Gwai Ha will return from his committee meeting soon," Mrs. Chan said. "Meanwhile, Mrs. He next door will come running if you call out." Her eyes darted about nervously as if she had more to say. She fiddled with the heavy curtain, rubbing a finger up and down the fabric absentmindedly. "Have him make you some weak tea," she said sternly.

"I can do that," Ying Fa whispered, looking up at her.

"Oh, no. This event has tired you. You must preserve your strength for my grandson." She reached out and pressed a hand to Ying Fa's abdomen, her expression warm. "He will come any day now." She closed her eyes briefly, and then mumbled something about Boss Li that she couldn't quite hear.

Too tired to ask her to repeat it, she turned over, vaguely aware of her mother-in-law stepping away. She heard the door close softly and sighed as the apartment's echoing silence enveloped her. Within moments, she was fast asleep.

Blindly, she followed the familiar path to work the next day, keeping pace with the other workers, apologizing for jostling someone, stepping in rotted vegetables and other unsavory items, spattering her shoes.

164

Surprisingly, Mrs. Chan had risen early to prepare breakfast: undercook eggs and overdry rice, for which she was grateful. It was her initial attempt at cooking; and even Gwai Ha had pitched in by carrying the wastebasket out to the hall, arranging pickled vegetables on a small plate, and carrying the condiments, bowls, and chopsticks from the kitchen to the table. It was all great fun to him and he had made them laugh with his antics.

If only she could have slept another hour, or ridden in a car or stayed at home. The last thought hung like a ripe peach, inches away from her sleep-parched brain. She breathed deeply as she walked, weaving around other pedestrians, attaching herself to groups of people as she crossed each street, a wry smile on her face as she imagined the awkward vision she must present.

"Why gripe?" she said with a little laugh. Her outburst caused an old man beside her to move away slightly. She expelled a tired sob that sounded much like laughter. Better to laugh than cry, as Yutang often said.

Bogged down and heavy, she managed to find her place in the factory's courtyard, her shadow lumpy beside her. Her legs ached dully and she needed the bathroom, but she would stand for the morning exercises; and she would stay awake at her machine. No child of hers would complain of a mother who laid down on the job.

Chairman Mao's words came to mind, that 'in difficult times we must not lose sight of our achievements; but we must look forward to a bright future and pluck up our courage.'

She nodded firmly to Chung and Baak-Hap. There was little chance to gossip with them these days; though the sight of them reminded her of a magical time when romance had bloomed between her and Gwai Ha.

She leaned forward as her baby moved, warming her heart with his sweetness. He was her happiness now—an exquisite promise that vanquished all fear of the birth to come.

The spring sun shone brightly because half the refinery chimneys in the city were shut down for their annual cleaning. She imagined the China Number One beach crowded with refinery workers, enjoying a brief and pleasurable respite from their grimy jobs. A fresh breeze blew; and she pictured herself sitting in a chair, sipping a frosty drink, gazing at the clear blue sky over the shimmering, aqua horizon.

There was a commotion at the guard's stand, a dramatic flourishing of arms and legs as the new guard, He Tien, a stout young man with deep-set, dancing eyes saluted Uncle Li.

It was rumored that Anwei had been promoted to another assignment in Mongolia, leaving his mother suddenly frail and old, like the shadow of dust. Many claimed that his untimely interest in a certain young woman had caused flying papers to land on important desks. She supposed it was true, considering Gwai Ha's possessive nature.

Too bad for Anwei and his mother—she had never wished them harm. Somehow, out of Anwei's bad luck, good fortune had come to Baak-Hap.

She caught a glimpse of her friend, gazing in Tien's direction. Her mother was already consulting an astrologer, and had begun tentative discussions with Tien's parents in Changsha. She'd even consulted Uncle Li.

Ying Fa smiled and nodded in Baak-Hap's direction, silently wishing her many years of contentment. Baak-Hap was too enthralled to notice her; but it mattered little. They were all moving into adulthood, each going her separate way.

As if in a fog, she straightened for the morning exercises, and then followed behind the others, barely conscious of Baak-Hap's hand pressing into the small of her back. Her stomach churned at the acrid stench of wet cleaning solvent, still drying in the corners of the embroidery hall. Her belly hung like a ripe watermelon, heavy and unwieldy as she took the simple pillowcase instructions from Chen Ming before lumbering over to the supply table. The forewoman's pitying gaze touched her like raindrops scattered across the sea.

"You don't look well," Chung whispered, taking her arm. "You should be home resting."

Beyond tired, Ying Fa giggled, causing Chung to look even more concerned.

Suddenly, a commotion at the door caused all heads to turn.

Ying Fa struggled to look up through a watery mist to see Mrs. Chan whispering to Uncle Li, one delicate hand pointing in her direction.

Trouble had arrived, causing a vague fear to rise like smoke tendrils in the pit of her stomach. Her legs began to spasm, and she sat quickly at her station, hoping to ease the pain. She didn't care that sweat dripped from her forehead. Her stomach pressed against the sewing machine, creating an unmovable shelf. She reached for some silk and began to thread her machine, realizing as her hands moved that she had selected the wrong colors from the supply table. Unable to think straight, she burst into tears.

A strong hand pressed on her shoulder and she looked up to see Uncle Li hovering over her, his expression formidable. She gasped, her hand clutching her stomach in protection. She tried to stand, but her stomach had wedged her into the chair and her legs had no strength.

"You should have admitted that you needed to rest," he hissed. "Your son should be your priority now. What were you thinking, you foolish girl?" He grabbed her shoulder, and she cringed at his touch.

"You will leave now," he said, his tone harsh as he removed his hand. "Mrs. Chan has agreed to escort you home in my car."

Ying Fa nodded as hot tears dried on her face. She gripped Mrs. Chan's proffered hand, sickened by her helplessness, then struggled to rise. Uncle Li pushed from behind, until she rose like a surfacing whale.

"Aren't I the strong and efficient one?" she murmured, snorting a laugh. The women tittered around her.

"Don't be ridiculous," Uncle Li said, backing away, shooting the women a disparaging look. The silence was immediate. "Your job can wait," he hissed.

"What a plump pigeon I have become," she whispered to Mrs. Chan.

Uncle Li shot her a hard look, while Mrs. Chan covered her mouth with a hand, suppressing a giggle.

She limped along on aching legs, vaguely aware of Chen Ming's furious hand signals telling the other women to get back to work, and of Mrs. Chan's surprisingly strong grip.

"You'll be fine, little daughter," her mother-in-law whispered, making her tears flow once again. "Men can be so obtuse," she hissed. "And that big lummox needs instruction on the frailty of pregnant ladies. You will soon be safe and warm in your own bed. I should never have permitted you to leave this morning."

Murmuring her thanks, Ying Fa leaned her head against her mother-in-law's and limped to the waiting car.

Chapter 9 – Mid-April

As Ying Fa's strength slowly returned over the next two weeks, it didn't come as a surprise that Mrs. Chan learned how to cook savory soups, gently stirred eggs and crisp vegetables. She was bright enough: she had never been taught.

Gwai Ha slept on the sofa now, lest he disturb her restless, uncomfortable sleep. Everyone was concerned. They tiptoed around her with half-excited, half-frenetic expressions. Uncle Li had even had a telephone installed, so they could contact him when the baby arrived.

All she wanted was to be able to turn over in bed without two people having to heft her like an overfed sow; eat her fill without having to run to the bathroom, and put her own shoes on, hers being two sizes too small.

She buried her head in her pillow, trying to drown out the telephone's incessant ring as she lay in bed, summoning the strength to rise. Then, with great effort, she heaved her legs over the side and gripped the edge.

Suddenly, water gushed between her legs. A deep pain overwhelmed her followed by another. She rode with it, closing her eyes against the silencing void.

At last, the time had come. She must bend to fate and produce her child.

"Ying Fa?" A voice sought to penetrate her concentration. She glanced up to find Gwai Ha and Mrs. Chan standing over her, their faces pinched with worry.

"It's time," she grunted. Panic bloomed in Gwai Ha's eyes and her gaze caressed him. "It's okay," she tried to say. But no sound emerged as pain once again took its grip.

"Get the midwife," Mrs. Chan said, sending him a sharp glance.

For a moment, the pain subsided and Ying Fa stared up at her mother-in-law in horror. "But I need to get to the hospital. I still have time." Another pain was starting to form—a trickle, a bellow, a scream.

"Yes, she must," she heard Gwai Ha say as if from far away.

She gasped aloud, trying to catch her breath.

"It is too dangerous," Mrs. Chan replied. "We are too well-known. She must give birth here, without the authorities involved."

A flurry of words entered Ying's Fa consciousness that had no meaning—high-pitched in anger and low-pitched in conciliation—as one contraction bled into the last, and another and another until she lay panting and heaving, a wounded animal climbing a mountain of pain.

Sounds echoed around her—a door closing, feet scurrying and water rushing—but she paid no attention. Pain came and went and she lay still, too dizzy to rise, awaiting more. Minutes leaked into hours. Laughter moved far away, a distant memory that made no sense.

She found herself in her mother-in-law's bed among starched linens, naked and drenched with sweat. Time held her suspended in its grip as disembodied hands soothed and stroked, not quite touching the core where she lay struggling, her strength abating.

Gwai Ha's worried face was replaced with that of a stern, middle-aged woman with greedy eyes.

She wanted to ask why she hadn't been taken to the hospital. She and Gwai Ha had spent many laughing moments rehearsing the short trip. And where was the taxi? And Poh Poh? A subtle breeze tickled her hot skin, then goose pimples rose and she shivered.

"Poh Poh!" she cried weakly, and within moments her grandmother's beloved face appeared. Familiar hands now rubbed her back, calmed her fears, trickled water between her parched lips, and sang soothing songs from a distant childhood, giving her something to cling to.

At last, the room gave a great shudder as she pushed and pushed until finally, the child emerged.

There was a moment of silence followed by a piercing cry. There were no shouts of joy, no laughter, no happy tears.

"What's wrong?" she croaked, struggling to rise. A strong hand pushed her back. It was Mrs. Chan. Then the afterbirth came and the cord cut and tied. The midwife lingered between her legs, wiping her up, removing soaked cloth, humming tunelessly.

Poh Poh stood with her back to her, cleaning the child in a clay basin on a small, polished table. With a cool cloth, Mrs. Chan wiped her face and neck. There were tears in her eyes and grief. With strong hands, she helped Ying Fa don a thin, cotton gown, pressed cloth between her legs, then stuffed a pillow behind her head.

"Give me my baby," she cried, ignoring her grandmother's downcast eyes as she held out her hands for the tiny, shrieking bundle swathed in soft cotton. "Now," she pleaded, ignoring Mrs. Chan's strained silence and the midwife's sneer; desperate to hold him. Was he deformed somehow?

Poh Poh passed her the baby and she settled back with a long sigh, cradling the precious bundle. "Oh, my," she breathed, taking in the tufts of black hair, the intelligent high forehead, and the perfect rosebud lips, and sighed with relief. He was the image of his father.

His crying ceased as she held him close. She crooned to him softly, gazing into sparkling, jet eyes that peered straight into her soul. Though the image of Gwai Ha, he was as beautiful as an exquisite little girl. On his left hand was an oval mole, the same as hers.

Girl!

Frantically she stripped away the blanket and discovered the reason for their silence.

"No!" she wailed, clutching the baby close, causing the child to cry out in pain and fear. "You can't take her!" she cried, knowing that they would.

"Please let me see her?" Mrs. Chan asked, binding her to her forever with her humble, heartfelt request.

Slowly, she turned her precious child, holding her so that her mother-in-law could inspect each tiny finger and toe, each inch of porcelain perfection. Mrs. Chan's hands stroked and touched in mute adoration, calming the child, while Poh Poh watched with tears streaming down her face.

"Good morning, Mooi Mooi," Ying Fa whispered, not daring to acknowledge that she was more than a little sister. Without a name, she would be less than real, hardly permanent; though in her heart the child would always be part of her.

"Get Gwai Ha," she said, forcing sound through her raw throat as she scanned Mrs. Chan's devastated face.

"No. Please. We must spare him this," Mrs. Chan begged. She moved toward the door as if to bar it.

Gwai Ha was already opening the door. His puzzled expression called out to her. She needed him to see, to grieve with her over this loss.

"It's a girl," she blurted out.

His expression change from joy to sorrow as his gaze fixed on the small bundle. He had wanted a boy, and there could not be a second child. His committee meetings often brought him in contact with the most powerful local officials as well as representatives from Beijing. There was no bending the rules. Then there was his uncle.

"Come," his mother commanded. "Come see her while you can."

Gwai Ha lurched sideways into the room, his expression pinched. He moved carefully to the bed and glanced down, a smile blooming softly at first, and then he sighed.

He knelt beside Ying Fa and draped an arm around her and the baby, keeping them safe, if only for a while. They huddled together in silence, breathing each other's breath. His wounded gaze touched hers. She reached out to wipe a tear.

"She's so beautiful," he breathed. He brushed their daughter's rose petal cheek with a long gentle finger.

"Is this what we dreamed about?" she whispered harshly, wanting to hurt him as much as she wanted his protection from this grinding pain. "Is this the kind of progress China needs?"

He closed his eyes briefly and shook his head. "It can't be helped," he whispered, his face an icy mask. He touched the baby one last time, then rose and left the room.

The midwife followed, probably looking for money.

The three women took turns holding the baby, staving off the inevitable. Time rolled past, one moment collapsing into the next, bringing the child's fate ever closer. Morning shadows played discreetly against the room's far wall. Suddenly there was a loud rap at the outer door followed by muffled voices. Uncle Li had arrived.

Mrs. Chan wiped her face with her hand, then lifted her chin and strode from the room. Not taking her eyes off her daughter, Ying Fa strained to hear.

"We have already decided," Uncle Li said. He was trying to whisper, but his harsh voice rumbled through the wall. "The girl's strong and fertile. She'll try again."

Mrs. Chan mumbled something unintelligible.

"Foolish woman," he scolded. "Always sentimental. Edicts are coming down, as you know. Even more stringent measures are coming from Beijing. Age restrictions. Marriage requirements. We must set an example, yet we must survive. What purpose does this useless female serve?"

There was a muffled sob.

"Impossible!" Uncle Li shouted. "I will not see this child, this girl. As far as I am concerned she doesn't exist. You know what to do."

A door slammed and Ying Fa felt a draft, indicating Mrs. Chan's return.

She looked up through a blur of tears and saw the apology on her mother-in-law's face, her eyes pleading for forgiveness.

"Daughter?" she whispered, reaching to touch Ying Fa's shoulder. "It's time."

Sobs escaped her throat as Poh Poh took the child from her. Already her arms ached from the loss. "Please help me!" she cried, grabbing wildly at her grandmother. "Take my baby away somewhere . . . care for her . . . please!"

Poh Poh shook her head sadly.

"Gwai Ha will be taxed three times his salary or lose his job," Mrs. Chan said softly. Tears streamed down her beautiful, angry face. "His future will be lost if you keep this child and produce another." Her face turned a furious red as she took a wavering step closer. "Do you want your second child—your son—to be unregistered, uneducated?" She reached out a hand. "All because of a useless older sister?"

"But I want her!" Ying Fa cried, hugging herself to stem the pain, imagining her daughter's tiny hands forming cabbage dumplings by her side, bright, innocent eyes crinkling with laughter and love, and sturdy, naked legs running beside her across a stretch of golden sand. She sobbed, her dreams evaporating.

"Of course you want her; but I would have him divorce you first," Mrs. Chan spat. A strand of hair escaped from her tightly bound chignon, brushing against her shoulder.

Ying Fa sucked in her breath. It was as Poh Poh had warned. She only half-listened as Mrs. Chan went on about the importance of waiting for sons; that one of her

176

daughters had shown great courage by waiting twice for hers.

"Such is the burden we women must bear," Mrs. Chan said. Then she began to cry. "My daughter passively accepted the loss of her girls . . . and now . . . with a son in her arms, she is but a shadow of her former self. Or so I hear." Her voice trailed off.

Through a veil of tears, Ying Fa saw her shake her head. "She'll never tell me. Never. I only learned this from letters from my other daughter . . . They will never forgive me."

The three women were sobbing as Poh Poh handed the baby to Mrs. Chan.

"Please let me keep her for a few days," Ying Fa pleaded, her heart shattered beyond redemption.

"Act quickly," Poh Poh instructed Mrs. Chan, ignoring her. Then she gripped Ying Fa's hand, tears falling down her wrinkled face onto the bed. "It is better this way. The longer she holds the child, the deeper the pain."

Ying Fa sobbed, scarcely able to believe what was happening.

Mrs. Chan stared at her for a long time, hugging the baby, her face a map of grief. Then, without a word, she left.

Sounds from outside were starting to fill the chilly, early morning air—horns beeping and bells clanging—as workers began their day. Ying Fa closed her eyes, relishing the aches and pains of tired muscles and torn flesh—the only proof that she had just given birth. Life would go on around her. She would return to the factory soon, a ghost of her former self, an empty shell.

She stared at the ceiling, imagining a public place, a bathroom or restaurant, perhaps the doorstep of the hospital, where Mrs. Chan would leave her child. She pictured her backing away to watch from a safe distance.

Someday, when her little son raced across the golden sand, leaving his grandmother and mother in his happy wake, she would ask Mrs. Chan where she'd left the precious bundle and who had picked it up. But not today.

A terrible ache engulfed her. Never again would she let love rule. Gwai Ha's glorious plans of success were for nothing. How could she ever let him touch her again, much less create another child with him, another girl who would only be ripped from her arms.

Baak-Hap's sister had given birth to yet another girl. How many times would she have to endure the same?

Through her tears, she looked up at Poh Poh's bowed head, awed by her perpetual acceptance, her relentless patience, her compassion. Who could describe the pain of losing a beloved daughter, of hopes cut short, snipped before they'd had a chance to bloom? What did it matter if one had known the sweet joys of a child for a minute, a day or ten years?

Poh Poh lifted her head and smiled at her sadly. "Do you want Gwai Ha again?" she asked.

Ying Fa shook her head. Her tears drying, she turned her face to the wall.

Chapter 10 – May

One day dragged into the next, with only the dim light that filtered in through her mother-in-law's bedroom window signaling the passage of time. Unable to speak, she allowed her body to be washed and the bloody towels replaced. In a fog, she felt strong arms lifting her from the bed, toting her to and from the bathroom. From time to time, familiar hands spooned broth between her parched lips and then piled blankets upon a sheet to cover her. The blankets were scratchy and the sheets rasped loudly with every tired move; but she uttered no complaint.

Couldn't they just leave her alone?

Each intrusion was like a million pinpricks burning her soul. Her body ached and her heart was sorely wounded. They went through the motions; but she was merely a womb to them, a vessel through which they would gain a son. Divorce or death—it mattered not. They would find another strong, young female who would be grateful for Manager Li's notice.

She had to leave. She had to.

How she hated their wordless crooning, as if meaningless words could heal her broken heart. She had to get away, to flee their guilty ministrations. They did not love her.

By dawn's light, she watched Gwai Ha leave for work, stealthily grabbing his briefcase and coat. He looked at her sadly, surreptitiously, the dutiful nephew, his face haggard in the gloom, his love a farce.

She wished him old and gray with a harridan for a wife and an ungrateful son rioting in Beijing—just like his uncle. The thought made her smile, probably for the first time in what seemed like weeks. Had it been that long?

Rain pelted the windowpane. She strained to hear the sounds coming from the kitchen. Mother-in-law, or Yanru, as she called her now, splashed in the sink, clanged pots, then opened and closed the refrigerator door. Soon, she would hang the damp towel on the hook below the sink, grab her purse from the chair beside the door and leave for the market. They still had to eat and pay their bills and honor their commitments. It seemed that Mooi Mooi's entrance and painful exit was already fading into the family's illustrious past.

She stared up at the ceiling, vowing never to forget. Mooi Mooi would never be a mere part of her past. She would divorce herself from those who had stolen her child along with her dreams. She would build her own dreams and then carry them out in quiet revenge. Shame would be her bedmate and failure her cloak. Harsh whispers would follow her for the rest of her life. No man would want her now.

The apartment door closed softly and she waited. Yanru had become forgetful of late, often returning minutes after she had left to retrieve money, a handkerchief or a list. She was a great one for making lists.

She held her breath, counting the seconds.

Cold damp air blew through a crack in the sill. The sound echoed dully in her ears.

Finally, she shuddered and then sat up, bracing herself with wobbly arms as the room spun around her. The time was now. She shook her head, refusing to give in. She had to do this. She had to. She would pack a few things and be on her way. Her marriage was over. She would recover in her own bed with the help of Poh Poh's proven remedies. Surely, her family would welcome their grieving daughter.

She took a deep breath, stood and then sat back down.

"This won't be easy," she said, chuckling at the awkward picture she must make. She bit her lip; surprised she was able to laugh and smiled grimly. She had shed enough tears for a lifetime in the past few days. She felt her heart warming a little; very different from what moments ago had been ice.

She stood again, this time widening her stance. She had to do this, if only for the sake of her sanity. Poh Poh spoke of women returning to their crops just hours after giving birth, their newborns strapped to their chests. Her own full breasts ached and her head hummed from the hormone surge caused by her milk coming in. And her child was gone.

She vaguely recalled spitting out the herb broth they had given her to stop her milk. Did they think they could remove every bit of evidence that her precious daughter existed?

The short walk to the kitchen was brutal, but she regained her strength with each step. With one arm supporting her swollen breasts, she scrounged in the refrigerator, searching for leftover; and made a fine meal of several cold dumplings, a few scrambled eggs and a pot of hot tea. After a trip to the bathroom, she dressed, threw a few things into a bag, wrote a short note and left.

An hour later she stumbled, sodden and weeping, the remaining few steps to her family's apartment. The rain had pelted her uncovered head. Her skin still crawled from the press and shove of the other faceless pedestrians. Her breasts were stretched to the bursting point, leaking rivulets down her chest. Her stomach heaved from the stench of human waste and rotting food she had smelled along the way. The stagnant pond in the nearby park, with its stench of mold and algae, had compounded the problem. Choking down bile, she knocked on the door.

She prayed that her parents and Yutang were already at work. What a loss of face for them to see her in such a sorry state. Soft steps padded to the door. With a sinking feeling, she realized it had been a mistake to come. But what choice did she have? She swayed as she stood, wondering what to do.

Then the door swung open and Poh Poh stood before her, her eyes brimming with tears.

"My sweetheart," she said, and grasped her arm and pulled her inside. The door slammed shut.

"Poh Poh," Ying Fa whispered and closed her eyes as she lead her to the bathroom. "Home at last," she said, ignoring her grandmother's odd silence. She welcomed the ministrations of her soft hands as she tended her needs and put her to bed.

Gradually, she became aware of Hsiao's angry presence. Usually calm, her sister-in-law was clanging spoons against crockery as she made the tea. She clattered pots, lids and bowls as she heated some food; and scolded Anji, who clung to her legs, crying.

Hsiao was angry?

She snuggled deeper into the soft, fragrant pillow, bitter disappointment souring her mouth. This was her home, her family, where she belonged. Couldn't Hsiao understand that?

Then a baby cried—not Anji's deep-throated little-boy protest—but a familiar kittenish, newborn sound. She sat up, searching the room, looking for the source of this cruel joke. Was there no mercy in the world?

She watched, confused, as Hsiao passed Anji to Poh Poh and then stomped to her bed, still curtained off, though morning was long past. She ripped aside the curtain and plucked a wiggling bundle from the middle of the bed.

"I believe this is yours," she said with such quiet rage that Ying Fa could only stare at her, unable to speak. Hsiao held out the bundle with one hand, her nose turned up as if the object stank; and made no move to come closer.

The baby's cry intensified, filling the apartment. Not knowing what to do, where to turn, Ying Fa clutched at her hair with both hands. "You're my best friend, and I've just lost my child. Why do you torture me?"

She started to rise, and then Poh Poh was beside her, pushing her down onto the bed. With a few smooth motions, she popped a dumpling into Anji's open mouth and his cries ceased.

"You know better than that," she hissed at Hsiao, her face haggard. "She's family."

Ying Fa looked from Poh Poh to Hsiao, realization dawning; and gasped as Hsiao stepped toward her and thrust the screaming bundle into her arms.

"Can it be?" she breathed, the sudden weight calming her as nothing else could. "Mooi Mooi?" she cried, pushing aside the swaddling, seeing her daughter's red face, her tiny fists shaking with rage.

She stared up at Hsiao in disbelief. "Why?" she asked. "Who did this?" Then she saw that the front of Hsiao's blouse was soaked with milk, let down by the baby's cry. The baby kept howling.

Moving on instinct, she unbuttoned the top of the nightdress she had borrowed from Poh Poh, positioned her daughter and helped her latch on. She winced, the first pull like a slice; but she held the child loosely, trying to relax, to meet her needs.

Silence filled the apartment—time and place melting into background noise as she lay back, watching her little daughter at her breast—her own precious child, wrenched from her arms and now returned.

"Who brought her?" she asked, her mind a jumble of questions. She didn't care who answered. Had Yanru done the unthinkable by thwarting Uncle Li? And what part had Gwai Ha played?

"This cannot be," Poh Poh said, shaking her head sadly. With her face in her hands, she hobbled to Zhaodi's room and closed the door.

Ying Fa gazed down at Mooi Mooi, enraptured by soft pearly skin, the shape of downy, crescent lashes, perfect rosebud lips and a cap of soft black hair that graced her tiny head. Her Mooi Mooi was a beauty. It didn't matter who had orchestrated her rescue; it was enough to hold her, skin to skin, ignoring the pain of first feeding, breathing in her deliciously delicate scent.

"You have to deal with this," Hsiao spat, shattering the silence. She glowered from her bed, a vengeful matron nursing her fussy son.

"What's wrong with you?" Ying Fa asked, tears filling her eyes. "I have her back now. Isn't that all that matters."

"Chan Yanru made me nurse her and it upset Anji." Hsiao's eyes glinted with tears. "You forget that I have to return to work in less than two months. That's not much time to wean Anji; and now your baby is making it impossible. I cannot nurse her. I won't."

Ying Fa looked away, stunned. "Who brought her?" she asked again, too tired to remind Hsiao that until a few moments ago, she'd thought her baby was gone forever. Hsiao's rage was like a high black cloud running to the sea. What had turned her against her?

"Chan Yanru barged in with her," Hsiao said, throwing a hand up in the air. "What a scene that was . . . yelling and crying and banging of doors."

"Barged in? What do you mean?"

"She was cold as ice," Hsiao replied. "Ordering us around like she was Manager Li's wife. Grandmother almost fainted from the strain. Your mother just kept bowing as if an empress had arrived; and then she threw the baby at me when it . . . when she started to cry."

"But why?" Ying Fa asked. "Did she say?"

Hsiao lifted her chin. "Manager Li claims you had a miscarriage. Everyone's talking about it." Her eyes narrowed. "Can't you see that Chan Yanru has stuck us in the middle of this controversy? Your father is sick about it, Yutang's furious and Zhaodi is frantic. What do you want from us? Can't you wait for a son like a good wife? You have your own family now, and this is mine."

Ying Fa gulped and looked down at her daughter. "You wouldn't say that if Anji had been a girl."

"But he's not." Hsiao whispered, her expression cold. Was that fear she saw in her eyes? Hsiao cradled her son as she nursed him, his sturdy body curled beside her on the bed. The sight of Anji's little leg tapping with pleasure filled Ying Fa with such longing that she burst into tears.

She looked down at her own sweet baby, pain clogging her throat. There was nothing to be said against her friend's honesty. Each moment with Mooi Mooi was but a borrowed joy. She sneaked a look at Hsiao. Unlike the Lis, the Wong's would probably have welcomed a girl.

"You've put us all in grave danger," Hsiao hissed.

"It just isn't fair," Ying Fa moaned. "Only moments ago, I was mourning my child, seeking a quiet place to heal my wounds. I didn't plan this. I didn't."

"Manager Li will learn about it soon enough," Hsiao said. "He has ears everywhere. He will make you pay. He will make all of us pay. You wait and see."

"That's enough," Poh Poh said sternly as she emerged from Zhaodi's room, her eyes red-rimmed, her expression gentle. "Ying Fa needs us now, child, even if it's just for a few hours." Her tone softened. "Like all women, she has no say in what happens to her. The same as with you, my little Soong Hsiao."

186

Hsiao blushed and then clamped her lips together as she always did after being chastised. Her hair fell across Anji like a soft shield.

"Poh Poh," Ying Fa whispered, then closed her eyes and sighed deeply.

"Get some rest," Poh Poh urged. She laid a cool hand on her forehead. "We'll eat later and share some tea. Thing's will look better then."

Ying Fa flashed a grateful smile and snuggled Mooi Mooi. Maybe now she would name her, making her a real, true daughter, someone to sing to and take to the market. She took a deep breath, feeling better already.

Poh Poh's nightdress, soft against her skin, smelled of safety and love. She had been right to come home. She would rest for a few days and then make plans with a cleared head. Perhaps she'd hire a woman to nurse her child. For a few Yuan, surely someone could spare a little milk. But Mooi Mooi was so little and helpless. How could she bear to leave her?

She shuddered at the thought of seeing Gwai Ha or Uncle Li at the Silk Factory. Of course, they would be there, hounding and harassing her, acting as if they hadn't ripped her heart out with their dreams. They wanted her to be Gwai Ha's assistant, traveling with him to places like Shanghai and Guangzhou. What had seemed like a wondrous opportunity just months ago now loomed like a prison sentence.

She brushed such worries aside. A few selfish men would not spoil her precious time, each moment to be savored and remembered.

As her fears gave way to exhaustion, she slept; and then rose a few hours later to eat the meal that Poh Poh had prepared.

During the meal, the three women limited their conversation to neutral topics such as friends, household chores and cooking. Even Hsiao's worried expression relaxed as they shared the deliciously prepared food and tended their children. Over her teacup, Ying Fa took covert glances at the two women, knowing the peace to be a mere respite. She was under no illusions as the quiet afternoon waned and the time for reckoning approached.

Just after sunset, she lay in bed nursing Mooi Mooi, trying to soothe her frazzled nerves. Her parents and brother would soon arrive.

The table was set for the evening meal. Poh Poh was in the kitchen downstairs preparing spicy shrimp and squid, mixed vegetables, lemon chicken and rice—a feast fit for an imperial family, hopefully a loving family. If only they would let her stay.

Hsiao, who should have been helping Poh Poh lug the food upstairs, was in the bathroom washing Anji's hands and face. He'd recently become a bossy tyrant, throwing tantrums typical of a bright one-year-old. It was obvious that he resented Mooi Mooi's presence.

She caressed Mooi Mooi's cheek, marveling at its softness, her heart overflowing. This was her own baby, her reason for living. How could Gwai Ha have let his mother take her away? She inhaled deeply, telling herself not to cry as she gazed down at the child.

"Eating and eating," she whispered, then gasped when the baby flashed a ghost of a smile. "My little greedy one," she said, loving how a tiny hand curled into a fist atop her breast. Her heart ached at such innocence and trust.

Then, like shattering glass, Zhaodi exploded into the apartment.

Ying Fa sat up, clutching Mooi Mooi to her breast, ready to flee.

Hsiao poked her head out of the bathroom, her face flushed. Quickly she ducked back inside.

All fantasies of a quiet family meal evaporated as Zhaodi approached, her chin set in a rigid line, her back straight, her dark eyes flashing. "I can't believe you have the nerve to come here!" she screeched.

Mooi Mooi started to fuss and Ying Fa shifted her to the other breast, ignoring her mother.

"You selfish girl!" Zhaodi shouted, her fist in the air. She loomed over the bed, making Mooi Mooi cry. Ying Fa struggled to get her to reattach, but the baby was having none of it.

"I told you that you belonged to those Lis. How dare you bring this upon us? How dare you plot and scheme with that haughty old woman to bring us down? Do you have any idea what you've done?"

With hands shaking, Ying Fa stroked Mooi Mooi's back, trying to soothe her. She made little sobbing noises as the baby finally latched on.

"I had no idea Mrs. Chan brought her here," she said, tears filling her eyes. "Ask Grandmother or Hsiao, though I'm glad she did. This is your granddaughter, not some stray dog you can kick away. And what about me?" Her words ended in a sob.

"This is pure bad luck and you know it," Zhaodi said. She turned as Hsiao ran through the room with her head bowed; deposited Anji on the floor beside Zhaodi, then fled the apartment. Zhaodi reached to shut the door.

"I had no idea Mrs. Chan kept her," Ying Fa repeated, lowering her gaze, too worn out to deflect her mother's blame. After all that her family had accomplished, it was indeed bad luck. "Please. It will only be for a few weeks or so." She caressed her baby's arm. Seeking some semblance of reassurance, she looked up at Zhaodi.

"A few weeks or so?" Her mother's screech echoed off the walls.

The apartment door opened and Zhaodi moved quickly to help Hsiao and Poh Poh carry the platters, baskets and pots over to the table.

Ying Fa watched as if from a great distance, as if seeing a play, with actors mouthing meaningless words, pretending that all was right: the harried grandmother popping tidbits into the beloved grandson's mouth, the daughter-in-law watching her own little grandson with loving anxious eyes, her dreams fulfilled. She laughed humorlessly, earning a few sharp glances. She was the unnecessary aunt with an unnecessary daughter, a pebble in their respective shoes. How carefully they avoided her gaze, their pinched expressions shouting her unwelcome. There was no compassion on anyone's face. Tears filled her eyes, as she looked at her daughter, frightened for her future.

"Hello, my daughter."

She looked up into her father's worn face. She hadn't heard him come in. Neither had she heard Yutang, who stood near the table, his hand on Hsiao's shoulder. Hsiao whispered to him, her sibilants like crushed ice in a glass.

Ying Fa wiped her tears with the back of her hand and sniffed loudly. "Hello Father," she said softly, awaiting his verdict. If anyone would have mercy, it would be him.

He laid his hand on Mooi Mooi's head, his expression softening. "You can stay the night," he said, looking deep into her eyes and smiling sadly.

"But . . . just one night. What about—?"

"Say no more." He touched her face, a long remembered endearing gesture that brought more tears to her eyes.

And then what? Must she leave this home too? Then where would she go and who would want her? She dared not ask.

"She can stay the night," he repeated louder, making sure that everyone heard. "And tonight, I'll hear no talk of this." He looked from Zhaodi to Yutang. "She's our daughter and our sister after all. We can spare her shelter for the night."

"Then out she goes," Yutang muttered over his shoulder. Father's expression froze.

"No talk of this," he repeated harshly and Yutang shrugged.

Hsiao scowled and grabbed Yutang's arm, as if for support. Then she leaped after Anji who was crawling into the bathroom.

They ate their evening meal in silence, its delicious promise flattened by the specter of Uncle Li's discovery. The aroma of the rich food sickened her. If it hadn't have been for Mooi Mooi, she wouldn't have eaten a bite—but she needed her strength.

She felt like an outsider watching Zhaodi and Hsiao cart dishes, bowls and chopsticks down to the kitchen for scouring. It was their home, their life. They waved her help away. Though she had her own spotless kitchen, mere steps from her apartment's main room—its luxury and convenience was nothing against the familial companionship they refused to share.

Here, she dared not show her face downstairs in the public kitchen, much less in the apartment's window where someone might see her. Mrs. Fa, still grieving the loss of Tsang Anwei, would be the first to notify Uncle Li. A mere knock on the door would send them all to unemployment.

She fled to her old bed and held Mooi Mooi while the rest of the family gathered around the television in Zhaodi's room listening to some silly game show. She was falling asleep when Mooi Mooi started to cry.

"Hurry. Hurry." Poh Poh said, appearing at her side, frantically helping her unbutton her nightdress.

Then Zhaodi was at the door. "Quiet her," she hissed. The baby stopped crying as Ying Fa's milk filled her mouth.

Day after day she'd have to quiet the child. Their lives would depend on it. Her hands shook as the impossibility of her situation came crashing down.

Zhaodi wrung her hands as she approached the bed. "It isn't you," she said in apology. Ying Fa started to rise.

"It's alright," Poh Poh said, gesturing for her to stay, then backing away a little, her gaze watery.

"I know," Ying Fa said at last. She smiled sadly, as she looked from one woman to the other. "Getting her back was a big surprise. I thought she was gone forever." Her smile faded. "But now I realize . . .."

Zhaodi's lower lip trembled. Even now she kept her distance, not reaching out to pat or touch, not asking to hold the baby. Never a beauty, her ravaged face had aged ten years in the past few weeks. Her skin looked sallow, an unhealthy shade of gray.

"I cried when the one-child law was enacted," she said softly, exchanging a knowing look with Poh Poh; making

192

Ying Fa yearn for her own mother-in-law's attention. "When the law came down from Beijing, we didn't know if it applied to children already born." She put a hand out, her look was imploring. "I didn't want to have to choose which child, yet I had chosen." She closed her eyes briefly. "We lived in fear for weeks that you'd be taken—especially your father. I could not bring myself to care for you, or even look at you more than was necessary. I thought. . .." She choked and then started to sob; her face in her hands.

Ying Fa shook her head, unable to speak. How unbearable it must have been for her, how hopeless. What was worse, she had had to live with her decision, seeing it in the flesh each day as she had grown. With the threats associated with the one-child law reinforcing old beliefs, Zhaodi must have been desperately afraid of loving her. Now she was finally free to lavish her love on Hsiao.

Poh Poh hugged Zhaodi; and it came to her that Zhaodi had always leaned on Poh Poh—when it should have been the other way around.

"What about you, Poh Poh?" she asked. "What should I do?"

"Your new family must decide your fate," she said, her expression unreadable. "Only Gwai Ha and Yanru can protect you from Li Zoumin. They are the only ones who can help us, too—though it may already be too late. You must leave tomorrow, as early as possible. There is no other way."

Ying Fa nodded sadly, then gazed at her child, too tired and confused to argue. Why was it already too late? She'd only been here since morning and Mooi Mooi . . ..

Mooi Mooi's crying. Someone had heard. Someone had reported them. Of course.

She looked up, horrified, seeing Poh Poh leading Zhaodi back to her room. They sat side by side behind the others watching the television, their backs to her in quiet solidarity.

The next day Father, Mother and Yutang left for their respective jobs after a hurried, tense breakfast. Holding Mooi Mooi, Ying Fa opened the windows to let in the cold spring air. Horns beeped, bicycle bells clanged and vendors shouted, hawking their wares. It was just another frenetic, desperate Maoming day from which she would like to disappear.

So what if the baby cried? What was the sense of hiding now, of pretending the neighbors hadn't heard? Surely, someone had already called Uncle Li.

How ironic that in months past Hsiao had gloried in her newborn's piercing cry.

She stared into Mooi Mooi's eyes, seeing with startling clarity a fully formed soul, a living, breathing human being, full of wisdom and strength. For a long staggering moment, she stared into Mooi Mooi's eyes, love filling her heart as the connection between her and the child seeped into her bones.

"You're mine," she whispered, and then the connection dissolved.

She saw baby eyes, heavy with sleep, looking up at her with such trust that she wanted to cry. How she hated Hsiao and the Lis, the terrible family into which she had married. How dare they take her child from her? How dare they make such an important decision about her life?

194

Heated by fury, she relished the cold air blowing in from the open window.

With renewed energy, she went to the bathroom, where she bathed herself and Mooi Mooi, then returned to her bed, cradling the child. There was nothing for her to do.

The others had cleared away the meal, as if she were a guest, as if she didn't exist. She lay quietly for a while, attempting to plan her next step while Mooi Mooi slept.

One path after another formed and then faded in her mind, each attempt ending with Gwai Ha and Yanru, and Mooi Mooi nowhere to be found. There was no getting around the fact that Uncle Li ruled them all. How could she hope to get a travel permit, a work reassignment or even an extension of her leave without his permission?

She jumped at the sound of a knock at the door, startling the child awake, making her cry. With quick fingers, she unbuttoned her nightdress and tried to soothe her; but Mooi Mooi, probably sensing her anxiety, screamed louder.

The knocking intensified.

She rose and bounced the baby lightly, pressing her red, round face into her shoulder. She whispered endearments as she inched toward the door, terrified of who stood behind it.

Then, thankfully, the baby stopped crying.

"Ying Fa. Please." It was Gwai Ha. "I know you're there. Please let me in. We need to talk."

"So at last you've come," she murmured, "my soon-to-be ex-husband." She shook her head in disgust, realizing why her family had cleared out so fast. She had to stop being so trusting. This was too much like her first date, with every second planned.

She flung the door open and gestured for him to enter. He looked exhausted. His clothes were rumpled, as if he hadn't slept in days. Yet he still managed to look like the beloved son, a person of importance.

He scanned her and the child without surprise.

"So you knew about this?" She closed the door, wondering what pathetic excuse he would make, what sad tale he would tell. The fact was he had betrayed her. He had let his uncle win. He'd just turned and walked away after crushing her in the cruelest manner possible. She would give him five minutes and then he'd have to leave.

"Ying Fa?" He held out a hand. Tears filled his eyes as he looked at Mooi Mooi. "I had no idea my mother kept her. I didn't believe my uncle until she admitted it herself. And now . . . ." He raked a hand through his hair.

"And now you're sorry," she said, glaring at him with all the venom she could muster. "Uncle Li must have his heir, so hand over the useless girl—isn't that right?" She spat as she spoke, then wiped the spittle off her lips with the back of her hand. "Over my dead body, you coward!"

"That's not what I've come to say."

She backed away as he came toward her. "Stay away from me, you monster!"

He held his hand out and took a deep breath. "Look, Ying Fa, I came to say I'm sorry, that I was wrong." His lips trembled.

She bit her lip, needing to hear his plan, not his excuses. No matter what he said, it was already too late.

She hugged the baby closer. What kind of man would throw away his child?

"Go on," she whispered, detesting the very sight of him, though some dark, traitorous part of her warmed to the quick light in his eyes. She cradled Mooi Mooi and kissed her face, watching him out of the corner of her eye.

"After you left, I began to think about her." He gazed at the child with a combination of awe and yearning—a sickening display. "She is ours—yours and mine." He clenched a fist and dropped it to his side. "Uncle can't do this to us. He is dead wrong. With our retirement pay, we won't need a son to provide for us. We can pamper our daughter; provide her with travel and abundance. If only he could see it our way, the way it's supposed to be in modern China."

"You sound like a propaganda film," she said coldly. "Who thought it up for you—your mother?"

He stepped back, shaking his head. "My mother? No."

She looked at the baby, recognizing her striking resemblance to Gwai Ha, and shook her head. Gwai Ha was as handsome as a paper doll, but Mooi Mooi was real. She was innocence personified, her own heart. How could she ever have loved this man?

"You come up with alternatives far too late." She wanted to slap his face. "What if your mother had done as she was told? With Mooi Mooi gone, would you still be here begging? Sounds like she's trying to justify her actions."

"Mooi Mooi?" He folded his arms across his chest.

"What about me?" she asked, wanting to cry. "How do you think I feel? And when was your mother going to tell me that my baby—my Mooi Mooi—was with my parents? Does she have any idea the danger she's put my family in?"

"When you left . . . I—"

"You what—missed my cooking? Your mother knows how to cook now. I made sure of it. You haven't listened to a word I've said."

She felt a draft and looked down to find that she had left her nightdress unbuttoned. Her left nipple was no longer covered by Mooi Mooi's face. Mortified, she turned aside to button it, then laughed harshly. It wasn't like he'd never seen it before.

"Let me hold her?" he asked, now a meter away.

On command, she handed her over; and then instantly regretted her obedience. For a few seconds she could only stare at him and their child, seeing a vision of hope—as it should have been in their baby's first moments of life.

Instead, she had endured a shameful, dragged out drama that had been worse than death. Now she must face yet another loss, this time involving others, with lives and livelihoods at stake.

Gwai Ha's expression was tender and curious. She moved closer, compelled by an urge to be part of her own little family. Her hands shook as she reached for her child.

Incredibly gentle, Gwai Ha handed her over, just as tiny pink lips parted in a perfect cat-like yawn.

"She looks like you," he said, gazing at Ying Fa with a boyish grin that he had no business wearing.

She glared at him in disbelief. Playtime was over. It was time to be a grown up. Never again would she laugh with this foolish man.

She held Mooi Mooi to her chest, feeling the pressure of her breasts letting down. "You have to leave," she said, looking at his chin. She would never nurse in front of him. It was bad enough that she had forgotten to button her nightdress.

"I guess I just needed to be whacked over the head to finally realize what I've lost—what we've lost," he said sadly.

She peered at him through narrowed eyes. "Did you listen at all to what I just said?"

He pulled at his hair with both hands and grimaced. "Yes, Uncle knows that she's here." She took a step back. "He's furious," he whispered. "He watches me with that evil gloating of his that reminds me of a vulture. He's not even my father, so what right does he have to decide how and if I perpetuate the Li family name? There are millions of Lis scattered all over the world." He gestured wildly with his arms. "Whole families have been wiped out by invasions, famines and floods. It's time for China to break the ancient chains that bind us, alter the way it values sons over daughters, destroy the concept of Party Boss as overlord." He took a breath, preparing to say more.

"So the sage speaks," she muttered. Then louder, "You're so full of hot air, Gwai Ha. Uncle Li is our Party Boss. That is the only detail that matters. He can do anything he wants to us. His kind rules China, whether you like it or not. And you can bet that when you're his age, you'll do the same."

Gwai Ha shut his lips, looking disgruntled.

"You don't like what I'm saying?" she asked tiredly. "Well, let me tell you something else, husband." She took a deep breath, her eyes filling with tears. "My family is terrified." She lowered her voice. "Each time this baby cries they push me to quiet her. Hsiao has become my enemy." She swiped at her tears, finding strength in her words. "My mother says that this child is bad luck." She poked her finger at his chest. "Don't you dare talk to me about what should be. That's nothing but a waste of breath, little brother."

He reeled at the insult; but she wasn't finished.

"What can you or your mother do to change his mind? Go to his wife? Escape to Guangzhou and live with your mother's relatives? It doesn't matter that Beijing promotes the benefits of keeping daughters. Uncle Li wants you to have a son and he will get exactly what he wants."

"Please come home," he said, reaching out to her.

She moved away, unable to bear the sorrow in his eyes.

"Just go," she said, wishing she had never let him in. She hugged Mooi Mooi to her, hoping she wouldn't cry.

"I love you," he whispered, rattling her confidence. How she had longed for those words just hours ago.

"You agreed to abandon our child." She couldn't look at him. "You are complicit. You are a monster just like him."

"We need you to come home, little Ying Fa," he said softly, sending shivers across her shoulders. It was all she could do to avert her eyes. "We'll talk at home," he pleaded. "There has to be a way out of this. There just has to."

"Go!" she yelled, and then strode to the door and threw it open. He stumbled back, arms out, beseeching her as she poked him in the chest. "Out!" she cried, pressing him back. Her breasts throbbed with the need to nurse. When he was finally out, she swung the door closed, and leaned against it, quietly sobbing.

His horrified look was embedded in her brain. Now she had no place to go, nowhere to turn. What was she supposed to do?

❀   ❀   ❀

She would never forget the shock on Poh Poh's face and the anger on Hsiao's upon finding her still in the apartment, quietly nursing Mooi Mooi in her own bed, when they returned from the market a few hours later.

"What are you doing here?" Hsiao shouted as she came through the door, carrying her sleeping son. Poh Poh followed, pulling the laden cart.

Ying Fa laughed harshly. "I'm supposed to be the submissive wife, returning home with my forgiving husband? You should know better."

She watched them struggle in through lowered lashes, dreading what was to come; and begged the gods for another hour, another day. Her reprieve was quickly coming to an end.

"Ying Fa, this cannot be," Poh Poh said, shaking her head sadly. She gripped the shopping cart handle for support. Hsiao rushed to close the bedroom window. Then she raced back, her expression sour as she laid Anji on her bed and closed the curtain around him.

"Why are you still hear, you troublemaker?" she hissed, coming at Ying Fa with both fists flying.

Poh Poh grabbed Hsiao's sleeve but wasn't fast enough to block the blow to Ying Fa's ear.

"Get out!" Hsiao screeched, and Anji began to wail. Hsiao went to him, her face a brilliant red.

Tears sprang to Ying Fa's eyes as she clutched her ear. So it had begun—the division, the hatred. It was just what Uncle Li wanted.

As she looked about the place she had once called home, a misty peace, like an unexpected summer rain, pervaded her consciousness, filling the aching hollows of her chest. She watched Hsiao comfort her son, feeling nothing. Perhaps she did belong with Chan Yanru and her evil son, a choice poorly made one sunny, blue-skied day when the beach had been golden and life filled with promise.

"You can't stay!" Poh Poh cried, grabbing her arm and pulling her to her feet.

Thankfully, she had already begun to rise. Looking deep into Poh Poh's eyes, she nodded sadly. "I know, Poh Poh. I was just gathering the strength."

"No you weren't," Hsiao said, hands on her hips. "You were hoping for more time."

"Can I hold her while you get ready?" Poh Poh asked, sending Hsiao a withering look. She held out her hands, looking miserable.

Ying Fa handed her the baby, recalling the horrible moment after Mooi Mooi's birth when she had done the same. However, this time was for real. Poh Poh would never see or hold this baby again.

In a heat to leave, she changed quickly into the clothes in which she had arrived, grateful that Hsiao kept her distance, her hair hanging in her face, a sure sign that she was deeply ashamed of her outburst.

The room was charged with tense silence as she stuffed her few belongings into a bag. She was about to take

Mooi Mooi from Poh Poh when the door burst open and Zhaodi, sobbing heavily, fell through the doorway.

"You won't believe this," Zhaodi said with a long shuddering gasp.

Ying Fa flew to her, grabbed her arm, pulled her inside, and then closed the door. "What is it?" she cried as she took her bag from her. The she pulled her over to a chair. Hsiao hovered, as if unsure of her role.

"Please?" Ying Fa mouthed to Hsiao, wishing she never had to speak to her again. Hsiao's eyes lightened, but just for a second. She sprang to the bathroom and returned with a warm, wet cloth that she used on Zhaodi's face.

"You're still here?" Zhaodi asked, turning to glare at Ying Fa. "Your disobedience will kill us all."

Ying Fa backed away and took Mooi Mooi from Poh Poh, sick to her stomach. "What happened?" she asked, already knowing that Manager Li had begun his revenge.

"I've lost my job," Zhaodi said, and they all gasped. "After thirty years as the best dim sum cook in all of Maoming, I've lost my job." She took a shuddering breath and closed her eyes as Hsiao clasped her shoulder.

"How can this be?" Poh Poh asked. She laid a hand on Zhaodi's other shoulder.

"Trumped up charges, complaints from patrons." Zhaodi's eyes flashed as she looked at Ying Fa. "Someone told Manager Li about your baby. You know this is only the beginning."

"I . . . I was just leaving," she said as she grabbed her bag.

"It's too late," Zhaodi spat. "We've all been condemned by Yanru's foolish act. When will it end?"

Ying Fa hugged Mooi Mooi closer.

"Until that baby disappears," Zhaodi said, pointing at the child, "We're all as good as dead. All of us, I tell you. Rumor has it that Manager Li won't stop until you comply; and even then, he'll make your life as miserable as he can."

Zhaodi took the cloth from Hsiao and twisted it in her hands. "You should have married that Tsang boy. Then at least we would be safe. You reach too high, daughter, expecting all of us to dance to your tune. Bad luck surrounds us and will choke out our lives. But it's you who must pay—you and that haughty mother-in-law of yours."

"I'm so sorry." Ying Fa bowed her head, pressing her lips to Mooi Mooi's hair.

"Ba," Zhaodi spat, and waved an arm. "Get away from me with that wounded look of yours. Good thing your father is not here. He agreed to one night." She raised a fist, her face a mottled purple. "That night has long passed!"

Ying Fa reeled from her rage, from the truth of her words. She looked down at Mooi Mooi, her tears now dried. "For good or bad," she said, "I've chosen my path."

"What will you do?" Zhaodi asked, now sobbing. She closed her eyes. "You must get rid of her. You know that."

"I'll talk with Gwai Ha and Mrs. Chan," Ying Fa said firmly. "Maybe they'll have a plan."

She was at the door when Hsiao called out to her.

"What now?" she asked, annoyed as she turned, her hand on the door handle, her throat full to the point of choking.

"There are lots of babies just like her at the orphanage," Hsiao whispered.

Ying Fa shifted Mooi Mooi higher.

"She'd be considered a gift by Westerners looking to adopt." Hsiao's eyes pleaded. "When I'm back at work, I'll watch over her until she's adopted." She tilted her head questioningly.

Just then, Anji took his first few steps over to her, a laughing, happy child.

Ying Fa's heart froze as Hsiao reached down, her face beaming as she praised him.

Yet his cousin must suffer for being a girl?

"How dare you tell me how to abandon my child," she cried.

Blindly, she fled the apartment, her bag dangling from her elbow, bumping against her side. Head down, she shifted Mooi Mooi to her other arm, trying to hide her under a blanket, and ran down the steps. She paused at the bottom and laughed. It didn't matter that it was broad daylight. Someone had already reported her.

Her tears dried as she strode from the building. She looked down at Mooi Mooi who slept in her arms, her heart aching. A forest of tall buildings, replete with watchful eyes, surrounded her as she made her way down the street. At the first busy intersection, she took a deep breath and marked the moment. If she had been born a man, she would simply leave this place, cast her lot at the train station and begin a new life in Guangzhou. She would look up her grandmother's relatives or live day-by-day, with her daughter as her life. However, as a man, she would never have become an embroiderer, met Gwai Ha or given birth.

The blaring horns and smells of the city didn't touch her as she slowly, carefully made her way across town to her mother-in-law's apartment. She felt detached from it all, as if an invisible orb surrounded her and her child. Had she really made the same trip just the day before? This time it wasn't raining, though the sun barely shone though the pollution-fueled haze that painted the sky a sickly gray.

Gray too, were her thoughts as she crossed busy intersections and stepped over rotting fruit as if dancing across an open square, her feet light, Mooi Mooi weightless.

When Mooi Mooi stirred, she kissed her soft, round face and breathed in her heady fragrance, willing time to slow, needing the dance to last forever.

She approached Yanru's apartment building, her gut constricting as she quickened her pace; yet she refused to acknowledge her fears. They would take her back. Hadn't Gwai Ha begged her to come home? Hadn't Yanru tried to save her child? She had to relax. She was almost there.

Insidious doubts crept in as she walked. She had expected her own family's acceptance, and they'd turned her out. Nothing was as she had predicted.

She took a deep breath and grasped the handle to the building's massive door. White noise from the gleaming entryway filled her ears as the door swung closed behind her. She pressed palm to forehead, trying to stave off the beginnings of headache, imagining a cool cloth pressed to her face, and a hot cup of tea. Perhaps Yanru hadn't forgotten how to soft-cook an egg. Her mouth watered and her stomach rumbled. She had eaten little in the past few days.

"Mooi Mooi," she whispered, her lips curving into a smile as she gazed down at her daughter. Thankfully, the baby slept, oblivious to her surroundings.

She had almost made it to the apartment door when she heard him—Uncle Li. The sound of his voice rumbled from Yanru's apartment.

Swiftly, she ducked into an alcove around the corner, praying the child would sleep. Then she scanned the hall leading to the outside door, checking that it was clear. She stifled a shriek as she crouched, her whole body shaking.

"So this is it; this is the end?" Uncle Li asked with a harsh laugh. "After all these years, after all I've done for you; you're going to throw it away on a useless girl?"

"Leave my mother alone!" Gwai Ha cried. There came a loud slap.

Ying Fa imagined him rubbing his face and glaring at his uncle, too frightened to fight back.

"You have your own wife and your own home," Gwai Ha whined.

"Leave us," she heard his mother say in that familiar, curt tone that brooked no argument. "This is between your uncle and me. No. I said leave. Now. There are things I must say."

There was a moment of silence.

Ying Fa leaned against the wall, hoping to ease her aching back. When she shifted, the baby awoke and started to cry. With frantic fingers, she wrested her dress open and began to nurse. Glancing around, she realized how conspicuous she was in the dim hallway. Her shoes poked out from under her dress, her head and neck were bare. Quickly, she turned and faced the wall, took a large scarf from her bag and draped it over her head.

She ripped a dress and a blanket from the bag and piled them on, too; and then tucked her feet under her, hoping she would resemble a pile of rags. In the early days of her marriage, such piles had been commonplace outside Yanru's apartment.

"Zuomin. Please," Yanru was saying, her voice thick and sweet. She imagined her circling the stocky man, trailing her long, slender fingers across his barrel chest. Poh Poh said he had been handsome once. She shuddered, thinking of his beady eyes, bushy eyebrows and unsightly paunch.

"You didn't really mean for me to abandon the child," Yanru said. "She's tiny, insignificant, just a baby. She is so beautiful, so much like Gwai Ha. You have to see her for yourself."

"It won't work, old woman."

"But Zuomin, dear. She's . . ."

"I told you a month ago it must be a boy; and you promised you'd do your duty. You're only prolonging everyone's pain by dragging this out." His tone was low and urgent. Ying Fa strained to hear. "I'll not be dissuaded by your wiles," he continued. "Always. Always, I took second place to my illustrious elder brother, shouldering the work while he was away at school. I took him in when the Red Guards should have killed him for his arrogance. I risked my life taking you in, too, while my peasant in-laws watched and waited for an opportunity to bring me down. You hate my lack of manners? You hate my ignorant wife? At least she had the decency to protect you from her family, who wanted to stone you in the square. You're nothing but a pampered girl, a spoiled whore, and now you're ready to prostitute yourself for some worthless girl."

Yanru cried out. She pictured him grabbing her hands and shoving her away.

"I don't blame the child's mother," he sneered. "You've never set a proper example. Just look at your snotty son. He detests the sight of me, though he knows perfectly well how to act when he wants something. Maybe I should send the two of you to a work farm. Then you can watch each other degenerate while you wonder what I've done with the Wong girl. You are a pitiful excuse for a mother, Yanru. I should have listened to my wife and had them move in with us right from the start." There came another slap.

A single tear coursed down Ying Fa's face. She couldn't move, could barely breathe. Move in with them? Manager Li's apartment? The work farm held more appeal.

"Please. I can't abandon her." Yanru spoke softly, like a child. "You know it isn't right, Zuomin. The child belongs with us. With me."

"Belongs with you?" he laughed. "You should listen to yourself, you selfish old woman. You own nothing without my charity. When I tell you to do something, you'll do it gladly or I'll strip you of everything you hold dear."

"Promises, promises," Yanru spat.

She was baiting him? Ying Fa closed her eyes, praying she would stop.

"I'm glad Gwai Ha's not your precious son," Yanru hissed.

Uncle mumbled a response, an expletive she didn't quite catch. Was he talking about Gwai Ha's father? She couldn't be sure. She shivered, wishing she had worn a coat or a sweater. Mooi Mooi lay heavy in her arms.

"My father should never have allowed me to marry a Li," Yanru said, now sobbing. "First one brother, and then the next. You Lis have brought me nothing but misery. I rose above your brother's arrogance, his womanizing and selfishness, only to lose my beautiful girls because of his cowardice. Those soldiers would have let us out of Beijing; but he had to be sure. He made me watch while my daughters' husbands dragged them away kicking and screaming. Bullies and thugs they were—lower than pigs. They were just children, Zoumin. You thought you did me a big favor by finding their addresses. Why? So I can learn how poorly they've been treated? Now you want me to give up my granddaughter. That will kill my daughter-in-law, whom I have grown to love. You threaten me with removing her from my life? Whom else will you take from me? Isn't it enough that you've shamed me all these years, your elder brother's honored wife?"

"Honored wife?" Manager Li sneered. "And how exactly how did he honor you, Yanru. You know what he was."

Loved? Ying Fa could hardly believe it. Yanru loved her?

"Where's the child?" he asked.

"Don't cry. Please don't cry," Ying Fa whispered, looking down, touching Mooi Mooi's cheek with one trembling finger. The baby continued to nurse.

"As if you don't know," Yanru said, chilling her to the core.

Of course, he knew. He has spies everywhere—ears listening through doors and walls and beneath windowsills. Money and power were everything.

"The Wong's have only begun to pay," Uncle Li said. "They should have turned her in immediately; but like your late father, they care too much for their pretty spoiled daughter and want her to have everything. Well, this time they will pay dearly for their weakness. The mother's job is gone. By the end of tomorrow, father and son may as well be living on the streets. A few misplaced papers, contraband items found in the trunk of a car— who knows what kind of trouble will find them. Maybe the daughter-in-law will return from maternity leave to find her job eliminated. Then they'll have to live off the grandmother's pension. Funny how the other tenants in their building have heard things. A few stern lectures and the Wong's will be most grateful for that shack on the beach they used to live in. Too bad Beijing controls the grandmother's pension."

Ying Fa's head spun. He wouldn't.

"Of course," Uncle Li added, sounding conciliatory, "as soon as this little problem is corrected, all will be restored as if nothing happened."

He would. He'd do anything to get what he wanted, no matter whom he harmed in the process.

"Please don't make me do this!" Yanru cried. "Please, Zuomin, for me. Please. I can't bear lose any more of my family."

Ying Fa closed her eyes. Tears streamed down her face. Yanru had given her heart to a demon; and this wasn't the first time she had cried to him, begging for what should have been her's by right.

She shook her head trying to clear it, telling herself to be strong. Her family was about to lose everything. How they must despise her now—their lowly sister and daughter. She should have realized the extent of the danger she had put them in when she'd first held Mooi Mooi? They wouldn't survive long without their jobs or their home.

"Maybe now you'll do as you're told," Uncle Li said. "If I find the child, I'll take care of her myself."

Ying Fa shivered, and then looked down to find a big stain darkening the front of her skirt from Mooi Mooi's urine. She had soaked her clothes and blanket, too. The acrid fumes stung her nostrils, but she dared not move, lest she cause a draft and make the baby cry.

"Alright," Uncle said firmly, "Next week I'm transferring Gwai Ha to Huazhou and Ying Fa to a work farm." Ying Fa bit her lip to keep from crying out. "Maybe once they're separated, they'll begin to appreciate the life they could have shared. Maybe you'll run out of hiding places for that child. Then you'll come to me begging, until your knees bleed. Then, my precious Yanru, I'll do with you as I will."

There was the sound of a scuffle and Yanru cried out. Tears streamed down Ying Fa's face as she remembered the endless drudgery and stark loneliness of the work farm. A year would age her ten, and Mooi Mooi would be lost to her anyway. Without Gwai Ha, without a shred of hope for the future, she would surely die.

"Please," Yanru sobbed, "It's only a child. You would do all this because of a child? You must be insane."

There was the sound of boxes falling as if Uncle had thrown something against the wall. Then the door creaked open and heavy, measured footsteps approached.

Ying Fa froze, holding her breath as the air changed, her heart pounding. She loosened her hold on Mooi Mooi for fear of gripping her too tightly. Uncle Li strode past, loudly hawking his spit, souring the air. His spit landed on the wall mere feet from where she crouched.

She closed her eyes, letting the seconds pass.

Her heartbeat thudded in her ears. One cry and it would be over. The child wiggled, probably sensing her fear.

Then the air changed again. The outside door opened and closed.

She took a shuddering breath and peeked out from under the blanket, the taste of bile acrid in her mouth.

The hall was empty.

She tried to stand, but her legs wouldn't support her. Slowly, she stretched them out, pointing her toes. They had gone to sleep, and were useless lumps of flesh. Pins and needles shot through them as she leaned forward onto her knees and tried to push herself up against the clammy wall. The baby had fallen asleep again; her pink lips slack against her breast. Milk trickled down her naked abdomen, seeping into the urine-soaked dress.

Her breath came fast, and she faltered the first few steps.

She reached down and grabbed her bag, almost dropping Mooi Mooi; then moved in slow motion, her hands stiff and clumsy, as she buttoned the top of her dress.

She tried to hurry. Uncle Li could return at any moment; or a passing neighbor might see her.

"He didn't mean any of it," she heard Yanru say as she neared the apartment. "They were just angry words that we'll both regret," she added plaintively. "You'll see. He'll accept the baby in time."

"Mother." Gwai Ha's tone was as cold as winter. "Don't you get it? He's obsessed. There's no reasoning with him. The baby has to go and the sooner the better."

"You want her gone?" Yanru cried.

Ying Fa stumbled to the door and pushed it open a few more inches. The apartment was dark inside, the lights off. Gwai Ha leaned against the doorframe to his mother's room, his arms folded across his chest, light from her bedroom casting his shadow across the floor.

For some reason the midwife's wrinkled face came to mind; and she shuddered, remembering the way she'd run after Gwai Ha asking for her money.

She paused on the threshold, wishing she could back away, melt into the past where it had been safe and free from care. It was hard to believe she had just given birth a few days ago. There was no going back.

Exhaustion pressed behind her eyes, at the core of her joints and into the depths of her soul. With each heartbeat her genitals pounded. Walking had intensified her bleeding, but she didn't dare feel behind her for the raw evidence. Another wet spot was inconsequential, considering what she had been through.

Gwai Ha didn't see her yet: his gaze was focused on his mother. His white shirt with its sleeves rolled up gleamed in stark contrast to his black hair and pants.

"No, I don't want the child gone," he said tiredly, his shoulders sagging. "Don't even suggest such a thing; but how can you value a child over the livelihood of two families? It's not fair, but what is? What Uncle's done to Ying Fa and to me is unconscionable." He combed his hair back with one trembling hand. "Someday he'll pay for this, but right now he's too strong, too powerful. You should have abandoned the child when he told you to, and been done with it." His voice trailed off.

"No," Yanru whispered. "Can't you see that he's just blowing hot air?"

As Ying Fa's eyes adjusted, she saw that Yanru was on the floor, wearing an elegant navy dress with green piping around the collars and cuffs—paid for by Uncle Li, no doubt. She sat with her legs to the side, the picture of a fine lady. Her fine dark hair tumbled like silk out of a chignon, around her face and over her shoulders, taking decades off her purported age. How dare she look so feminine, so calm and self-composed?

Yanru spoke in a small voice, "Zoumin would never—"

"You're wrong," Ying Fa said, gripping the doorframe as she entered, refusing to give in to a wave of dizziness.

They gaped at her, both startled and relieved. They had worried about her after all. She drew some comfort from that. At least she was welcome somewhere.

"My mother's already lost her job," she said, stepping inside on legs now strong. Adrenaline surged through her. She felt their gaze upon her, taking in the baby, her sodden state. She cared little what they thought.

She scanned the apartment, seeing the clothing strewn about; the pictures askew on the walls, the wardrobes open, overflowing, disorderly, the encrusted dishes piled high upon the table. The air smelled foul, like burned peanut oil and spoiled meat. She leaned over to pick up something off the floor, and then stopped herself. There would be plenty of time for cleaning in the long, lonely months ahead.

"Ying Fa?" Yanru said at last, her eyes filled with longing and sadness. She rose swiftly and came to her. "Daughter-in-law, I'm so glad you're home."

Gwai Ha stood rooted, uncertain. There was a flicker of fear in his eyes, and shame. He swallowed heavily.

"Let me take her," Yanru said, and reached for the baby.

Ying Fa turned slightly, warding her off. She would hold her baby until that last, terrible moment, and no one would interfere.

Yanru moved back, hanging her head. Then she sniffed loudly and wrung her hands, her knuckles white against her dark dress.

"Uncle Li will stop at nothing," Ying Fa said softly, trying to lighten the blow. She owed Yanru something at least for trying to save Mooi Mooi. "He will follow through with all of his threats. In a week my family will be living on the streets. Gwai Ha and I will be gone."

"Zhaodi lost her job?" Yanru asked, cocking her head. "There must be some mistake. She's been making dim sum for what . . . thirty years?"

"The mistake was leaving this door open," Ying Fa said, and closed it behind her. She dropped her bag to the floor. "Anyone passing in the hall would have learned our business. I heard everything Uncle Li said. Everything."

Yanru's face blanched.

"What happened with your parents?" Gwai Ha asked quietly. "Did they kick you out?"

She sighed as she looked at him, her heart in her eyes. He moved closer, his gaze holding hers. The messy room and his tiny, childlike mother, who had only been trying to help, faded into the background.

"Uncle Li will know I'm here within the hour," she said, her gaze steady as she stroked Mooi Mooi's back.

Gwai Ha swallowed, his Adam's apple bobbing. He turned away slightly and rubbed his chin with the palm of his hand. "I imagine the neighbors have been promised something." He looked back at her.

She nodded slightly.

"Why did you take her to my mother?" she asked, turning to Yanru, her fury barely in check. "My family's torn apart with grief. They are beset by warring loyalties and are terrified. Even Hsiao—especially Hsiao—has turned against me. And what about me, Mother-in-law? Now that I've held her, it will be all the more painful to let her go."

Yanru face reddened. She backed further away. "I couldn't walk away from that child, any more than I could stop breathing. Believe me, I tried. She's my granddaughter, my only granddaughter, as far as I know." She folded her arms across her chest. "I can't bear to lose another girl."

Ying Fa looked down at Mooi Mooi. "But you'll have to," she said, her lips quivering as she held back tears.

"She's the image of Gwai Ha," Yanru said, so softly that Ying Fa could barely hear. "She reminds me so much of my own little girls. We've all lost too many daughters." She was crying now. "I can't bear to see her go."

"Mooi Mooi is my daughter," Ying Fa said, unable to look directly at Yanru. "The cost of keeping her is too high. It will destroy us. And then what? She'll end up in some orphanage anyway, too old for anyone to want her. This way, at least she'll have a chance."

"But you . . . you begged me to keep her," Yanru said. "You begged your grandmother. You cursed Gwai Ha." She threw her hands up. "I can't believe you'd be so callous, that you'd change your mind."

"Mother!" Gwai Ha warned, shooting her an angry look. "This is no time for recriminations. She's speaking the truth, and you know it."

Ying Fa sucked in her breath, seeing him eye her sopping dress, hating the pity in his eyes.

"When were you going to tell me where you took her . . . that you'd kept her?" she asked, tears rolling down her face.

"I don't know." Yanru shook her head sadly.

The chill of disbelief, its long icy fingers of calm, poured through her. She raised her chin in defiance. "So you had no plan?" she asked, seeing the hesitation on her face, the trembling of her lips. "You thought everything would fall into place, even Uncle Li's agreement? How could you have been so foolish, after all he's done to you? How powerful do you think you are? He and his wife want to take everything that you have. Can't you see it?" She took a long shuddering breath. "At least you know where your daughters are."

She swayed slightly, feeling suddenly weak, and closed her eyes against the image of Yanru's daughters being dragged away screaming.

"And now we must abandon her ourselves," Gwai Ha said, the fury in his voice the only thing that kept her knees from buckling. She could hardly believe he was agreeing with her. If he hadn't, she didn't know what she would have done. There could be no future without the both of them acting as one.

Something about the way his hair hung over his forehead managed to calm her. She wanted to reach out and touch him, and wrap herself in any comfort he could give.

"It doesn't matter what you think," Gwai Ha said to his mother, though not unkindly. "This is my decision."

Yanru fled to the kitchen, sobbing, where she proceeded to clang pots and pans, making a great noise to drown her sorrow and rage. Ying Fa's stomach rumbled, yet there was a sour taste in her mouth. Her appetite had fled.

"We have to do this," she said looking down at Mooi Mooi.

She felt Gwai Ha's warmth before she looked up. He was centimeters away, his lips nearly brushing her forehead.

"Ying Fa, how I have worried about you."

In his eyes, she found the welcome she had long desired. She leaned toward him, and in an instant, she and the baby were in his arms. It was like after Mooi Mooi's birth—safe and warm—a complete little family, just for the moment. She began to sob, closing her eyes, relishing his strength.

"We'll take her in the morning?" he asked, his expression grave as he pulled away slightly. There was a slight twist to his lips, evidence that he held back his tears.

"Tomorrow?" Yanru shrieked from the kitchen doorway. "You can't do this, Gwai Ha. Please don't do this." She ran in and lunged for the baby; but Gwai Ha warded her off with an outstretched arm.

"No Mother," he said. "I've listened to you long enough. You'll do as I say."

Ying Fa choked back sobs. She was shivering, the wet taking its toll. Gwai Ha gripped her with a steadying arm.

"Can't you see that she needs food, Mother, and some tea?" His eyes narrowed. His voice was hard with command. "She needs a bath, too and some rest. She's been through a lot and needs our help. Right now."

She exchanged shocked looks with Yanru. His tone was much like his uncle's. But he was not his uncle—he was a man of conscience and education, a compassionate man, and her husband.

Her vision blurred and she swayed a little as her worries took hold. Would he really take care of her? Would he stand by her after it was all over; or would he fade into a fog of self-delusion; like Grandfather Wong, leaving Poh Poh to pick up the pieces of their shattered family? Her shivering intensified. Soon, they would be working for his uncle again, under his control.

She looked down and her breath caught at the sight of her daughter lying in her arms. Mooi Mooi was beauty personified—a luscious fruit she dared not taste. The baby slept, her face pearlescent in the dim light. She was what Poh Poh called a good baby, an easy baby, with a sunny disposition.

She must savor this day, this hour, and recall it with joy. It was all she would have. With glazed eyes, she noticed that her damp dress and the baby's wet blanket had seeped into Gwai Ha's clothes, marking him. She managed to smile. Had the recent events truly made him hers?

"No. It must be tonight," she said, looking at him, surprised by the strength in her voice. "It has to be," she added, forcing herself to breathe. "Or Uncle Li's revenge can never be reversed."

A warm rush flooded the insides of her thighs. Her knees started to buckle and she swayed. "I need . . .." Clinging to Gwai Ha's arm, she began to fall.

Quickly, he scooped her and the baby up and carried them to the bathroom. Her head spun as he took Mooi Mooi from her and laid her gently on the floor. Then, with strong arms and soothing words, he helped her remove her clothes and step into the tub.

"You don't have to do this," she said, trying to cover her nakedness with her hands.

"It's alright," he said, politely averting his gaze.

He ran the water for her, letting it flow over his fingers to gauge the temperature.

It was then that she noticed his hair. It was greasy, as if he hadn't washed in days. There were new wrinkles at the corners of his eyes.

He glanced at her and she lowered her gaze, but not before seeing the pity and disgust on his face. Filled with shame, she looked down at her swollen abdomen. Blood trickled down the inside of her legs. Her hair was matted and dull. The skin on her face felt dry and brittle, as if frozen into a statue, as if she had aged a decade. Would it crack if she dared smile? A sob rose to the top of her throat.

Desperate to be alone, she raised a hand in protest as he came toward her with a bar of soap and a cloth. "Please, go," she said, and waved him away when he looked about to refuse. "Take her," she said, glancing where Mooi Mooi lay. "I just fed her. Maybe your mother can give her a bath. There are some clothes in my bag."

A light bloomed in Gwai Ha's eyes, making her sob almost burst.

"You sure?" he asked. He passed her the soap and cloth; then set the shampoo beside the tub within her reach. At her nod, he scooped up the baby.

"Please," she said, unable to keep from smiling. "It will do your mother good. And you, too."

His expression softened as he looked down at the sleeping child.

"I love you," he whispered, his gaze locking with hers for a second. Then he was gone.

She sighed as she settled back into the steaming water. It was as if a huge weight had been lifted from her shoulders. Her arms ached from holding Mooi Mooi; and the constant worry had gouged a well deep in the core of her soul. She closed her eyes, grateful for the silence, the peace.

Later, with a full stomach and her baby cradled in her arms, she told them all that had happened since she had left the apartment, including Hsiao's offer. Gwai Ha asked many questions, while Yanru remained silent, her face downcast.

Though Yanru had earned Gwai Ha's censure for having endangered the two families, her heart went out to her. While she had bathed, not only had Yanru tended the baby, but she'd also removed her belongings from her bedroom, and piled them against the wall near her and Gwai Ha's bed; moving their things to the sole bedroom.

Gwai Ha retired to the bathroom to read as soon as the meal was finished, as was his custom.

"I know you're furious with me," Ying Fa began, looking over the sleeping baby at Yanru, who sat on the sofa beside her.

Yanru stared at her hands in her lap, her expression dour.

Neither woman had moved to collect the dirty plates or the soiled cups, napkins or chopsticks. The mess would keep.

With a breaking heart, Ying Fa handed Mooi Mooi to her, and then smiled softly, seeing the spark of joy cross her dispirited face. Yanru looked up, acknowledging the gift with a slight nod, but said nothing.

Ying Fa yawned as she rose to her feet. Affording Yanru a few precious hours with her grandchild was the least she could do. Beyond depletion, every muscle in her body screaming for rest, she headed for what was to be her room, then lay down amidst the piles of bedding, not caring if she ever woke up.

Chapter 11

Just after midnight, they slipped out, their footsteps echoing off the three- and four-story apartment buildings as they headed toward the inner city. Ying Fa was tired, but not in the bone-aching, mind-crippling way she had been a few hours ago. They headed for the Babies Welfare Building, a place where abandoned children were brought from all over the city and the surrounding countryside. According to Hsiao, a baby a day was the average; though sometimes in the summer they took in as many as ten, with toddlers often numbering among them.

Dark shapes formed and fled as she looked behind her into the gloom. She spied rats scrambling after garbage and an old woman sifting through a pile of rubble. It wasn't hard to imagine tiny teeth biting her ankles, pulling her down, making her lose her balance and flinging her child out into a sea of hungry mouths. She huddled close to Gwai Ha, more frightened by the bitter expression on his face than the shadows behind her. He was distant and cold, making her feel like an anxious young girl, a burden he had reluctantly shouldered.

At the last moment, Yanru had tried to stop them. Her final argument, coming just as they were about to leave, had been that Ying Fa was too weak from childbirth to be wandering around the city at night—as if she hadn't walked across the city twice in the past two days.

She had yelled at her then, venting her bottled-up rage on the poor old woman in such a way that she wanted to hide her face in shame. Yanru was faultless in what was about to take place.

They had left her at home, silent and weeping. She had cursed them with harsh looks before shrouding herself in what had once been their marriage bed. It was as if in giving up her room, she had transferred all adult responsibilities onto them.

Judging by how she could hold a grudge, she was unlikely to speak to them for weeks. Thank the ancestors she had let her hold Mooi Mooi one last time.

But were they doing the right thing?

The reality of her family's situation settled like three-day-old rice within her throat, choking off all questions. No matter how tired she felt, she had to go with Gwai Ha. She had to be the last person in the family to touch Mooi Mooi, though her heart would break into a thousand shards of glass.

Something cried out in a nearby alley and then was silent. She shuddered and quickened her pace, glad she had remembered to wear a jacket, and was able to zip it across her still rounded belly on this chilly spring night.

She shrank into Gwai Ha as they approached a group of men just let off from their shift at some mid-town factory. They joked with each other as they strode past, leaving the faint but detectable odor of sweat and grime in their wake.

An old woman hobbled into view and behind her, a young boy who whined tiredly until she stuffed something into his mouth. They disappeared through a doorway.

A bicycle bell sounded behind them in warning; and they moved aside to let a young woman pass. She wore a cheap-looking suit, dark high heels and hose—a prostitute, most likely. No honest businesswoman would dare be out so late at night.

The sky was ominously black from the belching oil refineries, and a dank rain threatened, matching Ying Fa's mood. According to Yutang, a deluge due later in the day promised to strip trees and take down buildings. Maybe like last year, the streets would flood up to twenty meters deep, shutting down commerce.

She smelled the rain as she walked, footstep by tentative footstep, following Gwai Ha, who cut through the darkness in his gleaming white shirt. In his hand was a simple bamboo basket; a small boat that would carry their daughter to a new life, hopefully a new family.

The few hours she had rested had done little to quiet her nerves. She held Mooi Mooi close to her breast with both tired arms, trying not to cry. When she stumbled over a stone, Gwai Ha clasped her by the elbow.

"Walk slower," he said, a little too sharply. Then he sighed in apology, sounding sad and resigned.

She closed her eyes briefly, his hurt intensifying her own. He was only trying to care for her in the best way he knew how. Hadn't he stayed with her, right beside her, throughout this ordeal? He had already offered to carry the baby, more than once.

But Mooi Mooi was not a burden. She would not hand her over.

In a side alley near the orphanage, Gwai Ha set the basket down. Then with gentle hands, she laid the sleeping baby in the basket. Her eyes burned as she memorized the crescent shape of perfect, black lashes. She touched a soft downy cheek, and then leaned closer to inhale the baby's powdery scent. Gently she took a chubby hand and kissed it. Then she signaled to Gwai Ha who kneeled beside her.

With trembling hands, he pinned a note to the baby's nightgown. On it, in his elegant script, was Mooi Mooi's birth date and time—invaluable information for the child's new parents.

She bowed her head, already distancing herself, and prayed to her ancestors, commending her child into their care. Then she secured the blanket around Mooi Mooi's tiny body. It was one of those expensive soft blankets with little bears dancing across it that she had purchased a few months ago in hopes of a son. She took a deep, shuddering breath. No son would ever replace this baby. She was her daughter, her firstborn, not some hastily buried miscarriage or stillbirth—but a living, breathing human being. In moments, she would be relegated to a family mystery, a painful, guilty one—like Poh Poh's daughters, the faded memories of grieving elders.

At Gwai Ha's nod, she helped him carry the basket to the orphanage steps, a nondescript brick building that had once served as the main house for some minor official. Hsiao had often described its dreary upstairs rooms and the dirty courtyard where babies took what fresh air they could get.

With steady hands, she smoothed Mooi Mooi's forehead one last time and then managed to stand. She placed her hands behind her back, looked down at her sleeping child and blinked hard, refusing to submit to a wave of nausea.

She must not give in to it, not when Gwai Ha needed her. One mistake and they would end up in jail. How ironic that this illegal act, resulting from a law designed to protect people from starvation, was caused by a powerful man's hunger for immortality.

"Go. Now," Gwai Ha hissed. He gestured for her to move and she ran as fast as she could, her legs wobbling and her fear mounting. She crossed the street and ducked between two warehouses.

From the darkened alley she watched him pound on the stout orphanage door. The sound of her own heartbeat filled her ears as he waited and then pounded again.

Hsiao claimed that doctors, nurses and a housekeeper were in attendance twenty-four hours a day. They must be asleep.

Zhaodi's tears came to mind, and she bit down hard on her lower lip, wanting to howl. There was no going back—lives were at stake.

She lifted a hand to her face, hoping for the scent of Mooi Mooi's skin; but could only smell her own.

Then Gwai Ha was running toward her and falling into the alley just as the orphanage door swung open. Out of breath, he sprawled beside her, his eyes closed, tears pouring down his cheeks. She watched in horror as a middle-aged woman, probably the kind director of which Hsiao had spoken, reached for the basket. The door opened further and another woman emerged, this one younger, probably a nurse or a nanny, like Hsiao. The women talked for a few moments and then took the basket inside.

Her sobs were silent as she collapsed, heartsick, against Gwai Ha. No one must see them. Her stomach heaved and she leaned over and vomited the entire contents of her stomach against the building's foundation. Gwai Ha rubbed her shoulders as dry heaves held her in their grip. As loose-jointed as a rag doll, she choked and sputtered, unable to catch her breath.

"We have to run," he whispered as he wiped her mouth with the tail of his shirt. Then he took her by the hand and pulled her behind him through the alley. Their footsteps pounded against the pavement as they navigated the tight maze of warehouses, apartment buildings, teashops and bicycle racks. They ran in front of the few buildings adorned with security lights; then slowed in front of the others. Most were pitch-black, inside and out, much like the moonless night.

"She's gone forever," she whispered, looking into his eyes as they came to a heaving stop at the entrance to a fruit-bottling factory.

"Yes, gone," he said, tilting his head sadly. His eyes were red-rimmed, his face wet. He was shaking from his own silent sobs. She clutched his forearm as they leaned against the factory's door, deep in the shadow cast by its iron gate. Her stomach was sore and hollow, her mouth sour. She began to rock, keening softly, her fist pressed to her mouth. This time the pain was as deep as a pit, more tortuous than she would felt after childbirth when his mother had walked out the door.

She had held her child, glimpsed her potential and savored her tightly bundled weight. The pull of rosebud lips upon her breasts would haunt her always. Poh Poh had been right. Losing her the first time would have been merciful.

She opened her eyes to find Gwai Ha crying silently, bowled over, his face almost to his knee, oblivious to her hand on his arm. With all of her strength, she pulled him into her arms; needing the muscular warmth of him, needing to give comfort. His arms came around her.

"He won't win," he said into her hair. "He's stolen my child, threatened to steal my wife, my livelihood, my future. He cannot win."

Tenderly, she brushed aside a strand of hair that had fallen over his eyes. "Come on," she whispered, taking his hand. "We need to get home. Your mother will be worried." He was all she had now—him and Yanru.

His expression hardened.

"What is it?" she asked, pulling away slightly.

"He'll pay," he said, throwing his shoulders back. A crafty light gleamed in his eyes.

She edged away, but he caught her hands, and then sat and pulled her onto his lap.

"Don't ever fear me," he whispered, and lifted her chin with gentle hands, forcing her to look at him.

She sighed, calmed by his familiar scent. He planted a brotherly kiss on her forehead, bringing a slight smile to her lips.

Then his eyes glazed over, his thoughts traveling to a fearsome place as reflected by the narrowing of his lids and the tightening of his jaw.

"We'll get that bastard."

"What can we do?" she asked. An ember of hate had caught wind: its slow fire burned in her heart.

"We'll wait," he said, focusing his gaze upon her again. "Uncle is sick and old, though he thinks no one notices. I'm supposed to be computerizing his factories. That's why I was assigned to him. Beijing has taken a strong interest in his operations. More is going on here than just a nephew assigned to his uncle. That's all I can say."

"Has he done something wrong?"

"Don't you worry about that, my little flower," he said with a tight smile, shutting out further discussion. "The best way you can help is by getting our home life back in order. My mother needs you; and so do I."

She looked at his chin, considering. "I have to return to work in a few weeks. I have to face him, see him each day. How should I deal with it?"

"I'm seeing him tomorrow," he said, his expression grave. "I'll tell him what happened."

She sucked in her breath.

"I need you for data entry, right away," he said, brushing a finger across her cheek. "I'll insist upon it." She nodded slightly. "That means no more embroidery, though I know how much you love it. I hope you don't mind."

"At least we have each other." It was a banal phrase, naïve in every sense of the word. She held her breath, awaiting his censure.

"We'll find a way to nab him," he said, as if he hadn't heard her. His nostrils flared, the artery on his neck pulsed visibly. "We'll watch for the right moment, for that singular opportunity that will certainly come. He's sure to make a mistake, and then we'll nail him."

He kissed her again, this time hard on the lips; softening a familiar place deep inside her.

Even now, with her bottom like an overripe tomato and the loss of their daughter a gaping wound upon her soul, he had the ability to reach her.

"Let's go home," she said a little too brusquely as she took his hand. Softening her words with a shy smile, she turned with him down the street.

Chapter 12 – September

A high iron fence surrounded the old park, the highlight of which was a large, algae-encrusted pond. Two iron gates stood open at either end, welcoming day strollers. Massive old trees provided a broad canopy. A worn dirt path encircled the pond. It was a place of quiet contemplation, once enjoyed by children and now favored by couples seeking a few minutes of privacy away from their cramped family apartments.

Ying Fa cast a glance over her shoulder as she hurried through the entrance. An early morning mist hovered over the path and spilled across the pond.

She stretched her legs as she walked, enjoying the pull of muscle, pleased with her vigor. Even a few weeks ago, she had felt dragged down, out of sorts. In the past five months, plentiful good food and a rigorous exercise schedule had restored her body, if not her mind.

Fear was never far away.

She shivered, seeing Uncle Li's beady eyes focused upon her last night at his wife's mahjong party. After hearing of Yanru's various successes, Auntie Li had borrowed her, insisting that she prepare the food for her party.

Their apartment was enormous, consisting of four massive bedroom, two bathrooms, an industrial-size kitchen and a massive great room. She had never seen such luxury, and had been desperately glad to leave. The party had been a great success; the apartment packed with guests, several of Maoming's most powerful officials counting among them. Such jostling for food and drinks, the stereo blaring, the reek of cigarette smoke filling each corner, reminding her of the Maoming Building's noisome disco.

Keeping her head down, she had prepared her juciest dumplings, most succulent noodles, most flavorful seafood with vegetables, and other expensive treats upon which Auntie Li had insisted. Even the rice had been steamed to perfection. She flushed, recalling Auntie Li's fleshy arm draped around her waist, as she had praised her in front of everyone.

Uncle Li had insisted she spend two days at the apartment, shopping for and then preparing the food under his wife's close supervision. As if Auntie Li even knew how to boil water.

She had kept her mouth shut and her eyes carefully lowered—sick to her stomach the entire time, unable to eat a bite—while the elder couple had watched and gloated. They had focused on Gwai Ha, too, lavishing him with food and affection, parading him as the adored nephew.

His smile had been tight, his gaze wooden. He had slipped into bed with her each night, turning his back on her, barely able to speak.

She hadn't minded using Auntie Li's kitchen or following her cryptic incomprehensible orders. Nor had she minded seeing Uncle Li for such long stretches of time. He never spoke directly to her; and rarely showed his face at the Silk Factory by day; even in the upper room where she and Gwai Ha worked.

It was the sly remark he had made to his wife, out of Gwai Ha's earshot at the end of the party that made her stomach roil. She had yet to tell Gwai Ha, fearing his reaction.

"Have them all the time?" Uncle Li had asked from one of the two massive leather sofas in the center of the great room. "Just imagine the life, what with her cooking and housekeeping skills and a small one running around."

About to enter the room to collect dirty dishes, Ying Fa had backed up, holding her breath, Auntie Li's profile within her view. "That's what I've been saying all along, husband," Auntie Li said with a braying laugh. "Now, finally, you see?"

Ying Fa had remained quiet, though she had wanted to scream in protest. How could they possibly move in with them? And what about Yanru? Where was she supposed to live? Surely, they didn't expect her to move in with them, too.

She flung her hair and stomped as she moved along the path, picturing her life as Auntie Li's servant, her child under her control.

Even worse was Yanru's continued obsession. Despite all that had happened, she still perked up at each mention of Uncle Li, her eyes begging for every detail. How could she still love him? He was supposedly intimate with his wife again, considering the kissing and fondling she had seen at the party—or had it been just for show?

No way could they live with those people. She walked faster, trying to vent her fury, unable to imagine being at Auntie Li's beck and call day and night, like a dutiful daughter-in-law. That was Yanru's right.

She searched through the mist, looking for someone, anyone. She had never felt so alone. Five months had passed since she'd last touched Mooi Mooi; and she'd finally convinced Hsiao to arrange a meeting. She had told no one. They would think her crazy, foolish, even stupid; but she had to see her daughter. She had to. Beijing had just notified the orphanage Director of her impending adoption. In a few months, she would be gone forever, on the other side of the world.

She hugged herself, wondering how she had made it through the past five months, painfully aware of her daughter growing up without her, just a few kilometers away; with her own sister-in-law holding her, bathing her, feeding her. Perhaps she would have healed sooner without Hsiao's weekly reports. Those reports had given her some semblance of peace. Short of visiting the orphanage herself, she had been able to visualize her daughter's little face, and imagine her in her arms.

She had become the model daughter-in-law, worker and wife. The mask of serenity upon her face had fooled them all. All except Gwai Ha, that is, who had suffered in silence beside her.

Her eyes watered. What a mess they had made of their marriage—the persistent awkward misunderstandings, the silent accusations that they just couldn't seem to transcend. Sex had become a furtive thing that she avoided—a painful joining that left her in tears and Gwai Ha stewing with rage. She had to hope that their impending trip to Guangzhou would help in some small way. It was a dream trip, visiting Poh Poh and Yanru's hometown, getting away from Uncle Li and the factory and their memories.

If only Hsiao would appear.

Hopefully, she had convinced the Director of the many benefits of taking the soon-to-be-adopted children for a brisk walk in the park. Didn't Beijing want their orphans to be seen as healthy, thriving little ambassadors—perfect representatives of their country? Four little girls would be traveling to America soon: a five-year-old, a toddler and two infants, Mooi Mooi being one of them.

She was supposed to bump into Hsiao, introduce herself to the Director, chat for a few minutes, and then ask to hold the babies. With the scarcity of children, everyone wanted to hold babies these days, didn't they? It would hardly seem out of order, even to the strictest of Directors.

A bird perched on a nearby branch, sang a few warbling notes and then flew away. Through the clearing mist, she watched it swoop and soar as it spanned the sky. It lit on another tree at the far side of the pond. She took a deep, shuddering breath, glad for the distraction. The tiny bird's family was probably grown and gone, ahead of the impending rain.

Gone, like her family.

In the months following Mooi Mooi's abandonment, Hsiao had become her only link to her own family. Though Zhaodi's job had been restored, she had suffered a heart attack and was recovering at home. Thus Poh Poh had banned her from visiting, said it upset her.

"Too much stress," Poh Poh had said at the doorway, hiding the apartment's interior from her view. Managing not to cry, Ying Fa had nodded sadly and walked away.

Apparently, they blamed her for marrying into the Li family, for birthing a girl and for inciting Yanru's desperate act. Her only connection to them now was Hsiao's weekly update and Yutang's charitable invitation to dim sum on a rare mutual day off.

She had never imagined becoming close to her brother or depending on Hsiao for family news. Now her patience would finally pay off. Clever Hsiao had charmed her way into the Director's good graces. She had even scanned Mooi Mooi's files.

Was that Hsiao up ahead? She peered into the mist.

That Hsiao could hold her precious son each night had been the perfect wedge to use; especially after seeing her little niece day after day, yet having to remain outwardly impartial, when she'd so easily fallen in love with her. Of course, she had fallen in love with her—Mooi Mooi was precious, lovely and sweet. At five months old, she would be plump and smiling, a mother's joy. Lucky Hsiao—at least she had gotten to hold her all these long, painful months.

Ying Fa grimaced. How like a Li she had become, using Hsiao as a tool to gain her heart's desire. No matter the risk, no matter the pain, she had to hold Mooi Mooi one last time, to inhale her baby scent and memorize each perfect line of her lovely little face.

She tripped over a downed branch and went sprawling. Not skipping a beat, she picked herself up, brushed off her pants, now with a hole in one leg, and moved on, ignoring the burn of her knee, the slight trickle of blood. Nothing would prevent this meeting.

Yesterday at lunch Hsiao had described Mooi Mooi's new mother—an accountant named Rena, married to a farmer named Mark. They owned a huge house in the country and couldn't have a child of their own. They were brown-haired, blue-eyed Caucasians with big noses—the man burly and the woman, tall and slender—both in their early forties.

"Hsiao!" she called out, seeing the women and children ahead.

Her sister-in-law turned; her back was rigid. Something was wrong. There was a closed expression on her face—a warning. Clinging to her skirt was the five-year-old girl, peeking up through long lovely lashes. She turned her attention to the baby in Hsiao's arms. She was bundled up, her face hidden.

A second woman turned with a sort of half smile. Her thick hair was pulled away from her face with barrettes, making her look much younger than she had the night of Mooi Mooi's abandonment. Up close, however, she appeared to be Zhaodi's age, her large-pored face evidence of a hard life. She held a fat, sweating baby who cried in a high-pitched tone. A blank-faced toddler clung to her skirt.

The woman's smile went only halfway up her face. Her gaze dropped away.

"Hsiao," Ying Fa said brightly as she moved closer, "so happy to see you."

"Hello, Ying Fa," Hsiao said, her gaze darting about her face, not quite landing. "Director Kuo," she said, inclining her head toward her superior, "this is my sister-in-law, Wong Ying Fa."

Though Hsiao was from a powerful family, she'd had to prove herself, like everyone else. It had taken her many months to earn the Director's trust.

"Nice to meet you," Director Kuo said, nodding at Ying Fa's outstretched hand indicating that her hands were full.

Ying Fa scanned the babies. Which one? She looked questioningly at Hsiao, unable to see the tiny faces angled toward the women who held them.

"I was on my way to our parents' apartment," she said, hoping to sound natural, hoping the Director didn't know of her family's estrangement. "How fortunate to meet you by accident." She scanned the group.

"Yes, how fortunate," Director Kuo murmured. She seemed distracted, nothing like the take-charge woman of that horrible night.

Ying Fa focused on the baby in Hsiao's arms "Can I hold her?" she asked, already inching toward Hsiao and pulling back the baby's blanket. Hsiao held out the bundle and she took it.

In an instant, she knew she had chosen wrong. The child in her arms was someone else's sorrow. Her eyes were narrower than Mooi Mooi's; her cheeks more pronounced. She was a beauty for sure, but not hers.

She looked up to find the Director watching her closely. There was a pained wrinkle over Hsiao's averted eyes.

They spoke of the weather while Ying Fa held the child for what seemed like the requisite time. Then she handed her back.

"I can't seem to get enough of babies," she said, and giggled behind her hand. "My husband and I you see . . .."

Director Kuo murmured something innocuous, her blush betraying her knowledge of Ying Fa's miscarriage.

"Can I hold this one, too?" she asked brightly, her hands out. "I've heard that holding a baby brings luck with conception. Maybe it's true."

Director Kuo handed the child over like a bag of potatoes.

Ying Fa held her breath as looked down at her child, drinking in the sight of her. Mooi Mooi had filled out in the past several months. Her cheeks were plumper, her head larger, her eyes huge and black. With gentle hands, she felt the crib sores at the back of her sweat-drenched head and saw that her beautiful eyes, her father's eyes, were dull and lifeless. What had they done to her?

She bit down hard on her lip, fighting the urge cry, fighting the urge to run as fast and as far as her legs would carry her to rescue her child.

It would be an act of gross stupidity.

She closed her eyes briefly, smelling the urine and something like greasy chicken soup. This was her child. So neglected? So dirty? All she could do was look at her and mourn.

It was painfully obvious that the child felt no connection to her, would never feel a connection. She would grow up knowing nothing about her.

Hsiao said the orphanage did their best to provide plentiful food, albeit not of the highest grade. She said the children were held, cared for and provided for as generously as the Director could manage. But obviously not her child.

Director Kuo cleared her throat and put out her hands. "Time to move on," she said.

Fighting back tears, Ying Fa quickly complied. Then, with all of the strength she could muster, she murmured a few complimentary words to the Director, nodded to Hsiao and continued on her way.

She was stumbling, blinded by tears, through the entrance at the far end when she heard someone call out her name.

"Wong Ying Fa!"

They said it again, this time shouting.

Her skin prickled at the too-familiar voice. Hastily wiping her tears, she turned to face Auntie Li, who stood beside the gate, as broad as an old tree in army-issue green slacks, a plain white blouse and sensible brown walking shoes.

"Come here," she commanded.

Ying Fa dropped her hands to her sides, her shoulders sagging. One step forward and then another took her closer. Time slowed as she wracked her brain for a likely explanation. With a sinking heart, she realized that Auntie Li, not Hsiao, had arranged the meeting with Director Kuo. Though Hsiao's mother was part of Auntie Li's circle, Hsiao would never have betrayed her. Or would she?

"Come with me," Auntie Li hissed. She grabbed Ying Fa's wrist, digging her nails in.

Ying Fa expelled air slowly as she allowed herself to be yanked back into the park and over to a stone bench. She sat beside Auntie Li, facing the pond.

"I don't have to tell you what I saw," Auntie Li said, her high-pitched whine piercing the quiet of the day. "Director Kuo loves the donations I give from time to time, and sweet little Hsiao will do anything to protect your thieving brother. Too bad he got caught last week with some black market scotch." She cackled like a crow.

Ying Fa's throat tightened. She gazed across the pond at the trees on the other side. She would admit nothing. How would she explain this to Gwai Ha?

"It's a disgrace that that dreadful woman has no control over you," Auntie Li continued, her high-pitched harangue like a mosquito's buzz. "She's always been trouble, never appreciating what she has, always wanting more, always wanting what is rightfully mine."

"What woman?" Ying Fa asked, ripping her gaze from a young couple that strolled along the path, hand in hand, their gazes ardent. If they only knew what heartache would find them.

"What woman?" she asked again, looking at Auntie Li fully.

"Don't play the idiot with me," Auntie shrilled, her black eyes rife with fury. Spittle flew from her thin, pale lips, spraying her face. Then her hand came out of nowhere, and before Ying Fa could move, she had slapped her aside the head, sending her to a dark place of startling pain, sending her to the dirt.

Ying Fa moaned, clutching her head; and watched as the startled couple quickened their pace. The man looked back once over his shoulder; and then they were gone.

"How dare you!" she cried, brushing the dust off as she stood. "What do you people want from me?" She held out a hand imploringly. "Isn't it enough that your husband forced me to give up my child? Isn't it enough that he has threatened my family? My mother's had a heart attack; and I'm not even allowed to see her."

The stout old woman moved surprisingly fast, grabbing her hand, twisting it behind her back with all of her strength, bringing her to her knees.

"Stop it!" Ying Fa shrieked, about to topple over.

"Now you listen to me," Auntie Li hissed. "My husband's well aware of your stupid little games. That baby is out of your life. I suggest you get busy making another. You will try and try again until you produce a son. Do you hear me? A male! And when you and Gwai Ha return from Guangzhou, you will move your things into our apartment. You will become my obedient niece-in-law and your son will be mine to raise."

Auntie Li lost her grip, and Ying Fa slipped away. Quickly, she crawled several feet and managed to stand, each muscle tensed and ready to flee. The thought of those puffy hands upon her again made her want to vomit.

Live with her, give up her lovely apartment, be relegated to a servant's role? How could she live without her wardrobes, her sense of serenity, her orderly cleanliness? How could she beg this woman for what she had already won from Yanru?

"But what of Chan Yanru," she asked, sickened by the subservience in her voice? She rubbed her wrist, resisting the urge to clutch her throbbing head, where a bruise was already pooling beneath her skin. Curses formed at her lips, but it would only make matters worse. Auntie Li was from a peasant family, low-class poor who scratched and scrabbled for their place in the world. She would be immune to crude language.

"What about her?" Auntie Li asked coldly.

"She . . . she'll be alone," Ying Fa stammered, already knowing that her words were futile. In the gamble of life, Yanru had lost, with her and Gwai Ha the unfortunate prizes. In fact, Yanru had never stood a chance against this scheming harridan; and Gwai Ha would be furious.

244

"Please," she whispered, tears springing to her eyes, unable to look above the woman's stumpy shoes. "Chan Yanru hasn't been well. She needs me."

"Good," Auntie Li said lightly. Ying Fa looked up, her breath caught by the ugly satisfaction on her wrinkled, rotted-squash face.

"She can't live alone," she pleaded.

"Then she'll go to a home for aged. I can't think of a better place for my husband's pretty whore." She dusted off her hands as if she had done a hard day's work, and then rose.

Ying Fa sucked in air, too shocked to speak. Chan Yanru was worth a hundred Auntie Lis.

"No one takes what's mine," Auntie Li said, then lunged for her.

Ying Fa moved fast, but was snagged by a hank of hair. She screamed, her hair tearing by the roots. Using all of her strength, she jerked away, leaving the hair.

Then she ran, feet and arms flying, startling a flock of doves, tearing out of the park, not stopping until she was almost home.

"Oh, dear god of my grandmother," she gasped, leaning over to catch her breath in a side alley off the main street. Car horns honked and bicycle bells jangled in the morning's warmth, creating mere background noise to her churning thoughts as she leaned against the crumbling building. An ageless woman dressed in rags swept dirt from a sidewalk in steady strokes at the far end of the alley. She glanced at Ying Fa, then lowered her eyes and continued sweeping.

Gwai Ha would never forgive her. She hugged herself, wondering if it wouldn't be better for all of them if she stowed herself away on a train bound for Guangzhou. By disappearing, she would become one less worry for both of their families. It was a silly fantasy, solving nothing. It would be better to confess her transgressions to Gwai Ha immediately and accept his wrath. He might even come up with a solution. Surely, he'd look beyond her singular mistake, and see how desperate she'd been to see their child.

She bowed her head, pressing her face to her palms, and prayed to her grandmother's god and then to her ancestors and any god who would listen, to make it right between her and Gwai Ha. She bit her fingers until she had drawn blood. Auntie Li would simply bide her time, just as she had said, waiting for their return from Guangzhou. Maybe by then, Gwai Ha would have forgiven her.

Chapter 13

They sat on either side of her at the table that night, enjoying the most succulent meal she had ever prepared. Unable to eat even a single bite of Gwai Ha's favorite—sea worms and spicy vegetables—she waited until she could stand it no longer, then told them all that had transpired, from her manipulation of Hsiao to her confrontation with Auntie Li.

Afterward, there was an ugly pause, a pool of silence big enough to drown in. She tried to read the looks on their faces, but could not.

If only they would say something. She clasped her hands on her lap, striving for patience.

"So Hsiao's been updating you on the baby's progress?" Gwai Ha asked tersely. He dropped his chopsticks with a clatter, soiling the fine, white tablecloth with a smudge of brown sauce. His look was frigid. The malice in Yanru's gaze was undisguised.

"Yes," Ying Fa whispered, feeling like a trapped insect beneath their scrutiny.

"You had the nerve to do this without telling me? Behind my back?" Gwai Ha shouted. He pounded on the table, toppling a serving lid onto the floor.

She nodded slightly, bowing her head, not daring to look at him.

"You idiot!" he shrieked, banging the table again, causing her to whimper. "She caught you holding the child; and now we're supposed to move in with them after the Guangzhou trip?"

She held her arms in front of her, locking her wrists between her knees, hunched over, wanting to die.

"Did you think at all about the consequences of your actions?" He lowered his voice. "Do you even care what happens to us? To you? You've been like a plastic doll for months, and in all that time you've been scheming?"

She kept telling herself that he would never hit, unlike some of the other men in their building, whose wives sported an occasional bruise or a split lip. Hadn't he told her never to fear him?

She looked at the platter of seaworms congealing in its sauce. The vegetables had melted into mush. Steam no longer rose from the fried rice. At least they had started to eat.

"I don't understand," Yanru said, looking up. She had barely spoken since Mooi Mooi's abandonment. Becoming childlike, she had made a habit of turning to Ying Fa for even the most trivial domestic decision. "You let that woman win?" she choked out; then began to clear her throat loudly.

"I suppose I did," Ying Fa said. "I suppose I just set myself up for it."

"You handed her an edge!" Yanru shouted. "What were you thinking?"

Tears burned Ying Fa's eyes. She shook her head sadly. Would they listen? Would they even try to understand?

"What was I thinking?" she began, her fury starting to build. "As if losing my daughter was my entire fault. Maybe I should just leave on the night train and never come back. Then you Lis can plan someone else's sorry life. Since when did I ever have a say in anything that matters? Since when did I even have a choice of a husband?" She looked pointedly at Gwai Ha as she rose. It was all too much. Her shoulders sagged and she dropped back into her seat. "Why should I bother to think at all?"

"Now wait a minute," Gwai Ha said, in a haughty tone she had grown to detest. "You're blaming us?"

"No, I'm not. But you're both in this with me, whether you admit it or not." She focused on Yanru. "You said we should keep the baby."

Yanru's upper lip trembled.

"And you." Tears welled as she looked at Gwai Ha. "Don't tell me you never wanted to see her again. Don't tell me you didn't cry when we left her."

"What's your point?" he asked through narrowed lids. Then he pushed away from the table, his fists like rocks against his thighs. "First my mother and now you. Must I forever be at the mercy of hysterical females?"

Ignoring his jibe, she leaned forward, elbows on the table, her fingers interlocked. "Mooi Mooi will soon be adopted," she said softly.

Gwai Ha sucked in his breath.

"Her parents have been selected and she's going to America—away from China, out of our reach." She watched Gwai Ha out of the corner of her eye.

"You sure?" he asked.

She nodded slightly.

"Adopted?" Yanru asked, tipping her head to the side. "To America?"

Gwai Ha took a deep breath, his expression resigned. "So you had to see her."

She nodded. "It was a set-up. They were just waiting for an excuse to have us move in with them." She told them what she had overheard at Auntie Li's party.

Gwai Ha leaned forward, his elbows on his knees, his face in his hands. "I should have seen this coming."

"So now you'll listen?" she asked, rolling her eyes.

"Now more than ever, we've got to nail him," Gwai Ha said through clenched teeth. "Don't you dare excuse him," he shot at his mother. Yanru looked away, her arms crossed beneath her breasts.

"What else?" Gwai Ha asked as he sat up, his gaze intent.

"The Director has already replied to Beijing's query," she replied, swiping at tears that she could no longer restrain. "I had to hold her one last time, Gwai Ha. I had to. Don't you see?" Hanging her head, cupping her empty teacup, she began to weep. "Imagine Mooi Mooi in the hands of strangers, speaking English, growing up in America, not knowing who she came from." She closed her eyes, despair wreathing her like choking black cloud.

Then a large hand was stroking her hair, and another, a smaller one, caressing her shoulder. She sighed, catching her breath, touched by their love.

"When?" Gwai Ha asked softly. She looked up, seeing the forgiveness in his eyes. She reached up and touched his face, and clasped Yanru's arm. They were her family, her life. Without them, she would have nothing.

"In about three weeks," she managed to reply.

"After you return from Guangzhou," Yanru murmured.

"Yes," Ying Fa looked at her sharply. She had been listening all along, hidden beneath her grief.

Gwai Ha stood and stretched, pulling his shoulders back. His gaze turned thoughtful. "If I didn't know better, I'd swear there's something odd with Uncle's books that deserve a second look."

"What do you mean?" Ying Fa asked. She took an embroidered handkerchief from Yanru's hand and dabbed at her face.

"The numbers just don't add up," he said, shaking his head. "I've been at it for months, checking this and that. But the more I look, the worse they look." He put his hands on his hips and looked at her, not really seeing. "I wonder . . ."

They both looked at Yanru, who was humming as she picked at the remains of the food, her expression sour. When she saw them looking, she smiled.

"Enough of that," she said, then delicately lifted a peapod halfway to her face between her chopsticks as if inspecting it. "The food's grown cold, children. You two can use that computer of yours tomorrow to solve this puzzle. The man is a crafty old beast, too stuck in the old ways to realize that he can't get away with certain things anymore. Times have changed; new skills are required. Old practices can get a person into a lot of trouble with a hungry central government. Seems there are few places to hide, with those computers tracking everything." She laughed, a pleasant easy sound, like a songbird in a tree.

Ying Fa couldn't help but smile. "You know something about him?" she asked.

251

Yanru waved a hand as if to brush aside a cobweb. "I know lots of things about that man. Too many, in fact." She smiled brightly, her face suddenly beautiful, youthful. "Let's finish this feast that Ying Fa has so skillfully prepared." She smiled brightly, her face suffused with joy.

Ying Fa nodded, her fears beginning to melt. Maybe Gwai Ha would find something in time, or Yanru would reveal a dangerous secret. At least they would have Guangzhou. That was a hope worth clinging to.

"I have a big surprise for you," Yanru said, her loving smile directed at Ying Fa.

"What is is?" Ying Fa laughed, and took in Gwai Ha with her glance.

He sat back, looking amused.

"I've made you some clothes with my sewing machine." Yanru said softly. "You will be the loveliest woman in all of Guangzhou."

"Sewing machine?" Ying Fa asked, unable to imagine Yanru even knowing how to plug one in.

"Beautiful things that will rival the clothes our Guangzhou relatives wear," Yanru said, nodding. "And believe me, they dress sharp."

Ying Fa looked from Gwai Ha to Yanru. "You know how to sew?"

Yanru smiled, once again the mischievous fairy.

"Of course," Gwai Ha said with a nod. He was also smiling. "It's her best kept secret. How do you think she affords all those expensive looking dresses?"

"But I thought . . .." Ying Fa blushed. "So Uncle Li didn't . . .." She giggled nervously.

Yanru laughed. "You just believed what I wanted you to, what I wanted everyone to believe." She made a dainty gesture with her hands." You aren't the only one who can run a machine. You've just seen no evidence."

"I'm so sorry," Ying Fa said. "And . . . and I thank you."

Yanru made no reply. She merely grinned and served them the remains of the meal.

Chapter 14

They took the day train to Guangzhou, first class—a tight, comfortable compartment with two facing sets of bunks and a table between. Forward was the lunch car, containing several rows of tables and chairs, the kitchen at its head.

They settled in immediately, with their luggage on the top left bunk, out of the way. Gwai Ha sat below it, losing no time getting to work, while Ying Fa claimed the upper right bunk, diving into some computer manuals.

At noon, they broke for lunch—steaming rice plates loaded with tender chicken and crisp vegetables—sharing their repast with a carfull of talkative businessmen. Gwai Ha joked and laughed with a few, while Ying Fa remained silent, sensing all eyes upon her. They were the first to arrive and the first to leave.

Halfway to Guangzhou, three-and a half-hours into their trip, Gwai Ha was still tapping away on his laptop, racing its draining battery, desperate for an answer. They had planned to bring two extra battery packs, but in the haste and flurry of packing, had forgotten both.

At first, she appreciated his diligence, afraid he would be all over her the first chance he got. On the eve of their departure, he had been insistent in bed, trying to elicit more from her than her usual lukewarm response. His indifference today was ridiculous.

She looked down at him from her bunk, more than a little annoyed. He had promised to answer her questions, but for the past two hours, she had had to entertain herself with a thick book on the Internet. It was beyond unbearable.

She pressed her face to her hands, and sighed. He had refused to answer even one of her questions until he had found the perfect solution. When would that be? Their agenda was packed. When they arrived in Guangzhou, there would be little time for simple husband and wife dialogue. He had probably forgotten all about her. Would this be the pattern of their supposed marriage-rescuing trip?

She watched the countryside roll past the window; lulled by bucolic scenes of rice paddies, litchi groves and an occasional water buffalo. She'd had little time for nature since she'd thrown all of her energy into Gwai Ha's world; with computers, fax machines, email, and conference calls each becoming an integral part of her life.

Gwai Ha wasn't the only one with a head for learning, she'd discovered. Despite her lack of a university degree, she was adept at learning anything from computer internals to word processing software. The concept of debits and credits was still somewhat of a mystery, but she would eventually catch on. Though she performed all the tedious data entry tasks, little by little, things were becoming clear. It was almost as if she had known all along how computers and electronics worked; and was just now remembering.

Her new life was wonderfully fast-paced, but often unsettling. There was so much to learn; and not just about computers. She was meeting smart people, educated and well informed; who were bringing about a quiet revolution of international commerce within the constraints of Communist China.

Every day was different: working the books with Gwai Ha, typing correspondence, filling out the hundreds of forms for Beijing. She loved racing to Zhanjiang and Huazhou in fast limos; and taking notes while Gwai Ha met buyers, sellers and officials, many becoming strong allies. She had dined on the best cuisine offered in all the places she had visited; and arranged impromptu feasts in return—such as she planned to do in Guangzhou.

It was Gwai Ha's golden dream; and she'd been caught up in it, captured in ways she could never have imagined. She'd come a long way from the naïve silk embroiderer whose simple goals had been to master difficult clothing, win the forewoman's respect and please her doting family. At one time, she had counted many of the women in the factory her friends.

Not anymore. Her circle had shrunk to that of her husband and his mother.

She toyed with the collar of her blouse, her worries mounting. Hsiao had betrayed her; and Yutang, the thief, was consigned to leaving messages on her answering machine. Hsiao was sorry? She hadn't known? It made no difference now. Poh Poh still refused her entry, and she couldn't see Zhaodi. After the trip, she would lose Yanru, too.

The idea of Yanru being locked away in a home for the aged was preposterous. She had read that such nightmarish places were common in America. How savage to abandon one's elderly, how shameful. With Yanru in such a place, she and Gwai Ha wouldn't be able to live with themselves. It would be like abandoning Mooi Mooi all over again.

She sighed deeply and crossed her ankles, pulling her shoulders back at the sudden pain that rose between them. She set her book down and rubbed her bleary eyes, then flexed her aching wrists. The book was heavy, but she only had a few pages to go.

In some ways, her world had grown smaller and meaner. Sometimes she would see Forewoman Chen in the Silk Factory compound, hurrying to her post. She was always bowing now, her eyes carefully lowered, as if she were some great lady or a visitor from afar.

Baak-Hap and Chung were long gone: one married to Tien and living in Changsha and the other the wife of some Guangzhou official.

She closed her book with a loud thwack, not bothering to mark the page. She would probably have to read it again, anyway. Her mind wandered to the day she had returned to work.

Not quite believing she would be assigned to Gwai Ha, she had expected to be thrown back into her old job, ridiculed and pitied as a woman who couldn't bear a son. Yet on that terrifying day, it had been as Gwai Ha had promised.

Standing before Uncle Li in his office, with hands trembling and knees threatening to cave in, she'd heard his standard lecture about industry, prosperity and China's rightful place, almost mouthing the words. She had known the length and timing of his pauses, at what point he would comb his thick fingers through his sparse hair, and when he would touch the tips of his fingers together in front of his stomach.

His gaze had never met hers; his face had been expressionless. After clearing his throat loudly, he had said that her salary would double now that she was Gwai Ha's assistant. Then he had told Gwai Ha, not looking at him either, that he was to continue buying raw silk and selling finished goods, but that his priority was to computerize the factories in accordance with Beijing's requirements and recommendations.

They exchanged polite nods and then he had left. They stood gaping at each other for a long time, not knowing what to think. Henceforth, he had made himself scarce; using his office only in the evenings or early mornings, or when she and Gwai Ha were out of town.

Gwai Ha met with him weekly to present progress reports, but they were terse dialogs, his uncle refusing to look him in the eye.

"I've found it," Gwai Ha said softly, followed by a long drawn out hiss.

"What?" She sat quickly, and then swung her legs over the side of the bed.

"Take a look," he said, his gaze locked on the monitor. "I can't believe I found this." He looked up at her with a dazzling smile, making her heart beat a little faster. "You've got to see this."

She set aside the book, jumped down and knelt beside him.

"What is it?" she asked, trying to read where he pointed. It was a huge number—more than her family would earn in a lifetime.

"That's an estimate of what he's pilfered, embezzled and stolen."

"Wow!" She shook her head. "You sure?" She was suddenly afraid for him, for them. What if it wasn't true?

He nodded slightly, his lids going to jet-black lines of concentration.

"But what if you're wrong?" she asked.

"That's the accumulated total." His face was like stone. "For the past five years, he's been leaking money from various accounts. It's money owed to the government, money he's neglected to forward. Beijing's cracking down heavy on this type of behavior. This will nail him."

The laptop's battery light glowed red. With quick fingers, he saved his work to disk and then turned the laptop off.

"How could it happen?" she asked, trying to get him to look at her again. Despite the chasm that had grown between them, she had missed him these past few days. After her encounter with Auntie Li, he had worked practically around the clock, searching for an answer, often joining her in bed just before dawn. He sat back, folded his arms behind his head, deep in thought.

She watched him, wondering what he would do next. Contact Beijing? Keep it a secret and merely threaten Uncle Li?

He leaned forward and touched her thigh, sending a shiver across the small of her back. Exactly two months after giving birth, she had opened her body to him, feeling nothing beyond the scrape of skin against skin. He had become a stranger, his passion fraught with peril. She understood the needs of a healthy young man, but each time he finished with her she would turned away, untouched by his frustration, unable to help him, unable to feel anything.

Was he changing his tactic? Perhaps he had solicited someone's advice. She shuddered, not wanting to consider who that might be.

"It has to be his gambling," he said, and pounded fist to palm, his gaze locked with hers. "That's why he wanted me to computerize. That's why he pulled me from Beijing though he was offered more able technicians. It wasn't my class ranking or the lack of an heir—though that was pure fabrication. As if he could be my father. 'Keep it in the family,' he'd said. Ha! I'll keep it in the family alright. I'll send this to my friends in Beijing, and then he'll dance." His gaze was hot, intense.

She could only nod like an idiot, her throat close to choking. Suddenly she was hungry for him, unable to avert her eyes from the long, lean lines of his thigh so close to hers. His slender fingers flew before her face as he wrapped his cables and tied them, tempting her somehow. She wanted to catch them and hold them to her breasts. He slipped the laptop and cable into a specially made case, then set it on the floor.

"So, we've got him?" she asked.

There was longing in his eyes, and worship. "I think this discussion can wait," he said softly, moving to her, smoothing a hand up her thigh, over her hose, under her sensible black skirt. His other hand reached for the buttons on her blouse. "First things first."

She leaned forward, sick with need, and shook her head. "No, we can't," she said. "Not in this place. I don't want . . .."

"Liar," he whispered. She turned away. In the confines of their compartment, there was no place to hide.

"I'll be gentle," he said; then took her hand and pulled her beside him onto a lower bunk, his breath coming fast.

She closed her eyes, relishing the touch of his hands as he unbuttoned her blouse. It slid off her shoulders leaving her exposed skin tingling in the cool, airconditioned compartment. A warm, liquid sensation filled her loins as he unbuttoned her skirt, his hands sliding over her buttocks.

"The next child will stay," he said, lifting her chin with one finger, forcing her to look into his eyes.

"But what if . . ."

"Girl or boy, they will stay." His eyes glimmered in the shadow of the passing scenery. He reached to pull the shade.

"Please stop, Gwai Ha. I won't walk away from another baby. I can't." She squirmed beneath his roving hands. Her breath came hard and fast as he reached behind and unhooked her bra. Heat and fire, how she ached for him.

"We won't," he said, his smoky eyes frightening her a little. "I'll make Uncle promise. He'll never harm us again. And my mother will not live her remaining days alone. She belongs to us."

"Promise?" she asked, moving closer, her hands reaching for his shirt buttons, for the front of his pants, desperate for his skin upon hers.

"I promise," he said. Then his lips met hers and she kissed him back with all the love she had missed.

Warm days and cool, rainy nights met them in Guangzhou. They couldn't have asked for more perfect conditions for the Guangzhou Trade Fair—the Guangdong Province's biggest commercial event of the year. It was to be an exciting two weeks of trade shows, auctions, training classes, lectures and behind the scenes negotiations that spelled prosperity for those who were shrewd and took quick advantage. The convention halls were packed to capacity with buyers looking for sellers, suppliers looking for markets and exporters looking for goods to ship overseas.

That first night, shivering with excitement, Ying Fa stumbled into their hotel's banquet hall dressed like a princess. Unaccustomed to high heels, she clung to Gwai Ha's arm, her breath catching at the sight of the room before her. Red and gold welcoming banners hung from the dark-paneled walls. Seated around twelve red-draped tables were Gwai Ha's relatives. His aunts and female cousins were dressed in every hue imaginable, each gown stunning in its own right, like gorgeous flowers against a backdrop of black-suited men. Children of all ages scampered about, dressed as elegantly as their parents were. The littlest one, a tiny girl in a violet confection of a dress, her black patent shoes shined to perfection—stole her breath away. There were boys in suits matching their dads', and old old ladies in muted silks. She watched in awe, seeing small hands clasped, round faces wiped and padded bodies hugged.

She sucked in her breath as Mooi Mooi came to mind, and fought the urge to flee.

She told herself to focus. She must not surrender to this sadness and fear. She breathed slowly in and out. She would bear another child. She had to.

262

An army of waiters placed steaming platters of appetizers on the tables, while others scurried about filling teacups from tall pitchers with long-reaching spouts. The older children helped themselves, while the adults claimed seats, forming tightknit groups.

Her mouth watered at the delicious aromas wafting through the hall.

Chan Lieu, Yanru's elder brother, had gone all out to welcome his beloved nephew.

She smiled up at Gwai Ha, and then blushed and looked away, recalling what he had done to her in their room just an hour ago. The sight of him made her breathless. In a black tuxedo, his natural beauty eclipsed every other person in the room.

A small orchestra tuned their instruments in the corner. Lively chatter erupted nearby and curious faces peered at them before looking away. She smiled, knowing that her aqua strapless gown, with its deep back slit, shimmered as she walked, showing her newly rounded curves to perfection.

She smiled, thinking back to that first night out with Gwai Ha and the green cocktail dress Hsiao had loaned her, the memory dissolving some small part of her ire. Hsiao certainly knew how to dress. She would give her that.

Yanru must have had learned how to sew to keep pace with her affluent relatives, though, according to Gwai Ha, such lavish banquets were given only once or twice a year.

It struck her that this was Yanru's family and not the Lis, the family both she and Yanru had married into. If only her own family would be as accepting.

A dull ache rose in her chest as she thought of Poh Poh. Yutang's last message was that Zhaodi had fully recovered; and that she was welcome again. It wasn't enough. She wanted a letter, an apology and an explanation. Yet Poh Poh remained silent.

Must Yutang forever act as interpreter? Was she a daughter only for the good times and at the family's convenience? Must she pay for Mooi Mooi repeatedly, each time things got rough?

Gwai Ha looked at her with concern, his arm going around her shoulders.

"Let it go," he mouthed, smiling at her warmly; the twinkle in his eye warning that he was itching to throw her onto the nearest table, if only he could.

She squeezed his arm, giving him her full attention, for this event marked the beginning of their auspicious future. It was up to her to make a good impression, to help ensure his smooth entry into Uncle Chan's chain of command. She smiled at him slyly. Even without her, he would do just fine.

She took a deep breath as she scanned the room, fixing a benign smile upon her face. The warm aromas of food promised much. What delightful treats would be served: sweet mammoth shrimp, a Guangzhou specialty, rice noodles, or even spicy squid? Her mouth watered in anticipation.

"So these are your mother's people," she said, wondering which were the brothers, sister-in-laws, nieces and nephews. Everyone was eager to welcome her and Gwai Ha. Only Yanru's gracious presence was lacking.

"Uncle Chan must really want me," he whispered. He wore a pleased expression, the likes of which she had rarely seen. How different from the tight, fake smile and false obeisance he habitually showed Uncle Li.

Uncle Chan had been badgering him to join his small group of exporters; which would mean moving to Guangzhou—but only with Uncle Li's permission—making the prospect less likely. As powerful as Uncle Chan was in Guangzhou, he could not circumvent Uncle Li's prerogative as Gwai Ha's Party Boss.

"There's always hope," she said, looking at the strange faces, wondering about the inevitable rivalries, jealousies and alliances typically invisible to a newcomer such as herself.

"There's Uncle Chan," Gwai Ha said, nodding in the direction of a group of men deep in conversation against the far wall.

"You lucky boy," said a middle-aged woman who sidled up to Gwai Ha with a smirk. She snagged his arm.

Ying Fa, a little unnerved, stepped closer to him.

From Yanru's description, she had to be her brother's wife, Auntie Tsien, the family's powerful matriarch. She was about Ying Fa's height, but broad, with huge, deep brown eyes that tilted up from her nose, giving her a surprised expression. She wore a light-gray, high-necked brocade gown that was simply adorned, with a matching chiffon scarf about her neck. Her hair was straight, graying and chin-length. She wore silver bands on her earlobes.

"Auntie Tsien, this is my wife, Wong Ying Fa," Gwai Ha said with a pleased smile. "Many of my teenaged summers were spent in her home." His hand rested briefly on Ying Fa's waist, making her blush. Though her shoulders were bare, inviting his touch, his doing so could bring censure, cause offence and otherwise shock the elders.

"You were forever teasing my sons," Auntie Tsien said with a braying laugh. Her eyes narrowed as she scanned Ying Fa. "You managed to marry this lovely creature?"

Ying Fa smiled shyly. "Nice to meet you," she said, lowering her lashes.

"From quaint Maoming, of all places?" Auntie Tsien said, teasing gently. She extended a hand that Ying Fa took, looking into her warm, welcoming eyes. Deep lines on her face defined her as a woman who had worked hard for success, while maintaining her sense of humor. She patted Gwai Ha hard on the shoulder, making him wince.

"Tough guy," she said with mock severity. Her eyes sparkled. "Don't stay away so long. We've missed you and your mother. Maybe you'll stay this time? Or the next?" She smiled hopefully.

"Auntie Tsien Lieu," he said softly, making her laugh, a guttural sound that brought a tickle to Ying Fa's throat.

Tsien? Lieu? Who was this woman? She looked from one to the other in mild confusion. Were they playing with her?

"I am Chan Lieu's wife," Auntie Tsien explained, taking Gwai Ha's hand. "But one of his brother's wives is also called Tsien. This lug has always called me Auntie Tsien Lieu to keep us straight. So disrespectful." She laughed and rolled her eyes. "One of my daughters-in-law is a Tsien, too. . . Oh, I keep forgetting about them." She extended her hand, palm up, gesturing to three young women, who stood to the left of them.

"A curious trio—sometimes troublesome, though lovely," Auntie Tsien said. "I often envied Yanru her single son."

Ying Fa smiled blandly, and nodded, though Auntie Tsien's words reflected false modesty. How could she help but be inordinately proud of bearing three sons and seeing each of them to manhood. What woman would not? Their wives were a trio of rare beauty in peach, off-white and red silk gowns. Three pairs of dark eyes were scanning the room, gauging the other women's gowns, observing the guests in attendance. The slender one on the left pursed her lips, watching intently as the shortest one in the middle spoke to the tallest. The tallest, stark elegance in a luscious peach gown, grinned as she hugged a fat baby. They were definitely trouble. What a wealth of stories they could tell.

"They are lovely, Auntie Tsien," Ying Fa said, catching Gwai Ha's approving smile. She stood a little straighter.

"Your mother-in-law has told us much about you," Auntie Tsien said, her eyes filling with sympathy.

Ying Fa blushed and quickly dropped her gaze. News of Mooi Mooi must have traveled to Guangzhou. She gripped Gwai Ha's arm, hating the pity. Her skin prickled as she imagined every person in the room staring at her, horrified at what she had done, judging her as a pretend woman, an object of contempt. Would she never escape it?

When she looked up, Auntie Tsien was gesturing excitedly to another woman about her age.

"Stay there," she said, clasping Ying Fa's arm for a second. "I'll find out where you're supposed to sit." Then she was off.

Ying Fa smiled sadly at Gwai Ha. This family could become theirs if they were to move to Guangzhou. Scanning the crowd, she realized that most of the children were boys. More than one woman, like her, must have lost a precious girl. If she hadn't just seen her glamerous reflection in the room's floor-length mirror, she would have bolted.

"Relax," Gwai Ha whispered in her ear, his breath clean and minty from toothpaste. "This is only the beginning." He had read her all too well.

"Don't worry about me," she said, forcing a smile. "I'll be fine." With the smile came a tickle in her throat, then a giggle. "This could be fun, actually."

Yanru had often hinted of rambunctious older cousins neatly outdone by her mischievous son. Perhaps it was time she learned a few embarrassing things about him.

"What secrets will I learn?" she whispered, raising her chin, looking at him coyly.

"What do you mean?" he asked. "I have no secrets. Not from you, anyway."

"Sure. Sure. A big, strapping guy like you? You've probably had lots of little childhood incidents, of which you've never told a soul—little things that I can tease you about later." Her gaze lingered on his full lips, and she licked hers.

His jaw dropped. "Ying Fa—"

"When will I ever get this rare opportunity?" she asked, opening her eyes wide, looking at him over a bare shoulder.

"Don't you dare," he said, shaking his head and laughing. "I—"

"Come on," she said, now gripped in Auntie Tsien's strong hand. She laughed as he sauntered after them, his composure solemn, ever the diligent executive. The eyes of every woman in the room followed him closely.

Auntie Tsien came to a jerking halt at what seemed to be the main table.

"Chan Lieu, this is Yanru's daughter-in-law, Wong Ying Fa." Auntie Tsien smiled fondly at her husband, who at first glance, seemed an older, masculine version of Yanru. He sat with a group of men of various ages. Looking around at the bright eyes and sly measuring glances, she sensed a warm welcome for Gwai Ha and a keen interest in herself.

She faltered, finding herself lost in the gaze of the blackest eyes she had ever seen. With salt and pepper hair and a firm chin, Chan Lieu was Guangzhou's version of Uncle Li—not a man to be trifled with. Though his resemblance to Yanru was startling, unlike Yanru, his gaunt face was a map of deep vertical grooves that spoke of years of command: first in the Red Guards and then later in business. His eyes sparkled with humor, making it easy to see why Gwai Ha adored him.

If they moved to Guangzhou, would he take control of Gwai Ha's personal life? With three grown sons, would he force Gwai Ha to abandon a child? If only she knew. Perhaps one of his daughters-in-law had already sacrificed a daughter—maybe the tall one, with her precious son. At her age, she could have had three or four children by now.

"Pleased to meet you," she said, dropping her gaze, seeing that he was also a man of strong passions. His perusal moved like a warm glove over her body, making her thankful for Yanru's lovely gown. Blushing, she peeked at Auntie Tsien through lowered lashes, hoping she took no offence.

Auntie Tsien laughed, looking thoroughly pleased.

"I hope you enjoy your stay in Guangzhou," Uncle Chan said softly. She glanced up to find absolute sincerity, as well as love in his eyes as he turned to Gwai Ha.

"Ah, my favorite nephew," he said, then rose and hugged Gwai Ha unabashedly. With an arm slung around Gwai Ha's shoulders, he took her hand as gently as if she were made of porcelain.

"What a lovely flower you have picked, eh boys?" He nodded at the other men at the table. They nodded and grunted in return.

A tall man, a younger, leaner version of Uncle Chan, stood at his gesture.

"This is Chan Lee, my eldest son," he said, exchanging nods with his son.

Though his expression was hard, Chan Lee took Ying Fa's hand gently and bowed over it. His gaze softened at the approach of the shortest sister-in-law, probably his wife.

"My eldest daughter-in-law, Tsien Ming-yi," Uncle said, nodding at the young woman.

Ying Fa smiled at her, pleased by the subtle way she appraised her gown. She looked friendly enough and delightfully curious.

Then, one by one, as food was served and tea poured, Uncle introduced each relative, old and young. Ying Fa clasped hands, smiled, kissed babies' cheeks, smiled, nodded and smiled some more, while tea flowed and an endless array of delicious dishes was served for three of the most pleasant hours she had spent in many months.

After the formal introduction to Gwai Ha's family, Uncle Chan quickly immersed him in the intricacies of his import/export business. He arranged meetings, product demonstrations and meals, leaving plenty of time for Gwai Ha to conduct his own business transactions, while he tended his vast network of contacts and enterprises, reaching from Beijing to Hong Kong.

After his father, Boss Chan died; Chan Lieu had grown his sphere of power ten-fold. His eldest son, Chan Lee, managed the family's network of rental properties; his middle son, Chan Shou, an engineering professor in Beijing, managed several lucrative development projects; and the youngest son, Chan En-Jien, like Gwai Ha, dealt with the import/export business. To tempt Gwai Ha to relocate, Uncle Chan involved him in meetings touching upon all of these areas.

Ying Fa learned during their welcoming banquet that Chan En-Jien, two years older than Gwai Ha, was the tallest sister-in-law's husband and the father of the baby boy. She had wanted to get to know this particular new cousin-in-law, but the meetings with En-Jien were strictly for business. Once Gwai Ha explained that she was his official assistant, both men completely ignored her.

She sat beside him in all his meetings, quietly taking notes while he begged, bargained and wrangled, playing perfectly the role of smart executive in his crisp, tailored suit. She liked to watch his face, the way his eyes narrowed when getting at the truth or concentrating; or growing wide with practiced cordiality when shaking a foreigner's hand.

She became used to his daily exchange of telegrams and emails with contacts in Beijing. Each time a missive came, she would wonder at friends in high places, allies of whom his Uncle Li was blindly unaware. He sent her shopping once with a client's wife so he could meet alone with a Beijing official. Not surprising, he had refused to answer her questions; and she learned not to ask.

She found herself becoming a social creature, delighting in the endless rounds of dinners with prospects and clients, alternately playing hostess and guest. She received high praise for her menu selections and for Yanru's lovely dresses, each gossamer jewel-toned creation lifting her confidence. In them she was articulate and witty, everyones darling.

Dinner conversation was high-spirited, usually about literature, technology, sun-drenched vacations, life in Europe and America and politics. Never had she enjoyed such discourse.

Then later, when conventionally acceptable, she and Gwai Ha would retreat to a sensual oasis of their own making within the quiet confines of their room. Behind closed doors, she liked to mimic his contacts: the balding German businessman who wanted cheap embroidered tablecloths; the terse, silver-haired Japanese silk trader, who insisted on dealing directly with the factories, going so far as to arrange an inspection; and the Shanghai fast-talker, who didn't know what he wanted.

She often had Gwai Ha rolling on their bed, gripping his middle in mirth, while she puffed out her stomach and rubbed her head, or minced across the room, her buttocks held tight, shouting orders.

He didn't laugh when she attacked him, though; practically tearing the clothes from his body, so hot was she for him after a particularly harsh and frenzied sales session. She whispered dirty words into his ear, and told him what she would have liked to do to him that day while she had taken notes. Nor did he laugh when she slipped into the shower with him one evening, sending him into such heights of ecstasy, that he claimed she surpassed every woman in Beijing.

On the eve of their departure, long after the glittering cocktail party they had hosted for his adult relatives, they were slowly undressing, getting into their nightclothes, both in a tired mood of quiet contemplation. Within a day, they would be back in Maoming, facing their fears, and their future. If they failed, they could lose everything; but if they won . . ..

Gwai Ha was sitting at the desk; having just removed his shoes and socks, and was rubbing his tired feet.

From under a bed, she withdrew some papers, which she quickly sorted. In one hand, she held a summary of dates, times, purposes, participants and action items of his various meetings. The other papers, she stuck behind her back. Keeping her face devoid of emotion, she set the summary documents on the desk and stepped back a respectful distance, awaiting his verdict.

He glanced at her questiongly and then picked up the papers. "What's this?" he asked, then began to read.

Their clothes were packed and waiting on the second bed; their toilet articles, except for their morning's needs, were stowed safely away; the silk sample case was locked and beside the door. All that awaited them this evening was a simple meal, to be delivered by room service within the hour.

"You are amazing," he said at last, shaking his head as he looked at her. "How did you do all this and everything else you've had to do?" He blinked hard. "We've accomplished a lot in the past two weeks." He shook his head again. "But we've still so much to do." He put the papers down on the desk and rubbed his forehead. "Well done," he said. "I can't imagine how you did it."

She bowed to him in the old way, not as a servant to a master, but as a peer, worthy of respect. His nod was automatic.

"Keep in mind that I've made no mention of your meetings or transactions with Beijing," she said gently, knowing that she had just ruined their evening. His response was of little consequence. He had to accept that she was with him, every frightening step of the way.

"What do you know about it?" he asked and spun away from her angrily. He folded his arms across his chest. "You've been spying on me?"

She refused to react. It was too important. "You've been busy ruining your uncle, finding yourself a new job and securing your mother's retirement, all of which most definitely affects me. You are not a free and easy college student anymore, Gwai Ha. And I am not your meek, stupid little wife."

"My uncle's none of your business." He sent her withering look. "Haven't you done enough?" he asked, then fumbled in his pocket for a pack of cigarettes, a clear sign she had rattled him. He had acquired the habit from his cousin, Chan En-Jien during late afternoon bargaining sessions with Hong Kong trade representatives.

"Done enough?" she said sadly, her mouth stretching into the travesty of a smile. "So you still blame me for Mooi Mooi, is that it?" She rubbed the side of her face. "You just don't get it, do you?"

She bit her lip and moved to the window. A fog had settled in her brain. What was she supposed to do now? What questions could she ask; which complaint could she lodge? It made no difference if he refused to listen.

Blindly, she pushed aside the filmy curtain and looked out at the city lights. How had she managed to botch this so badly? With their future at stake, she couldn't think of a single defense. Couldn't he see how insufferable he was being? How selfish? Zhaodi would say it was her flapping tongue, uncontrollable temper and haughty attitude. But she had only taken an interest in her future. Meekness had never gotten her very far.

"You know," she said quietly, hearing his ragged breath as he drew on a cigarette. "All I ever wanted was a husband who loved me and a family to care for. I know you want to do this thing with your uncle alone, but you can't. Don't expect me to sit by when our lives are at stake."

"How can you help?" he sneered, looking her over, a scathing reminder of Yanru.

"How can you ask that?" she replied. "You just finished telling me that I'm amazing, and yet you wonder how I can help?"

"Yeah," he said, looking down his arrogant nose at her. "I don't want you around when I confront the old man. It's between him and me, man to man, and I'll do it alone."

"But what if I happen to be there?" She was getting frustrated. "What am I—some kind of fixture? That's what I feel like when you have your status meetings with your uncle. I'm like a piece of furniture at the far end of his office, a pair of hands to enter data, a woman to go home with. What do you see when you look at me, Gwai Ha?"

He grinned lasciviously. "You're curvy and—"

"Please," she said, waving a hand, stopping him. "Do you realize how much I've learned in the past few months?" She took a step closer. "How much I've changed?"

"So?" He folded his arms over his chest.

"I'll be there with you, as your assistant, won't I? What if I say the wrong thing and cause us to lose our advantage? You have to tell me what's going on. I need to know."

"So you've known all along about Beijing," he said, and threw his head back and took another drag on his cigarrette, his eyes going to slits. "You've really been spying on me?" He looked at her out of the corner of his eye. "So what do you know about it then?"

"Oh, that's right; change the subject," she said, putting her hands on her hips. "Ask a question for a question. Show your contempt. Don't even bother to sway me, husband. I've studied your tactics for weeks. Do you think that because I'm a woman, I can't possibly figure you out?"

"So you've known all along?" He glared. "Then what's your prognosis?"

"Still, you underestimate me." She moved to the bed, dropped the papers she had held behind her back at her feet and sat with her head in her hands. "How much do I have to do, learn or become before you see me as I am?"

"And what are you," he asked with a soft chuckle, "my lovely enigma—demure by day and wild by night. What am I supposed to think? I don't know another married woman who acts the way you do."

"As well you don't!" She threw a pillow at him and he caught it. There was relief on his face, and no small amount of respect. Maybe she had gotten through to him after all.

"I'm not used to having help," he said with the shrug, his version of an apology.

It wasn't enough. She had to know all of the facts surrounding his uncle's position; and she had to know that he truly saw her, and not as a retractable extension of himself.

"Do you really see me?" she repeated, her gaze boring into his.

"Sometimes I wonder," he said with a quick shake of his head. "You were supposed to be a meek little silk embroiderer: smart, quick, a great cook, the perfect wife. Now look at you." There was a twinkle in his eye.

"This won't work," she said, looking away. She folded her hands together, trying to stop their trembling. "I think I'll take a walk and clear my head. You are not taking this seriously. You aren't taking me seriously." She rose from the bed.

"Why? The food's coming any minute. You barely ate a thing all night." He strode to the door and barred her way. "Tell me—what am I supposed to see?"

"That. I. Am. Just. Like. You." She poked him in the chest, emphasizing each syllable. Then she spanned the distance to the bed, and reached down and grabbed the papers.

She shoved them at him—the papers she'd carefully crafted—detailed financial statements of each of his uncle's factories, illustrating debits and credits, income and expenses, and sources and uses of funds.

His low appreciative whistle was better than a plate of hot, savory noodles on a cold winter's night. She gazed into happy eyes that matched her own.

"I see you," he said, now grinning. "Now what would you like to know?"

Chapter 15

Twenty-four hours had passed since she had confronted Gwai Ha; and now they were in his uncle's office, finishing the last data feed into the factory's desktop computer. Within seconds, the data would be available to every other computer on the network; and on its way to the Ministry of Commerce in Beijing.

She scanned the vast, ugly room that had become her life's focus. It was cave-like with ancient plaster walls and a brown, stained linoleum floor, cracked in several places. Cheap calendar posters and faded prints of white-capped mountains hung beside silk shipment schedules on the dreary walls, adding to the gloom. At the other end of the room, near the door, was Uncle Li's desk. Their work area was at the opposite end, near the windows.

Piles of flapping papers held down by rounded stones were stacked on their desk and a nearby table, representing the factories' bills, invoices and correspondences, all categorized and now entered into the computer. They had worked practically all night, returning home for a few hours to wash and grab a bite to eat.

It was dismal and overcast outside. The refinery stacks belched out clouds of soot, spreading grime over the sprawling city, making it difficult to see that rain threatened.

They sat together, hip to hip, his hand gripping the mouse, the cursor hovering over the enter button. Aside from the click of keys on the keyboard, the only sound in the room was the whine of the massive floor fan, a pedestal affair that threatened to topple over with the slightest push. It pumped damp cool air through the room, but her skin was on fire. Every second counted.

Uncle Li would walk in at any moment, demanding to know the status of their trip. At any moment their plans could turn to ash from some detail they hadn't considered. Her heart raced as she typed. They had to win. They just had to.

Gwai Ha tapped his fingers impatiently and she typed faster.

Then, finally, with the last file copied and the corresponding log entries made, she removed her hands from the keypad and nodded.

"Ready?" he asked, his expression grim.

"Do it," she said.

He clicked the mouse.

Closing her eyes, she pictured the transfer as a bolt of light streaking its way to Beijing.

Gwai Ha expelled a long hiss and they sat back to watch the send icon pulse and then disappear.

"Now comes the hard part," he said, resting his hand on her knee. Even through thick black pants, she felt the moisture of his sweaty palm. Her face burned as if from fever. She was edgy, her skin hypersensitive. She resisted the urge to push him away. It took so little to hurt his feelings.

"What can he do to us?" she asked tiredly.

"I don't want to hear it," he mumbled. Looking annoyed, he moved his hand away.

She stared at her hands, twisting them in her lap, wishing she had kept her thoughts to herself. Bickering was a waste of vital energy; especially when they were walking on such a fine edge, ready to fall and desperately in need of each other. Tears filled her eyes, but she refused to cry. Her dry mouth tasted of fear; but it was too late to sip from the bottled water she had set on the floor an hour ago. There would be no bathroom trips until the matter was finished.

"Sorry," she said softly, knowing he would refuse any comfort she offered. Sometimes, like now, she recognized a younger version of his uncle upon his face; though he wouldn't thank her for saying so. Did he always have to be the strong one, the one in control?

He gripped her shoulder gently, startling her. She looked up.

"It's okay," he said, with ove in his eyes. "Let's not fight."

She touched his hand, pressing it against her shoulder, curling his fingers tighter.

Suddenly, the door swung opened and then closed. She giggled nervously, her hand to her mouth. Gwai Ha sent her a meaningful glance.

They stood together and he touched her hand with one finger, begging her to hope. Their plan had to work. Uncle Li must not defeat them.

"Let's go," he whispered and handed her the stack of papers she was to pass him during the meeting. They had rehearsed this many times on their return trip, often to the point of exhaustion.

They stood before Uncle Li's desk and watched him enter, his movements deliberate. He didn't make eye contact. His heavy metal desk was to the right of the door, away from the wall, facing out into the room. Upon it was a green felt blotter, upon which sat two black rotary telephones and a stack of paperwork held down by a stone in the shape of a dragon. To the left of the door were boxes of toilet paper stacked to the ceiling, a special shipment for a favor owed. Behind his desk and to the right was a standing garment rack upon which hung a gray wool coat, a beige trench coat and a large black umbrella, hooked by its handle to the rack.

He seated himself with a loud groan—from hemorrhoids most likely. According to Yanru, he was a walking medical text. She hoped he hurt, inside and out.

His gaze raked them as he settled behind his desk—as if they were of no account.

She looked at her feet, sick to her stomach at the sight of his beady, black eyes. For years, she had feared him: she had obeyed his least command. This was not going to be easy.

Ignoring them, he took up his morning newspaper and began to read.

Though Gwai Ha had warned that he would play it this way, the gall stung. Yanru would have been at his throat by now, forcing him to pay attention, commanding his courtesy.

But Yanru was on her way to Shanghai to visit her eldest daughter, safely out of the way. She was too weak when it came to Uncle Li. He would try to manipulate her, given the chance.

According to Gwai Ha, last minute plans were the most difficult to foil. In Guangzhou, he had pulled strings on the morning of their departure, calling his estranged sisters, calling Beijing to secure his mother's retirement pay, and then calling his mother with travel instructions. He had wired her the passage fee.

Though fearing her daughters' condemnation, Yanru had tearfully agreed. She had cried when Gwai Ha had said both women were eager to see her. In another month, she would visit her youngest daughter in Changsha. Hopefully, at the end of all this, she would join them in Guangzhou.

Gwai Ha flashed a warning look and she nodded slightly, bringing her attention back to the present. He had known she was daydreaming; had probably done it himself on many occasions. Today they could ill afford even the hint of weakness.

They were supposed to wait for Uncle Li's acknowledgement, though always before it had been Gwai Ha alone, waiting and daydreaming, until Uncle Li finally decided to listen.

She caught a small movement. The door opened a crack, showing Uncle Li's scrawny secretary, a smooth-faced, bird-like woman who was hovering outside, probably waiting for this interview to end. She was an instrument, a business tool, utilitarian to a fault. Unbeknownst to Uncle Li, she was also his wife's loyal spy.

The door closed softly.

Uncle Li's hand hovered over the weighted-down papers, his fingers lightly touching a corner of a page.

Grumbling under his breath and expelling gas as if he were alone, he continued to read.

She closed her eyes briefly, slightly nauseated. The odor mingled with that of damp socks and burnt tea, the floor-fan being too far away to have much affect.

Uncle Li scribbled something on a piece of paper. Then his eyes rolled up in his head, like a hungry shark, as his mind darted here and there making plans—as if he were alone. He picked up the phone and barked a few orders. He dropped the receiver and then wrote some more.

A quick glance at Gwai Ha showed that he was struggling to stay in control, his face reddening, the muscles in his jaw tightening. It was all she could do to keep from screaming.

They had agreed he would start the conversation, lulling his uncle with the expected. In his world, a woman dared not speak unless asked.

A phone rang, but Uncle Li ignored it. He scanned Gwai Ha's face and then hers, his fathomless eyes missing nothing. He put the newspaper down.

"I assume your trip was successful," he said with a nervous smile. "What could be better than having exquisite goods to sell and a lovely young woman to warm your bed? Eh, nephew?"

He snorted in the semblance of a laugh, his broad, peasant face looking placid, almost simple.

She wasn't fooled. There was a slight movement to his jaw, much like Gwai Ha when annoyed.

"Yes, Uncle," Gwai Ha said, his head held high. "It was very successful. And in ways I never expected."

Uncle Li leaned back, his look long and measuring.

Gwai Ha continued. "The Germans, in particular, wanted to—"

"Before we talk about Guangzhou," Uncle Li said, his eyes narrowing, "My driver's ready to move your things. Tomorrow would be a good day to pack." He rose from his chair slightly, looking Gwai Ha in the eye, ignoring Ying Fa, and then sat back down. "I suggest you be ready."

Was he aware of their investigation? How had he learned of it? She resisted the urge to hug herself, suddenly chilled.

"Go on," Gwai Ha said, maintaining his composure, though his hand trembled slightly as it touched hers.

"I've found a slot for your mother in an elderly home, so you needn't concern yourself with her," Uncle Li said smoothly. "I want you moved in with us by the end of three days. Is that clear?" A telling flush rose from beneath his collar.

"Three days?" Ying Fa blurted out, wanting to laugh. He couldn't possibly know about Yanru. What else didn't he know? She shot Gwai Ha a scornful glance.

His eyes held a warning.

"We'll not be moving in with you," he said softly.

"Excuse me?" Uncle Li said, scowling, keeping his steady gaze on Gwai Ha, like a snake on a mouse. "I said you're moving in with us; and you'll do as I say. Your wife needs guidance, and apparently, so do you."

"No," Gwai Ha said, drawing out the word as if speaking to a child. "You no longer make plans for us, Uncle. We are moving, but to Guangzhou, and in about three weeks."

"What!" A crimson blush spread across Uncle Li's face.

"I'm taking a position with Government exports, working for Chan Lien, my mother's elder brother. Ying Fa will remain my assistant."

"What!" Uncle Li knocked his chair back as he stood abruptly.

"The job starts in three week," Gwai Ha said with a smirk. "To learn more, call your friends in Beijing." He raised his chin slightly. "Ask for Lien Chiang, my old professor. He'll tell you everything, from one uncle to another. Pretty sweet, eh?" He took Ying Fa's hand.

"I'll tell you when and where you work, boy," Uncle Li said as he scrabbled behind him for his chair with one hand, pulled it closer and sat down. He stared at their clasped hand, glowering. "You belong to me, you work for me, and so does she." He pointed at Ying Fa.

Gwai Ha laughed. "Are you ready to talk business, old man?" He looked at Ying Fa, released her hand, and nodded.

She returned his nod, keeping her face stern, though she wanted to laugh at the easy victory.

Uncle Li glared at her, yet she refused to lower her gaze. He was an ugly troll, foolishly wallowing in past accomplishments.

"You need this woman here for some reason?" he asked with a slight lift of his chin. "Hiding behind her skirts like you do with your mother?"

"She has become . . . useful," Gwai Ha said slowly, a muscle twitching on the side of his face. He extended a hand, palm out, and she handed him a document. He placed it on the desk.

"Take a look at this." He said, turning it so his uncle could read. He pointed his finger at a number on the page. Uncle Li leaned closer, squinting.

"Over the last five years," Gwai Ha said, "this significant amount of money has . . . let's say . . . become lost to government controls."

"And?" Uncle asked, his face reddening as he stood back, scowling.

Ying Fa's hands trembled. She prayed to her ancestors that she wouldn't drop the other documents, detailing the mess that Uncle Li had made of his finances, of his life. She imagined papers fluttering from her tired fingers in slow motion, and blowing about the room with the fan's strong breath.

"We've traced it to your gambling," Gwai Ha said, looking at him squarely. "It's been confirmed in writing by many of your so-called friends, who are tired of waiting for your payments." He leaned against the desk. "Now we have you, old man. Now you'll leave us alone."

"No," Uncle said, shaking his head. "You must not do this, Gwai Ha. You can't."

"I can." Gwai Ha looked at Ying Fa and she smiled. "And we have."

Uncle sat heavily in his chair and stared at the document. Then, one by one, Gwai Ha took the other papers from Ying Fa and laid them on the desk for his perusal.

Ying Fa clung to the last remaining sheet.

Uncle read each one, muttering loudly, shaking his head. After several long moments he began to tear the pages, one-by-one, into tiny pieces. He threw them into the air and they blew about the room like confetti. A few pieces settled on the top of his hair, making him look ridiculous.

"You have nothing now," he said with a taut grin. "It's your word against mine now, boy."

Gwai Ha smiled, a wolfish look she had seen across bargaining tables in Guangzhoua, a look that chilled her. "It's in the computer, you old fool," he said softly, his voice like silk. "You know—those books you asked me to computerize, the reason for Beijing's agreement? Didn't it seem too easy to get me; considering I was third in my class. What a waste of talent for fifth-rate Maoming."

Color drained from Uncle Li's face. He rose heavily and lumbered to the nearest computer. He kicked it with all of his might. Breathing heavily, he tore about the room until he had found an odd piece of pipe, leftover from a recent building repair, behind his coatrack. Hefting it, he smashed the monitor first. Then he ripped out various cables, permanently damaging the precious and expensive equipment, his behavior exactly as Gwai Ha had predicted.

Finally, he stood keeled over with his hands on his knees, breathing laboriously, his hair flopped over his mottled face.

"Are you finished?" Gwai Ha asked. He sat at Uncle Li's desk, his feet propped up. She stood behind him, every muscle tensed, ready to flee.

Uncle Li rose to his full height and turned, still gasping, looking confused. "Why?" he asked, tipping his head to the left, peering at Gwai Ha out of one eye. "What do you mean?"

Ying Fa held her breath.

"We've stored that data in many places," Gwai Ha said. "The hard copy was just for you, you ignorant, old fool. Once computerized, the information stands for itself. Forever. See this?" He took a disk from his pocket. "This is just one copy. There are many others in safe places.

Just say the word and Beijing will know everything. Otherwise—"

"What do you want?" Uncle Li gasped. He raked his fingers through his hair, looking pathetic and old.

She felt nothing for him but scorn.

"I want you to stay out of my life," Gwai Ha said. "This woman is my wife." He took Ying Fa's hand. "Not some vessel for the next generation. You have no interest in getting to know her, yet you have taken her child—my child. You will never interfere with my family again. Do you understand? We are moving to Guangzhou to get away from your influence. You will sign this document, granting your approval."

Ying Fa held out the paper.

"In exchange for?" Ice and steel filled Uncle Li's face.

Ying Fa's pulse raced.

"I'll doctor the books," Gwai Ha said, smiling, waving a hand expansively, sounding reasonable. "I'll cover your losses, like a good nephew. But that's where it ends. My new contract will be for the entire Guangdong Province. I'll see you once in a while, but for business only."

Uncle Li closed his eyes as if weighing the cost. Then he sauntered over to his safe behind the coat rack, sending chills down Ying Fa's spine.

"You can't do this to me," he said; and shot her a look of quiet glee.

A card not shown; a hand not revealed. What was it? She caught Gwai Ha's eye, and he glanced at her nervously, then dropped his feet to the floor.

Kneeling down, Uncle Li fiddled with the tumblers and opened the safe. Then he reached in and extracted an envelope.

"Here," he said, with a large expulsion of breath. He threw the envelope on the desk. "It's your turn to read."

Ying Fa peered over Gwai Ha's arm as Uncle Li extracted two documents from the envelope.

"Your birth certificate and Li An's death certificate," he said, folding his arms over his chest. "Most interesting reading."

The documents looked complete with all the official stamps. Gwai Ha had asked his mother for them a few months ago, but she had claimed ignorance. Looking closely, she saw why.

Li An had died more than a year before Gwai Ha's birth, proving irrefutably that he could not have been his father. She stared at Uncle Li, and then back at Gwai Ha, realization hitting her like a slap.

"This can't be," Gwai Ha said, shaking his head. His eyes watered. Then he turned and pounded the wall behind him, knocking a calendar off with a crash.

"Ask your mother to deny it," Uncle Li said, his eyes glinting with victory, his lips curling.

She gaped at him in shock. He had remained silent all these years? She grabbed Gwai Ha's arm, hoping to calm him, trying to bring him back from his rage. The fantasy father he had worshipped had been his uncle all along—and his father . . . the crude peasant?

"My mother's not here," Gwai Ha said, his face ashen. He waved Ying Fa away.

"Tell the truth." Uncle Li sneered as he moved closer. "Did your mother ever let you look at these documents, particularly my brother's death certificate? Of course she didn't. She was too ashamed. Her child a bastard, and not

290

the precious only son of her illustrious cultured husband? I suppose we all have our illusions."

Gwai Ha moaned and buried his face in his hands.

"She has copies, you know, buried deep in the drawer of her precious sewing machine," Uncle Li hissed. "Go see, if you don't believe me. You will find them. She made me promise not to tell you."

"Then why did you?" Ying Fa asked, pushing aside her fear. This man was nothing but a poor loser, a liar and a thief. He would not stop them from leaving. "You talk about it now when you have everything to lose, but couldn't bother with Gwai Ha when he really needed you? You are pitiful."

Uncle turned, his calm malevolence shocking her.

"If you had only done your duty," he said, shaking his head. "I suppose I should blame your grandmother and those insipid parents of yours. Just like poor Yanru who always thought too much of herself, you've never had a proper example to follow." His face clouded as he looked at Gwai Ha. "So where is she? Where is your mother?"

Was that all he cared about? "Is he really your son, or is this another one of your lies?" she asked, moving in front of the desk, placing herself between the two of them.

"Am I?" Gwai Ha cried, shaking his head, already accepting the truth. Just looking at the two of them together removed even a thread of doubt.

"Oh, he's my son alright," Uncle Li said, his eyes gleaming as he looked at Gwai Ha. "My love child," he sneered. "After An died trying to rape some peasant girl, Yanru was quick to seek my protection." Uncle Li grinned. "What satisfaction—my elder brother dieing without a son."

"Nooo," Gwai Ha moaned.

Ying Fa's stomach clenched. "All the more reason for us to hate you," she said softly, wanting to knock the smile from his face. "What kind of man are you, anyway? What poor excuse for a father. If he is your son, how dare you throw away his child, your own granddaughter? How dare you scorn him, your so-called lovechild? You didn't even know he existed until you lost your bully sons."

"Ying Fa," Gwai Ha warned. His back muscles rippled as he shifted position. Was he was about to concede?

"No!" she cried, refusing to be censured. "I will talk. I'll say what I must. He will not rule our lives."

"Shut her up," Uncle growled. "Or I will." On surprisingly quick feet, he lunged at her with an upraised hand.

Gwai Ha sprang over the desk, with one kick knocking him down.

"Please!" she cried, afraid for both of them. "Violence is not the answer." Especially beween father and son, she'd almost blurted out. "It solves nothing."

Uncle Li lay sprawled on the floor, holding his knee, his face pinched with pain. "I'm just an old man," he gasped.

"Then leave us alone!" she cried. "We don't want anything to do with you, no matter who you are."

He picked himself up off the floor and rose to his feet. "You can't mean that," he said, scratching his head. He looked at Gwai Ha sadly. "I am your father." He held out a hand. "I've always only wanted the best for you; but sometimes your mother doesn't—"

"I don't want to hear it," Gwai Ha said, his arms folded across his chest, looking away. "Just sign the release, so we can go to Guangzhou. I want nothing more to do with you."

He took the paper from Ying Fa and slapped it on the desk. "Sign it." He placed a pen and his father's private stamp beside it.

Ying Fa held her breath as old man rose with as much dignity as he could muster, and signed the paper. Then he stamped it, making it official.

Gwai Ha glared at him as he walked away.

"You don't know," Uncle Li said sadly from the doorway. "You can't know what I've sacrificed for you. My brother had all the gifts, all the honors, while I slaved to pay his way. He scorned and reviled me. He even took the woman I loved, as if she were a ripe plum from some roadside tree. A little understanding was all I asked, a little hope for the future. But then you two had to go and do this." He gestured at the computer, and then let out a tired sob as he shuffled out the door.

Tears spilled from Ying Fa's eyes. She let out a long shuddering breath. Though he had taken Mooi Mooi and tried to destroy them, filial devotion had been instilled in her from the moment of her birth. There was no getting around that he was Gwai Ha's father; in his own selfish way, he had loved him.

When the door closed, she closed her eyes briefly. How would they live with this?

"He's just a tired old man," she said, shaking her head sadly.

Gwai Ha was crumpled against the desk. She went to him, but he pushed her away with the swipe of his hand.

"My father?" he whispered hoarsely. "How can it be?"

293

"What will you do?" she asked, aching for him. She clasped her hands together, unsure of herself.

"Nothing has changed," he said sadly. "He's never really been my father. He would turn on us in a second, and take as he sees fit. He is finished; and my friends in Beijing are thrilled at the fine catch they have made. The wheels have long been in motion, and cannot be stopped."

"Wheels? What are you talking about?"

His expression was implacable as he took the signed document from the desk and folded it carefully. Then he reached into the desk drawer, removed a blank envelope and slid the paper inside.

"Let's go home," he said, then took her arm, his expression closed, warding off the numerous clamoring questions that he knew that she had.

She nodded carefully.

Chapter 16

A week later, Ying Fa sat cross-legged on her bedding on the floor, enjoying the rare, warm breeze that blew in her apartment window. Not a stick of furniture remained; and she was alone, her nimble fingers guiding a steel embroidery needle in and out of scrap of white silk.

She inspected the luscious purple bird she was creating, looking for mistakes; but found none. The cloth glimmered in the dingy light. She had designed the jacket from memory using Yanru's cast-offs as a pattern; and had forgotten how comforting it was to embroider. Weaving in and out, carefully padding the satin stitch, each thread a perfect line against the rest. She clipped a loose thread with tiny scissors and smiled at her work fondly. The jacket would warm Yanru this winter in Guangzhou.

She sighed. Without Yanru, the place had seemed especially empty.

Outside, car horns beeped, truck engines roared and bicycle bells clanged—the normal sounds of the busy city. They were the familiar sounds of what had been her life; and she would miss it. These final lazy days in Maoming had granted her a serenity she couldn't have dreamed of a year ago.

Gwai Ha would be home soon. He had left after breakfast to visit friends, grab the daily newspaper and stroll through the market for today's lunch. Like her, he was tired of eating out and craved the warmth of a meal both cooked and eaten at home. At least they could eat at home.

The apartment walls echoed now, in the absence of his husky male voice and his overwhelming presence. His resilience, more than anything, gave her reason to smile.

Just three days following their confrontation with Boss Li, he had returned to his happy, scheming self, eager to move on. The shattered look was gone, replaced by a determination that amazed her. He was in control now and growing stronger every day.

So he'd kept few secrets.

She closed her eyes, savoring the memory of that day. On his orders and unbeknownst to her, soldiers had waited in a nearby alley. When Boss Li had stormed out, they had snatched him, and he had gone, kicking and screaming from their lives forever. Meanwhile, another smaller force had plucked Auntie Li from one of her committee meetings. She had used the embezzled funds for bribes; and to furnish their lavish apartment. Now both were gone and the government had confiscated their belongings. In a decade or so, they might emerge from some muddy work farm, grateful for a shared hovel.

New management was already in place at the factories. Except for a few last-minute conferences, there was nothing for her and Gwai Ha to do but relax and wait for the day of their departure.

Meanwhile, they had partied at the Maoming Building by night, made love at all hours, sampled the best restaurants and attended the local Ping-Pong tournament. Gwai Ha had even played a few matches, all the while complaining that he was too stale to bother—though he had won two rounds. She smiled as she set aside her work, remembering the cheers and the celebratory banquet that had followed.

He had promised to take her to the beach tomorrow, no matter the weather.

Most of their furnishings were already loaded onto a truck headed for Guangzhou. All that remained was a small teapot, two sets of chopsticks, a few bowls, plates, cups, blankets and pillows, toilet articles and a week's change of clothing for each of them.

Footsteps sounded in the outside hallway, and then retreated. She listened closely as a peppy love song came on the radio. Their new neighbors were from a poorer section of town, though such distinctions were supposedly part of the past. The family was touchingly grateful for this singular advantage, reminding her of her own family, like them, sharing an ambition for the future and a passion for each other.

For a moment, she gave in to the old pain, yet unhealed, of her family's estrangement. Fighting back tears, she pushed sad thoughts aside. In a week, they would leave for Guangzhou. No bad memories, no regrets or shameful secrets must follow them there.

A wave of darkness overtook her, stunning her with its intensity. Plans, dinners and even lovemaking could not fill the need she had to see her family one last time.

"Zhaodi," she keened, rocking gently with her arms across her chest. Tears coursed her cheeks and she brushed them away. Never again would she touch her own mother, argue with her or even hold her hand. Since the incident in the park, she had not seen nor heard from any of them—except for Yutang's increasingly frantic phone messages, to which she had refused to listen.

He always phoned when Gwai Ha was out. So far, she had erased each message. Gwai Ha would never understand. He thought Yutang's intentions were good, fool that he was. He hadn't grown up with the liar, the womanizer, the thief. Nor had he been the victim of his relentless teasing, or had to sacrifice his education to send the fool to trade school.

Yet somehow, Yutang had been talking to Gwai Ha, feeding him tragic stories, telling him what to say. Why else would Gwai Ha be broaching the subject on a daily basis, poking ever so lightly at her reasoning, trying to get her to visit her family, to make amends?

She had her reasons and it behooved Gwai Ha, for the sake of family harmony, to respect them. How frustrating to have to constantly articulate her family's betrayal. He just did not understand.

There was a knock at the door; and then there was silence.

The knock came again, this time louder, more urgent.

Who could it be?

If only Gwai Ha were home.

The knocking stopped, replaced by voices that spilled into her main room, voices that argued. Was that Gwai Ha, Yutang and Hsiao? What nerve! What gall!

She rose and looked out the window, gazing without focus at the dreary building across the way, struggling with her rage. Maybe their apartment in Guangzhou would have a view of the Pearl River.

She ran a trembling finger along the window frame, making a line in the sooty grime, and sighed. The wait for an apartment would be long, so Uncle Chan claimed, maybe six months or more. Even Uncle Chan's influence couldn't change that. Especially when Gwai Ha refused to settle anywhere but Shamian Island, a strip of land once reserved for Westerners. Meanwhile, they would keep most of their things in storage and make do with some third-rate apartment.

How Poh Poh would love to hear about Guangzhou.

She sighed heavily. She would probably never see Poh Poh again, and her last memory would be painful and strained. She closed her eyes, remembering the beloved face as she had seen it on that day. Were her childhood years worth nothing? Would she become a faint memory to her supposed family, a phantom daughter, a story to tell Anji on a rainy day, like that of the Wong Aunts, half-secret and half-fantasy?

"Ying Fa?"

She turned.

Hsiao stood half in the doorway, wringing her hands, her face pinched with concern.

Ying Fa turned back to the window, blinded by tears. How dare she come here? She would never relent.

"Ying Fa? Please." Hsiao moved closer.

"Go away." She clenched her fists, fighting the urge to spring and hurt. "How dare you come here, you traitor?"

"I've brought you some jasmine tea." Hsiao set the cup on the floor beside the blanket. "Your grandmother begged me to bring it. She said you—"

"Leave me alone."

Her mouth was dry and her throat raw; and she spied the fragile cup out of the corner of her eye. Its scent was unbearably sweet. Only Poh Poh could make it the way she liked.

"Where is my husband?" she asked, hating to acknowledge this woman.

"He's just outside," Hsiao said. She had seated herself on the edge blanket, making herself at home.

Ying Fa swung around. "Don't you understand that I want nothing to do with you? You're a liar and a traitor, and worst of all, you've turned my family against me." Her voice broke and she turned back to the window, hiding her eyes with her hair as she leaned against the window frame, arms outstretched.

"I didn't betray you," Hsiao said softly.

"Can you explain then why Auntie Li said you did— something about Yutang getting caught with the goods?" She turned again to look at her. "Can you explain why my grandmother doesn't want to see me? Don't my parents want to say goodbye? I am leaving Maoming in a week. It will be months before we return. And tell Yutang to stop calling me? I don't want to hear about your perfect little boy, or how perfect little Hsiao takes care of us all."

"They won't come to you, you know that," Hsiao said gently. "Your parents would lose face and Grandmother can't write, or walk this far."

"No?" Ying Fa sobbed, hating that she was being reasonable. "But how could you have known nothing of

Mrs. Li's plans? Between Yutang's weakness for a pretty face and your stupid lies, you deserve each other."

"But Ying Fa," Hsiao said softly, infuriating her further with her practiced femininity, "Mrs. Li was my mother's most bitter enemy. She's the last person I'd help." Hsiao slurped her tea, her little finger upraised, reminding her of her family's affluence and status. "I knew nothing of the Director's plans," she said, fluttering her lashes demurely, reminding her of the times when, not long ago, they had practiced the effect together in front of the mirror.

"But what aren't you saying?" Ying Fa asked.

Hsiao set her teacup down. "It was only later that I heard of the substantial donation from Mrs. Li. What a foolish monkey I was. Looking back, I should have wondered why the Director agreed to take Mooi Mooi to the park so easily. Usually, I can hardly get her attention. If I hadn't been so intent on helping you, I might have been more suspicious."

"I wish I could believe you," Ying Fa said. She slumped to the floor, and sat with her arms wrapped tightly around her knees. "What about how you treated me when I came home? Didn't you see that I was desperate? I had just given birth, just lost my baby. Why didn't you support me? Why were you so quick to want me gone? You even told me how to abandon my child." She raked her fingers through her hair. Then she said with a sob, "I thought you were my best friend."

Hsiao rubbed her eyes with both hands, and then she dropped her hands into her lap and for a long moment just looked at them.

"Well?" Ying Fa asked. She pushed herself up off the floor, took a few steps, grabbed the other cup of tea and took it to the blanket's far edge. She took a long sip, relishing the smooth warmth as it seeped down her throat, the flowery fragrance soothing her jangled nerves.

"I was pregnant,' Hsiao said, and looked up at her.

"Pregnant?" Ying Fa shook her head. "You mean when I was with my baby, you were . . .."

"Pregnant." Hsiao nodded sadly.

She looked deep into her eyes, finding sorrow and truth. "Why didn't you tell me?" she asked.

"I thought I'd prevented it, but . . .." Hsiao turned away. "Your parents, Grandmother, Yutang . . . everyone agreed there was nothing else to do." She pressed a hand to her mouth as silent sobs wracked her body.

"You had an abortion?" Ying Fa asked, horrified. No matter what, Hsiao had been her friend, and was her sister-in-law still. A second child would have crushed the Wong's future, as much as Uncle Li tried to do.

"Yes, I did," Hsiao said and hung her head. "My mother doesn't know. She'll never know."

The image flashed of her elegant, overprotective mother. She would be crushed.

Silently, she went to Hsiao and held her close, rocking her on the floor of the echoing, empty room. They were just two grieving women, deprived of their children, caught up in their country's desperate need for survival. No herbs, pills or soothing words would ever ease the pain.

"You must come with us," Hsiao said at last, pushing her away. "Today."

"Come? Where?"

Still holding Ying Fa's arm, she wiped her tears with the corner of the blanket. "You must go with Yutang and me; and Gwai Ha, too. The Americans are here." She looked expectantly at her. "That's what we came to tell you. But you must hurry."

"What Americans?" Ying Fa asked. She sat cross-legged, hugging herself, her breath coming fast.

"They've come to take your daughter," Hsiao replied softly, her eyes full of kindness.

The jolt to her stomach was like a massive stomping foot. She stared at Hsiao, shaking her head, barely able to breathe.

"We thought you'd want to see her new parents; and of course see her one last time." Hsiao frowned. "Did we do right by telling you?"

"Gwai Ha knows about this?" she asked, and then looked up as the door opened, and he stuck his head inside.

Behind him, Yutang bounced from one foot to the other, displaying his anxiety. "Mooi Mooi, you must come with us now," he said, starting to move toward her. Gwai Ha gripped his arm, restraining him.

Ying Fa closed her eyes, loving and hating Yutang all at once. She was indeed his little sister, and once she had hurried to follow the sound of his voice calling her that name. But it was her baby's name; and today she must say her good-byes. She bowed her head, covering her confusion.

"Do you want to do this?" Gwai Ha asked. He squatted beside her, his face centimeters aways. He smelled of pork dumplings and green tea.

She threw her arms around him, holding him close. "Yes," she whispered, with more conviction than she felt.

"Are you sure?" he asked, gazing into her eyes as he brushed the hair from her face.

"We must do this," she said sadly; and he nodded.

"This will make it final," he whispered, "It has to, my flower; but please don't tell my mother. This must stay between you and me."

"As you wish," she said, though Yanru would want to know. And she would tell her—one day over tea when they were alone.

"We must hurry," Yutang said, his eyes darting from one to the other. "A friend of mine's taking the families for lunch. We need to get there first and look like the locals that we are."

Then in a rush, Gwai Ha was helping her to her feet, assisting her with her shoes and pulling her out of the apartment. They took the front steps two at a time.

"Their guide is taking them to the Black Dragon after they meet the babies," Yutang called out over his shoulder. She ran to catch up, and then linked an arm with his and caught Gwai Ha with the other, while Hsiao, her lips opening like a landed fish, hurried behind them.

They sped down a street parallel to the main traffic corridor, separating at intervals to avoid swarms of bicycles. They dodged mothers with children perched behind them, fruit peddlers burdened with inventory, couples in suits returning from work, and dozens of factory workers in the ubiquitous black pants and white shirts.

Her lungs ached and her legs wobbled as she tried to keep up. Halfway there, they just lifted her along, her feet barely touching the ground.

The Black Dragon was a dingy bar located off a side street close to the Maoming Building. By night, it was a reputed prostitute haven; by day, it served a decent rice plate. Inside was a long dark room with a small stage at the far end for a band, and twenty or so smooth round wooden tables lined up on either side, chairs all around.

For two horrible hours, they sat at a table in the depths of the shabby room, sharing a bottle of scotch. The women drank little, while the men chain-smoked Western cigarettes, clouding the room, obscuring the stage. Aside from the greasy looking bartender, who watched an old black and white cowboy movie from behind the cashier station, they were the sole customers.

Twice the women ran to the bathroom, returning quickly, fearing they'd missed the baby. With frequent nervous glances at the door, they spoke quietly of Zhaodi's improving health, Anji's antics, Grandmothers' arthritis and Father's impending retirement.

As they ordered food, Ying Fa took furtive looks at her brother and his wife, seeing a tired couple, already bowed down by life's worries. No longer the teased younger sister, she found it strange to speak with Yutang as a peer.

During what could have been awkward silences, Gwai Ha regaled them with tales of ping-pong tournaments and Beijing's brazen women, lightening the mood.

Then a sullen waitress appeared with their meal—a feast of noodles with chicken, steamed shrimp, mixed vegetables, white rice, and a pot of tea. She left on silent feet.

Gradually, conversation turned to Guangzhou and the life she and Gwai Ha had planned. Hsiao and Yutang agreed to visit in a few months, though it was an empty promise: they were needed at home, especially Hsiao.

The waitress returned and cleared the table, leaving the half-full bottle of scotch, which Gwai Ha promptly poured into four glasses.

"Please come for dinner tomorrow," Hsiao said, resting her hand on Ying Fa's arm. We've all missed you. Your mother is much improved, and longs to see you. Please. It will be pleasant. There will be no harsh words or reprimands. We all want to move on to better times."

Ying Fa smiled painfully. Despite the injustices life had dealt her, and the hurtful way her family had responded, she loved them dearly. Perhaps it was time to reconcile. She took a deep breath and said, "why not?" Then she smiled at Gwai Ha. A mended family would be her parting gift.

He took her hand across the table. "Good girl," he mouthed, making her warm all over.

Yutang laughed, baring gleaming white teeth, and clapped Gwai Ha on the arm.

Then his smile faded. He nodded in the direction of the door.

Gwai Ha's face blanched. "Don't turn," he whispered.

Ying Fa sucked in her breath, using all of her strength to keep still.

Hsiao took her hand; and Gwai Ha pushed her shot glass closer.

"Drink up," he said, and then took two gulps of his own, his gaze hardening.

She turned slightly. Out of the corner of her eye, she watched the Americans sit at a table not far away. There were two couples, the closest heavy-set with bushy brown hair and kind faces. The baby in the man's arms was not hers.

Steeling herself, refusing to shed a tear, she turned her gaze to the furthest couple. She saw the burly man first. He sat with his arm across the back of his wife's chair. There was a soft smile on his weathered face as he gazed at the baby in her arms.

"Must be the father," Hsiao whispered. Ying Fa nodded slightly, too numb to speak.

The man's slender wife spoke rapid English to their local interpreter, one of the Maoming Building's assistant managers, a tough, thirtyish looking woman, who shot Yutang a warning glance.

She was one of his friends? He must have gained some advantage over her, to achieve such a dangerous favor.

She stared at the woman holding Mooi Mooi. Her soft brown hair fell like a cloud about her face. Her stunned expression spoke of joy, fear and great weariness—perhaps from the long trip. She was in her early forties, according to the paperwork Hsiao had seen, but looked years younger.

Ying Fa looked down at her hands as the woman scanned the room, deeply ashamed. It was a bar after all; and they were a party of locals, drinking scotch too early in the day.

Then her curiosity got the better of her, and she looked at the woman, examining her face, seeing her kindness, generosity and pain. There were wrinkles in the corners of her round gray eyes that spoke of laughter. Then, for an awful moment, the woman locked eyes with her.

Hsiao grasped at her sleeve and tugged. "You must not," she hissed.

She couldn't look away. It was as if the woman knew exactly who she was. Then, for a brief moment, there was fear in her eyes. She looked down at Mooi Mooi, her gaze softening.

Mooi Mooi began to cry. Quickly, the woman pulled a baby bottle from a bag on the floor and began to feed her.

Ying Fa rose. She had seen enough. She stared at Mooi Mooi, wishing her a good life, a happy life with this loving couple. An evil man had stolen her heritage and family; but the deed was done and could not be reversed. She smiled sadly, seeing the fierce protectiveness on the woman's face that demanded respect. No one would hurt Mooi Mooi under this lioness's protection. According to Mooi Mooi's paperwork, she couldn't bear a child. At her age, to be granted such a gift? Perhaps it was fate.

"Come on," she said to Gwai Ha, now desperate to leave. He leaned over the table, fumbling with his money, while his shoulders shook. His hair had fallen across his face. She couldn't see his expression. Alarmed, she started to go to him.

"Easy," Hsiao whispered, taking her arm. "Let Yutang deal with him."

"I'll pay," Yutang said, pulling on Gwai Ha's hand.

"Will you fight over the bill," Ying Fa hissed. "Not now. Not here." She glared at her brother who was hurriedly stuffing Gwai Ha's bills back into his pocket, and placing his own money on the table. He took Gwai Ha by the elbow and hustled him toward the door.

Gwai Ha looked back at her, his eyes glossy with tears.

She looked away. It was all she could do to hold back her own sobs, to keep from running to Mooi Mooi and spiriting her away. She bowed her head, allowing Hsiao to pull her past the tables. Hsiao murmured words of endearment and encouragement as she half-carried her to the door; following the men.

Her legs threatened to buckle, as if she were drunk, playing into their disguise. Yet, the last few seconds in her daughter's presence should not spell dissolution, no matter that she was a baby. She straightened her spine; leaned forward and took Gwai Ha's hand.

"Let's go," Gwai Ha whispered into her ear. "I can't take this. It's too much."

She took in his haggard face; then bowed her head and moved with him to the door, pushing aside Hsiao's hand.

Gently, she pressed a hand to her abdomen, wondering at the miracle of life. The child born in Guangzhou would be theirs for all time. Girl or boy, no one would take it from them. Later, on the train to Guangzhou, she would tell Gwai Ha her news.

She turned at the door; taking one last look at her daughter's smooth, round face and the beginning of two families, each bound by hope and love.

Mooi Mooi would never know her sister or brother. She'd grow up far from her clan and her culture, in a world of unimaginable riches. She'd never hear the tale of the Wong Aunts, or how Poh Poh had learned to play mahjong, or how Yanru had pulled her husband in a cart all the way from Beijing, or how her parents had foiled a greedy uncle. She'd never learn to make dumplings at her mother's knee.

"Good-bye, beloved daughter," she whispered, raising a hand to her lips, pretending to send her a kiss.

Hsiao pushed at her back, sobbing loudly. Yutang took her other hand, and then one step led to another and she was running down the street.

About the Author

Wendy MacGown loves to write. She loves to read, too. Books fill her cozy house on Boston's North Shore. For many years, she has written for business: software user guides, training guides, white papers and brochures. Before that were short stories, opinion columns, and one summer stint as photojournalist for a small local beach paper. Literature is her passion, her driving force, bordering on obsession.

Two of her novels, "Little Sister" and "The Crystal Fish Bowl," won honorable mention in the Arizona Authors Association 2005 Literary Contest.

Her other passion is her family, her husband and their two precious girls, both adopted from China, who are developing an equal passion for the printed word.

LaVergne, TN USA
22 February 2011
217525LV00001B/45/A